RITUAL IN THE MIND

DOCTOR WISE BOOK 12

ARJAY LEWIS

MIND
BENDER
PRESS

II

Ritual In The Mind: Doctor Wise Book 12

Copyright ©2024 Robert J. Lewis

Cover Design: Marianne Nowicki, PremadeEbookCoverShop.com
Editing: Libby Broadbent

ISBN-13: 979-8989828104

Published by:
Mindbender Press
474 South Main Street
Phillipsburg NJ 08865
www.mindbenderpress.com

IV

DEDICATION

To Jeff McBride:
Master Magician, Teacher and Friend
Keep the mystery coming.

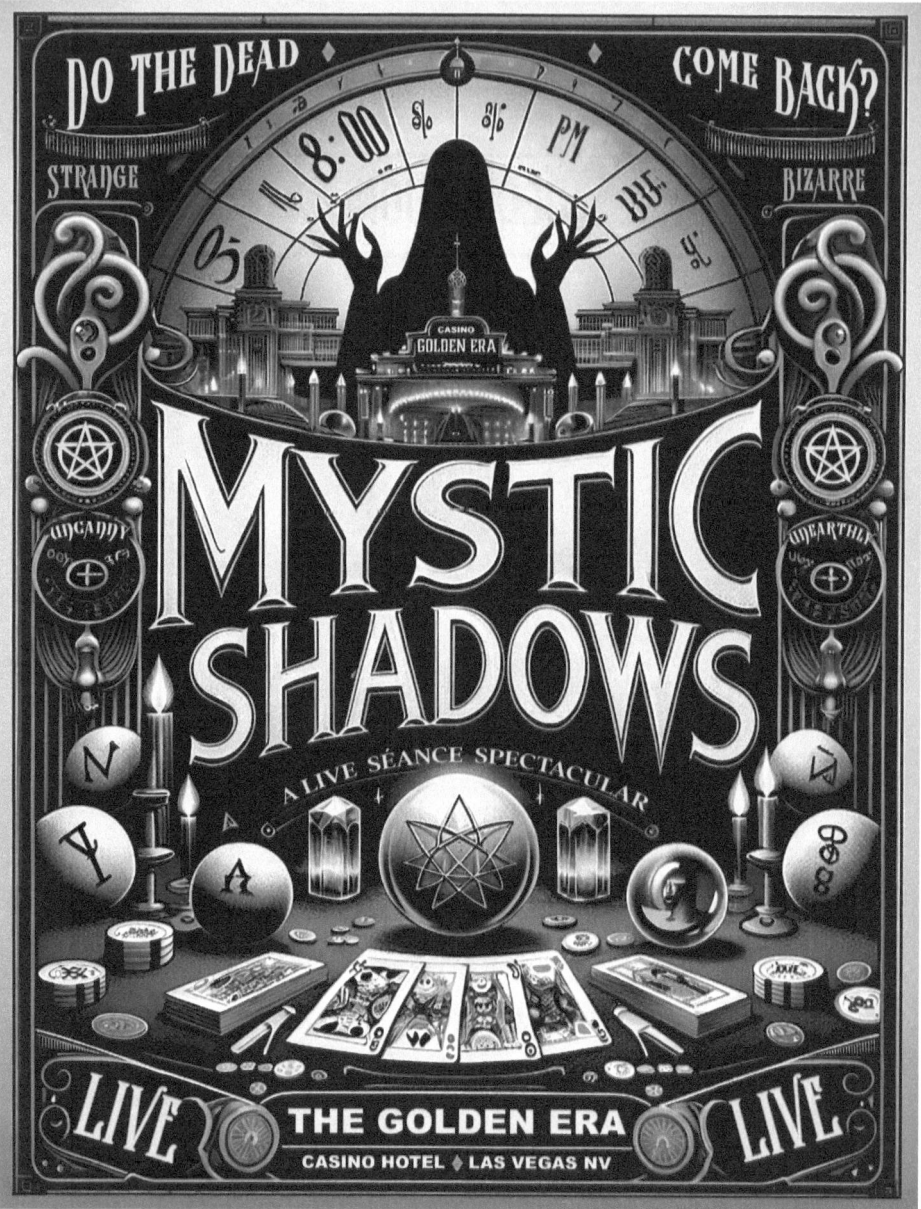

"Any ritual is an opportunity for transformation. To do a ritual, you must be willing to be transformed in some way. The inner willingness is what makes the ritual come alive and have power. If you aren't willing to be changed by the ritual, don't do it."

—*Starhawk*

"The sacred is not in heaven or far away. It is all around us, and small human rituals can connect us to its presence. And of course the greatest challenge (and gift) is to see the sacred in each other."

—*Alma Luz Villanueva*

PROLOGUE

I t had been quiet overnight, but now the men came again with their tools and began pulling down the walls — her walls.

Why wouldn't they leave her alone?

The constant pounding of hammers, the shrill screeching of power tools, and the ceaseless chatter amongst themselves was enough to drive her to madness. It seemed they had no regard for her in this place.

She hated this room, but she'd grown used to it over the years, became used to the solitude, where she simply drifted. Now it was suddenly a battleground of noisy invaders. They relentlessly tore down walls, the room filled with dusty debris and the incessant clatter of hammers and saws. Her sanctuary, her ethereal abode for years was being invaded.

It wasn't just the noise and destruction that angered her; it was their ignorance as well. They scoffed at the mere mention of a presence, dismissing the tales of haunting as nothing more than superstitious nonsense. They carried on with their work, convinced they were the sole inhabitants of this space. They did not know their actions disturbed the delicate balance between the physical and spiritual worlds, and she hated them for it.

Someone new came in, so much like the man she hated. His fancy suit and perfect haircut angered her. He spoke to the workers, laughing and joking.

She wanted to strike out at him, but it was daytime, and she was too weak in the light.

Among the group of workmen, a burly man showed him their unexpected find. He held out an old Colt 45 Peacemaker, like an iconic relic.

As the man turned it over in his hand, she saw layers of dust and neglect tarnished its weathered exterior. It had remained undisturbed for fifteen years. The once vibrant nickel-plating had decayed, giving way to patches of rust, but the gun's timeless elegance still held a charm that transcended its deteriorated state.

But there was more.

To her, the weapon glowed with an aura of dark energy, like a black ring surrounded it, as if it contained a secret power. She knew what it was. That handgun had been the instrument of her death. The cold metal delivering the fatal shot that left her trapped in this place all these years.

Death — after she had experienced terrible things.

Fear gave way to anger, and she felt a renewed energy. She glared at the weapon, her soul filled with fiery determination.

She would find the owner of that weapon, bring him here and take her vengeance upon him, upon all who did the awful things to her, and she would use that very weapon to do so.

The man in the fine suit smiled and took the weapon with him, leaving the men to their work.

She followed him as he went down the stairs and into the hotel. She sensed the glow of the weapon as if it were a beacon, pulling her onward.

She would have her vengeance.

1. ORDERED TRAVEL

J yanette and I dragged our luggage into the hotel room.
Our day was jam-packed, beginning with the plane trip from New Jersey to Las Vegas. After retrieving our luggage and our rental car, Jyanette drove us to our hotel while I navigated.

We'd left for Vegas on a morning flight, and I couldn't understand why I felt so exhausted. In the earlier time zone of the West Coast, it was still the afternoon. Regardless, my fiancée was brimming with energy and anticipation as she dropped her suitcase and dashed past me through the living room of our suite.

She vanished into our bedroom through an open door. Within moments, I heard her shout from the bathroom. "Len, come check out this tub! You could swim laps in it!"

I collected both Jyanette's and my luggage before placing my cane under my arm and making my way toward her voice.

As she emerged from the bedroom, a broad smile graced her features, but it quickly vanished, replaced by an expression of sheepishness. "Len, you shouldn't try to carry both suitcases," she chided.

She rushed to me to help, and I merely smiled. "I'm okay. My leg is supporting me better these days."

For nine years, I possessed no right knee because of the extensive damage inflicted from a car accident that left doctors with no choice but to fuse the leg, rendering it stiff and unbending. But thanks to the exceptional skills of a surgeon friend of my father, he implanted an artificial knee, which allowed it to function normally. However, because the original surgery removed some of the muscle mass, I occasionally experienced moments where my leg would weaken due to fatigue, making my cane an indispensable aid.

My usual cane had been my faithful companion for years, its brass handle shaped like a sleek cobra's head, a perfect fit for my hand. It could not accompany me on flights because of the hidden twenty-four inch sword encased within it. The solution: my sleek, foldable metal cane, used for metal detector checks and court appearances. It may lack the blade, but it was useful when my weak right leg needed the support.

"I was worried," she said. "You took two lessons at your dojo this week before we flew out. I was afraid you'd overdone it."

I studied Aikido, a wonderful and spiritual form of martial arts, from a tiny Asian man named Ashwan. He expanded on my training now that I had two functioning legs and I'd wanted to get extra lessons in before we went away.

I embraced her tightly and planted a kiss on her lips, eliciting a contented hum from her. We parted, and I looked around the room. "Pretty impressive."

Jyanette smiled. "It sure is. Did your brother arrange rooms like this for your entire family?"

"I'm sure he did. He's the star attraction at this hotel, so he had some pull in arranging the rooms for his wedding party."

Jyanette cast a look into the bedroom before turning her sultry gaze towards me. "There's an enormous round bed in there, bigger than our king-sized at home. Should we try it out?"

I smiled. "I intend to, but let's unpack first. Maybe take a shower."

"Tell you what," she purred while keeping her eyes fixed on me. "I've already started the water for that tub. We can get clean while we get dirty."

"Sounds like the perfect compromise," I said.

With a burst of enthusiasm, she ran off to check the filling bath.

As I walked toward the nearby desk, a gift basket caught my eye. An assortment of fresh fruit, cheese, crackers, and a bottle of champagne packed the basket. Attached was a note that grabbed my attention:

To Len and Jyanette
Thank you for coming!

My twin brother went to great lengths to impress, as he was the consummate showman.

He'd flown Jyanette and I, my sister and her brood, my parents, and his fiancée's parents from New Jersey to Las Vegas and provided luxurious rooms for all of us at the Majestic Odyssey Casino and Resort — the luxurious new hotel where he performed as a headliner, two shows every night, six days a week.

He'd come a long way from when we were teenagers doing magic shows for the neighbors.

As I had an unfinished case to wrap up with my detective friend Bill McGee at the Mountainview Police Department, Jyanette and I opted for a morning flight, while others had jetted off the previous day.

Jyanette's entrance into the room suddenly caught my attention — she was completely naked.

With a mother who emigrated from Africa, she inherited an extraordinary dark skin tone I could only describe as ebony. Standing at a height of five feet-eleven, she possessed an alluring beauty that started from the curve of her breasts and extended to her shapely wide hips - a sight so captivating it almost left me moaning in awe.

With a wicked smile, she announced, "The bath is ready, and it's nice to be appreciated."

"If I haven't appreciated you enough," I said, attempting to sound sexy. "I am more than ready now."

As I pursued her to the waiting tub, discarding my garments along the way, she let out a lusty chuckle.

Our ardor ignited in the spacious tub, but we completed the act in the round bed, both of us breathless and sated.

"I expect a lot more of *that* while we're here."

"You mean besides the family dinners, the rehearsals, and the wedding?" I grinned. "I have to provide stud service?"

She touched my face tenderly. "These last couple of months, with me working at the DA's office and you so busy, I feel like we didn't make love very often."

I looked away momentarily. "I knew they hit you with a large caseload, and could tell that certain cases were upsetting you."

She sighed, looking up at the ceiling. "Murder, child abuse, and rape — it makes me want to go live on an island somewhere far away from other humans. I'm afraid I neglected you."

"I'm just glad we could be here at the wedding."

"You're off for the summer, and I'm out of work since Jill came back from maternity leave. I want to unwind, relax, and get to know my fiancé again." She rolled over and caressed my leg. "I want to get away from you being the Mountainview Police's pet psychic."

I shook my head. "Jyanette, you know the police count on me —"

"I know, and your psychic abilities make you an asset to them. How about you not be a psychic for a few days?"

"I'll… um… try?" It was the only promise I could make. "I mean, it's not like I can shut it off with a switch."

"Do your best. I have a brilliant suggestion. When we're not navigating your family and attending all the events where our presence is required, we hide up here and stay naked."

"That'll raise eyebrows if we get room service," I noted.

She sighed. "Okay, you can put on a robe for the waiter, but I expect nudity once he's gone."

Eventually, we got up and transferred our baggage to the bedroom, where we unpacked. After some cajoling, I convinced

Jyanette we needed to put on clothes, despite her desire to do everything in the buff.

I found it too distracting.

Jyanette, looking proper in a green top with black pants, read the event schedule for the wedding from her phone. "Both families are having dinner together tomorrow night."

"Nothing tonight?"

"Not everyone is here yet. The Tannenbaum's aren't arriving until tomorrow."

"The last time I saw Mr. and Mrs. Tannenbaum was back in college when Julia and I were dating," I said, putting on a white shirt.

"Are you uncomfortable with this situation, Len?" Jyanette frowned. "Your twin brother is marrying the woman you dated throughout high school. You mentioned she was your first."

With a smile on my face, I shook my head. "No, I'm ecstatic. Julia is an extraordinary woman and the fact that she tamed my playboy brother is truly remarkable. He used to lecture me about the futility of marriage, but now he's settling down. It's incredible."

"Will you bring up your former relationship to the bride during your best man's speech?" she asked, her eyebrows raised.

"Not if I value my life," I said, which made Jyanette chuckle. "Besides, I already wrote it back in New Jersey."

"We have a night on our own. What shall we do?"

"I don't know. See a show?"

"I'd love to see your brother's show."

"Sorry, it's on hiatus for two weeks. We'll be back in New Jersey before it starts again."

There was a knock at the door, which surprised both of us.

I headed through the living room toward the door, saying, "Probably just Thomas or my sister coming to check on us."

As I swung open the door, a petite woman with a youthful and effervescent appearance met me. She stood about five-feet, two-inches in height. Long lashes framed her twinkling eyes, and she had a bright, infectious smile..

"Doctor Wise?" she said, and I felt she was forcing a bubbly tone.

"I'm Leonard Wise."

"Oh my gosh, I've read all about you!"

I frowned. "How can I help you Miss—?"

"Summers, Bonnie Summers. I'm the head of promotions for The Golden Era Casino Hotel. May I come in?"

She pushed past me. She was slender, and dressed in an unusual 1950s-style dress and white gloves.

Jyanette joined us in the living area. "And who is this?"

"Hi there!" She held out her hand. "I'm Bonnie Summers with the Golden Era Casino. I'm here to invite you to a show."

She turned back to me and went on. "You see, I heard you were going to be in town, and what with you being an expert and all, I wanted to invite you."

"Slow down," I said. "What is this about?"

Bonnie paused, seeming to force herself to take a deep breath. "Right, I got ahead of myself. I'm with the Golden Era—"

"We got that part," Jyanette said, crossing her arms and staring at our visitor. "Why are you here?"

"Right! In case you haven't heard of us, the Golden Era is known as the Haunted Hotel."

"The haunted hotel?" Jyanette repeated.

"What does that have to do with us?" I said.

"The hotel is presenting a new show for a select clientele and we wanted to invite you—" she turned to Jyanette, "and your — um—"

"Fiancée," Jyanette growled. "His *lawyer* fiancée, Jyanette Emery."

"Right. Ms. Emery, sorry I didn't know. We want you as our guests to come to the first show. We would really value your input."

I walked over to Jyanette and put a hand on her shoulder. "Why would you want my input? I know nothing about show business."

"Oh — I didn't tell you. It's a séance show. It's called *Mystic Shadows*."

Jyanette and I exchanged a glance.

Miss Summers went on. "You see, I know that you're an expert on séances and stuff. You teach parapsychology at that university in New Jersey, and you were the one who found all those things at a haunted house."

"Scudder House," I said.

"That's it! This is the trial run, the first show. It would be great to have you there. Plus, if there is anything you think looks phony, you could help us by making suggestions."

"So it's a fake séance," Jyanette said.

"It's a show," Ms. Summer said, her voice becoming even more bubbly, if that was possible. "But you never know what might happen. I mean, the hotel is haunted."

I was ready to show Miss Summers the door, and look online for a Cirque Du Soleil performance, but to my surprise, Jyanette piped up. "It sounds like fun."

"That's great!" Bonnie reached into her 1950s style handbag that matched her ensemble. She handed two slips of paper to Jyanette. "Here are two passes. The show is only open to a select group. See you tonight!"

She headed for the door. I let her out and returned to Jyanette, shaking my head.

She held up the passes. "There! We have a show!"

"I don't know. It all seems too convenient. How did they know about me, and that I was here?"

"Oh, come on, Len. We both have had to deal with the weird stuff you attract—"

"I attract?"

"You're a magnet for it. I think it will be fun to go to something that we know is fake! We can just relax and enjoy it."

She kissed me, and I decided she was right. It might be fun.

What could go wrong?

2. CEREMONIAL SCENE

We spent the afternoon relaxing, eating lunch at the hotel restaurant — the price of which almost made my hair stand up. Afterwards, I went to the hotel gym, as I had to keep working the muscles in my leg the way my physical therapist taught me.

Jyanette napped, and I woke her with kisses and we made love again. I came to Vegas for my brother's wedding, but it seemed like I was the one enjoying a honeymoon.

We got dressed to go out, me in a suit with a tie, while Jyanette poured herself into a shimmering dress that hugged every curve and made me weak in the knees.

We ate a quick dinner, and as Jyanette didn't feel like driving, we took an Uber to the Golden Era Casino.

We rode away from the huge monoliths they build in Vegas these days, and down several roads to the real downtown. This was old Las Vegas. Smaller casinos and the classic neon lights flickered and danced in the twilight. This had been the heart of the city for years, drawing in both locals and tourists alike with its vintage charm and allure.

"While you were in the gym, I did some research on the Golden Era Casino."

"Do tell?"

"It's a small hotel by today's standards, what they now market as a boutique hotel."

"Probably the suggestion of the perky Ms. Summers," I pointed out.

"Want to hear the history or not?"

"Sure."

"It opened as the Lucky Seven in the 1930s, and it was the biggest place in town and the first to have elevators and air conditioning."

"Quite a history."

"It gets better," Jyanette went on. "In the 1950s, the mob takes the hotel over, adds some games, and calls it the Lucky Seven Casino. The place is totally mobbed-up, but celebrities come and it gets a reputation. In the 70s, a former Chicago gangster, Salvatore Lombardo, buys the Lucky Seven, combines the place with a casino next door called the Ace Of Spades, does a big remodeling, and reopens it as The Sphinx."

"Wait. It's two hotels, but still small by today's standards?"

"Very. Lombardo managed to not get caught up in the busts in the 90s and early 2000s that cleared out the mob and brought the corporations in. Lombardo held on until six years ago, when he sells out to a group of investors."

"Most of the casinos are owned by corporations these days," I said. "At least according to my brother."

"The new owners renovate the place, to bring it back to its heyday. But the workers have all these stories of strange noises, things moving on their own, and some guys claimed they saw a lady walk through a room and right through a wall."

"That must have made the investors reconsider its financing," I said.

"Just the opposite. The CEO, Robert Wells, decides they should go all in. They promote the place as a 'haunted hotel' to bring in ghost hunters as well as gamblers. They even let guests rent instruments to track ghosts."

"What kind of equipment?" I asked. "Electro-magnetic field detectors, or maybe a Gauss meter?"

She grinned. "Len, I know nothing about that stuff. That's your line of work. I only know if you stay there, you can rent some gadgets."

We passed the original Golden Nugget and the wide Fremont Street walkway between the casinos. The Golden Era appeared frozen in the early 1960s, the historic brick building fronted with yellow and white metal siding that screamed 'old motel', with hundreds of neon tubes that were visible in the twilight. The hotel took up the entire block, and our driver pulled to the curb in front of a multi-level parking lot connected to the building. This also boasted the hideous metal siding on its exterior, but in an open pattern, popular in about 1971.

I tipped the driver, took my folded-up cane off my lap, and got out of the car, then offered a hand to my lady.

She looked at the front of the older building. "Not much to look at, is it?"

"Well, the tickets were free," I said.

We headed into the hotel, which, of course, took us directly into the casino.

The problem with being a psychic is mental energy is constantly bombarding my brain. Most of these gambling establishments force you to walk through the casino in order to get anywhere, so you'll stop and play a game or put some change in a slot machine.

They know how they make their money.

To navigate the hustle and bustle of a casino, I must battle against the frenzied mental chatter exuded by the gamblers. The adrenaline rush of winning and losing floods the air, amplifying the projected emotions of each individual. Focused concentration is the key to deflecting the overwhelming onslaught of thoughts, and being in that place put my practiced skills to the test.

"Are you all right?" Jyanette asked, noticing my discomfort as we navigated through the boisterous gambling floor, aglow with flashing lights and clamorous bells. More than anyone, she is aware of my abilities and the strain caused by crowds and places where there is a lot of emotion.

"I'll be better once we get out of the casino."

The lobby was resplendent with chandeliers and intricate plasterwork, new carpeting was on the floor, with a design that harkened back to the 1930s. Fine wood fixtures in the lobby oozed elegance and luxury. There were clear glass windows with intricate designs resembling stained glass handiwork.

Jyanette led me to an elevator, and we rode it up several floors.

"The casino looks new," I mentioned. "From the outside, I was expecting it to be worn and drab."

"According to what I read online, the investors insisted on a complete renovation. The place was closed for over two years, as they found asbestos in the walls."

"That must've been a mess."

"They took down old walls, updated the electric wiring and plumbing, and installed everything new, finished about a year ago."

"So why does the outside look so outdated?" I asked.

"According to the website, it's historic. They got a grant and tax abatements to maintain the older look. That's why they renovated only the inside and made it look like it did in the 1930s."

"Sounds like a corporate move," I smiled.

"The renovation is how they discovered the room we're going to. Apparently, it was the former owner's private office. Then one day, he has a work team close up the stairway, and builds a wall to hide it."

"Why did he do that?"

Jyanette shrugged. "The article didn't say. But it was when they uncovered the office that the workers experienced all the weird stuff."

The elevator door whooshed open, and we stepped out into a well-appointed hallway. The carpeting was luxurious, and the walls sported an old-fashioned wallpaper that matched perfectly.

Outside the elevator, as if waiting to leap upon the next arrival, stood Ms. Bonnie Summers, accompanied by an assistant with a clipboard. A reflection of the hotel theme, the assistant was also an attractive woman in a 1950s-style dress.

"Doctor Wise!" she gushed. "You made it! Emily, mark down that Doctor Wise and his guest have arrived."

"Yes, I have them," Emily replied, making a mark on the clipboard.

"Emily, we only have two more guests arriving. Can you handle them?" Ms Summers said.

"I will," Emily replied.

Bonnie turned to us. "Let me show you the way."

We walked down the hall, and passed a series of meeting rooms with fanciful names like Longhorn, Prospector, Cattleman, and Wrangler.

At the end of the hall, we turned to go through a doorway. There was a long staircase going down to our right and a blank wall to the left.

On the wall, there was a poster advertising the show in fanciful lettering declaring: *Mystic Shadows*, A Live Séance Spectacular. It looked like a poster from an old-fashioned Spook Show, which was a popular form of entertainment back in the 1940s and 1950s. On the poster was an illustration of a table with a crystal ball, candles, and a dark and frightening silhouette with the caption: "Do The Dead Come Back?" along the top. It was overblown and exactly what you would expect for a casino show.

"Neat poster," Jyanette said, staring at it.

"Thanks. We really think it captures the essence of the show," Ms. Summers said. "It also has a really neat feature."

She placed her hand on the crystal ball on the poster and murmured, "*Sim sala bim.*"

Jyanette and I exchanged a confused glance, only to be surprised when the wall itself swung outward, revealing a narrow set of stairs going up. Someone recently stained and varnished the wood, but left the walls plain.

"The room is at the top of the stairs," she said and gestured for us to go ahead of her.

Jyanette and I started up, and she followed, closing the wall behind us. The stairway was lit with spotlights focused on black and white framed photographs on the walls as we ascended.

"What are the photos?" I asked.

Ms. Summers spoke up from behind us. "Photos of the original hotel, and the renovations over the years."

"To give a sense of history, I take it," I said to her over my shoulder.

"That's what we're going for."

A blinding flash lit up the short staircase and made us freeze in place. I looked up to see someone standing on the upper landing with a camera in hand. I couldn't see their face because all I saw was an enormous pink spot before my eyes.

"Grace, easy on the guests," Ms. Summers said.

"Oh sorry about that," a woman's voice rang out. "I thought I'd turned the flash off."

We carefully walked up to the landing at the top of the stairs, as my eyesight cleared. I saw a tall woman in her 50s with sharp facial features and striking blue eyes. Her wavy gray hair fell around her face, framing her features. She wore a black leather jacket over a black t-shirt and dark wash jeans, and held a large camera in her hand.

Behind her, a tall black man in a security uniform shifted his broad shoulders.

Ms. Summers was still on the last step. "Jeez, Grace. That could've gone wrong if they lost their footing."

Grace shrugged. "Sorry, I was trying to get some casual shots. If I turn the flash off, can I get another?"

"I guess," Ms. Summers said. "I mean, if it's okay with you, Doctor."

"What's this for?"

"The Las Vegas Journal," she said. "We're covering the event."

Now I knew why they wanted us here. The entire production tonight was a publicity stunt.

"This is Grace Matthews, photographer and photojournalist," Ms. Summers explained. "The big guy behind her is Kofi Johnson. He's our security chief for the hotel and the casino."

I saw the man more clearly now. He stood about six foot seven inches tall, with broad shoulders and a muscular frame that spoke of a lifetime of discipline and strength training. His skin was a rich shade of brown and showed the signs of middle age with deep lines around his eyes and mouth.

He smiled with sparkling white teeth, and spoke with a Haitian accent. "Welcome folks. Glad you could make it."

Ms. Matthews directed us. "Could you two go down a couple of steps, point at a photo, and look a bit frightened?"

"That will be easy. Publicity events make me nervous," I said.

"Len, be nice. She's just doing her job," Jyanette reminded me, and guided me down a step. "Of course we can."

We posed and did our best acting, and she finished taking photos, then pulled out a small notebook and a pencil and spoke to Ms. Summers. "Bonnie, can I get their names?"

"Doctor Leonard Wise and Jyanette Emery," Ms. Summers said.

Ms. Matthews raised her eyebrows and looked at me. "Are you the psychic guy they were all excited about coming?"

"Grace!" Ms Summers exclaimed.

"Yes," I said. "But actually I'm a parapsychologist. I study odd phenomenon as a scientist."

"Great, glad you're here," Grace said. "I think you'll add a lot to the event. Head on in, I have to shoot our last guests as they arrive."

"Come along, Doctor," Ms. Summers said.

"I'll take you folks in," Mr. Johnson said, and we followed the pair down a short hallway also lined with black and white photos in frames. It was almost comical to follow the pair, as Mr. Johnson was so tall, while Ms. Summers was so petite.

"You're the security chief?" I said. "I would think you'd send a regular security man just to watch some guests."

"No, I must be here. We have important people tonight."

"Thank you, Kofi," Ms. Summers said as we reached the only door on this floor.

This received another of his big smiles. "Always glad to help, Bonnie."

The three of us entered the spacious chamber that served as the designated séance room. The ambiance exuded a dark and portentously gloomy atmosphere, heightened by a modest yet intricately designed chandelier suspended from the ceiling.

The air smelled of incense.

Thick curtains covered the sole window, imparting an enigmatic aura. An array of symbols and occult imagery decorated the walls, setting the stage for otherworldly communication. Positioned at the heart of the space stood a sizable round table, with ten chairs where participants would assemble to connect with the spirit realm. Twenty chairs faced the table in four rows of five for spectators, completing the total seating arrangement to a mere thirty.

"I thought it would be in a theater," Jyanette whispered.

"So did I," I said. In the room's corner there was a fine wood bar, where other guests sat on barstools, drinking and talking.

One man was talking to an attractive young woman. He looked over at us, said a polite word to the woman, and rushed over to greet us.

"Doctor Wise! Ms. Emery, so glad you could make it," he said. He was six feet tall, with a slim muscular build, wearing an expensive tailored suit with a power tie. He styled his dark hair in a slick, professional manner. His eyes scanned the room and missed nothing.

He held out his hand. "I'm Robert Wells, the CEO of the Golden Era. It is really a privilege to have someone of your standing here at our show. I am so interested in your impressions."

"Thank you, Mr. Wells," I said, surprised by his ebullience. "I'm glad we could fit it in to our schedule."

"Yes, your brother's getting married. I've read the stories about it. The Great Wizini takes a bride. Bonnie, show them our set-up and then I'll introduce you to the other guests for this performance."

"Of course, Mr. Wells," Bonnie said. "Doctor, Ms. Emery, let me show you where you'll be sitting."

She led us over to the large séance table. Behind it were shelves containing mystical -looking objects and figurines, and a large rectangular object covered by a cloth.

On the séance table were tarot cards, a pair of candlesticks with two white candles, and a large ouija board.

I froze, and Jyanette took my hand.

"You'll be sitting there and there," she said, pointing, then noticed the odd look on my face. "Is something wrong, Doctor?"

"No," I croaked and cleared my throat, my eyes still focused on the spirit board. "I just have a dislike of ouija boards."

"Oh, why's that?"

Jyanette spoke up. "Leonard's former fiancée died in a car accident the same night they experimented with one at a party."

I faced Ms. Summers. "I guess seeing it threw me for a second."

I didn't tell Ms. Summers the entire truth. Jyanette knew, but said nothing.

The night I last used a ouija board was the night when my psychic abilities first manifested themselves, like a lightning strike. My successful use of the board inspired others to experiment with the occult. Unfortunately, things took a dark turn when we inadvertently summoned a demon. This entity manifested before me on the road in front of my car and caused the accident that claimed Cathy Garber's life and left me with my injured leg.

I had not looked upon one of those accursed boards until this moment.

"I see. When you're ready, we can go meet the people you'll be sitting with," Bonnie said and headed for the bar.

"You all right?" Jyanette asked, concern written on her face.

"Yeah, I just hope that isn't a foreshadow of what's coming."

3. LETHAL LITURGY

T he bar reflected the mystique of the entire séance room, with rich, dark wood paneling enveloping the walls. Soft, atmospheric lighting cast an ethereal glow. Strategically placed antique mirrors adorned the walls.

"Attention everyone," Ms. Summers said. "This is Jyanette Emery, Esquire, and Doctor Leonard Wise, the esteemed parapsychologist."

With that, Ms. Summers headed for the door to take care of other duties.

The attractive woman stepped forward to shake my hand. She was striking, with long, dark hair that fell in loose waves around her shoulders. Her blue eyes sparkled in the dim light and her plump, full lips opened in a smile. She was tall, though not as tall as Jyanette. She wore a dress covered in glittering bugle beads, with a low-cut front that exposed her ample bosom.

"A real scientist," she said. She spoke in a little girl voice that sounded phony. Some men like that high-pitched 'girly' voice, but it grated on my nerves. "Hello, I'm Desiree Longing, and they invited me for my show business opinion. But you know all about ghosts, don't you?"

"I've done some work in the field," I said, keeping my eyes on hers, though with her low-cut gown, I had to resist the urge to glance down.

A tall and lean man, standing at six feet-two stepped toward us. He had brown eyes and dark brown hair kept short and neat, with a chiseled jawline and a small scar above his left eyebrow.

"Hey, I'm Connor," he said, taking Jyanette's hand. "I do lighting over at the Three Kings Casino Hotel. They brought me in to give my judgement about the lighting setup."

"What do you think?" Jyanette responded.

He gazed around the room. "So far, it's pretty good. The pre-show lighting gives a nice ambience and adds to the air of mystery."

"So?" Desiree asked, lowering her voice. "Have you seen any ghosts, like real ones?"

"Occasionally," I said. "But I'm just here to enjoy the show."

"That's all any of us are really here for," Wells said, getting between us. "We're just waiting for one last pair of guests and then we'll be getting underway." He moved to the bar. "Can I get you a drink?"

"Just water for me," I said.

"I'll have champagne if you have any," Jyanette said to the man behind the bar.

"I do," answered the bartender. He was a middle-aged man of around forty-five, average height, with a stocky build. He wore a burgundy vest with a crisp white shirt, and gazed at us with gray eyes framed by a pair of rectangular glasses, which gave him the look of an intellectual.

His nimble fingers danced across the bar, reflecting years of experience, and quickly poured Jyanette a flute of the sparkling liquid and a glass of water for me.

"Thank you, I said, slipping a bill into his tip jar. "And you are?"

"Oh, that's Will Anderson," Wells interjected. "He's a fixture in this place."

"That's right," Will said with an easy, disarming smile. "I worked here as a dealer and bartender before the renovation. I was glad when they brought me back."

"The place wouldn't be the same without you," Wells said.

It was then I noticed a woman in the corner, sipping from a glass with ice in it. She was about five foot four, with short blonde hair and bright blue eyes. She wore a dark suit with a burgundy tie, a pair of pentagram earrings, and a large silver ring with an amethyst stone.

On impulse, I stepped away from Wells and went to her. "Hello, I'm Leonard Wise."

"So I heard," she said, smiling. "I'm Rosie."

"Each one of us is here because of our speciality," I said. "What's yours?"

She sipped her drink. From the color of the liquid, I guessed it was scotch. "I helped rig the place."

"I'm sorry, what?"

She chuckled. "My fault. I just assumed everyone here is in the biz. Rig means I helped set up the lighting. I'm here to make sure nothing requires replacement or rehanging."

I looked over at Connor, still talking to Jyanette. "I thought Connor said he did the lighting?"

"He helped with the design. I'm the one who actually did the rigging."

"I see different specialties."

"Connor can rig too, and there was a lot to do here."

I gazed around the room. "I see little lighting."

"That's because it's hidden. That was part of the fun, rigging the room so it doesn't look like much. I tell you it's practically Disney level quality."

I smiled. "I look forward to it."

At that moment, the door opened, and a white-haired gentleman came into the room. He was a tall and imposing figure, even slightly hunched. Years of living had weathered and creased his olive skin, and his hair was slicked back in a classic 1970s style.

Another man followed him, six feet-two and at least three-hundred and fifty pounds. He had a thick head of gray hair, which was also slicked back like his companion.

"Mr. Lombardo!" Wells said with his booming voice and approached the older man, grabbing his hand and shaking it vigorously. "I'm so glad you could make it."

"We would've been here sooner, but the stairs were rough on Big John," Lombardo said. His deep, gravelly voice was smooth and captivating.

"You got to get an elevator," Big John wheezed.

"For one night, you'll be all right," Lombardo said.

"Everyone, I want you to meet Sal Lombardo, the man who took two hotels and turned them into the Sphinx, which is now the Golden Era. We follow in his footsteps."

The group all applauded, and Sal smiled and nodded.

Wells went on. "He's here with his former bodyguard—"

"Now retired," Big John added.

"Now retired," Wells repeated with a laugh, "He's Big John Rossi."

Rossi raised his hand and waved at the group.

Sal looked around the room and said, "I can't believe you turned my private office into a room for a séance."

Wells grinned. "During renovations, the crew reported that this room was haunted. What better place for a séance?"

Sal chuckled. "I didn't know you'd make it a selling point for my hotel."

"Marketing this as a haunted hotel was a great idea," Wells said. "We'll bring in people who rarely gamble. Sal, John, you two get a drink, and we'll get started."

The older man stepped up to the bar. "Is that Will Anderson?"

"The same, Mr. Lombardo," the bartender said, smiling. "Good to see you. The usual? Scotch with water and two cubes of ice?"

Lombardo's smile widened. "You always knew what I liked, Will."

I noticed Bonnie Summers and Grace Matthews both slipped into the room. Grace was snapping pictures, and Bonnie stood near her, quietly making suggestions.

After a few minutes, while Sal and Big John got their drinks, Bonnie Summers came forward and spoke. "Ladies and gentlemen, if you could find your seats, we are almost ready to begin."

Lombardo and Wells were seated at opposite sides of a large table, with Connor and Desiree on one side of Lombardo and Rosie and Big John on the other. I sat next to Big John, beside the vacant seat at the head of the table, while Jyanette sat on the opposite side of the empty chair next to Wells.

A bell rang, and we all turned to see a woman walk into the room. She was a slender woman in dark clothing trimmed with crystals and other spiritual trinkets. Her long grey hair hung loose, going down her back in a natural and carefree manner. Her eyes were green, and she wore an inviting smile.

Sal rose from his chair. "Celeste Moon! I haven't seen you in years. Are you running this show?"

Celeste embraced him, and he kissed her cheek.

"I am here to help the living contact those who have passed through the veil," Celeste said, then looked over at Wells. "Do we have the surprise in place?"

Wells rose. "Thanks Celeste, I nearly forgot. We have one more item that will make this event even more memorable."

He went behind the empty chair to the shelves that adorned the back wall and went to the cloth-covered object that was eye-level from where I was sitting. He pulled the cloth cover off of it, revealing a glass display case. Mounted upright on a wooden support was an imposing six-shooter revolver that looked like it came out of the old west.

Wells stepped away and gestured at the glass-enclosed weapon. "Sal, what do you think?"

Sal forced a smile, but I could tell from his expression that he wasn't happy to see it.

He knows that gun...

The buzz passed through my mind. A 'buzz' is my nickname for a psychic insight that pops unexpectedly into my mind. This one was strong.

"Where did you find that?" Lombardo asked.

Wells smiled. "A construction worker uncovered it behind a wall panel during the renovation. It's a classic Colt Single Action Army revolver, what they called the 'Peacemaker' back in the day. When we found it, it was pretty rusty and unusable, but we cleaned it up, restored it, and wanted to put it on display. Any idea whose it was, or how it got here?"

Sal's mouth grew tight, and he shook his head. "No idea."

Big John cleared his throat and said, "They've renovated this building so many times. That gun could've been here since the gold rush."

"That's why we called the place the Golden Era Casino," Wells said. "Come on, let's find our seats and get started."

Ms. Summers sat in one row of spectator chairs next to Grace Matthews who snapped photos of the event.

Celeste had gone to the bar, and Will handed her a glass of water. She placed it on the table, and with a gesture, the candles on the table lit.

Jyanette looked at me with a teasing grin. "I never see you do that."

I smiled and focused on Celeste.

The chandelier dimmed, and the burning candles became the primary source of light.

Celeste took a drink and put her glass on the floor, as did Robert Wells. I found this curious, but also moved my drink to the floor near my chair.

"Come, let us all unite our thoughts and energies." Celeste extended her arms, beckoning the group. "We must all join hands."

Sal took a quick nervous sip from his glass and set it down on the table so the ice clinked. He clasped Rosie's hand on one side and Connor's on the other.

I held hands with Celeste and Big John.

"All of us tonight must focus on the same goal," Celeste said, closing her eyes. "This intensifies our energy and increases our odds of success."

"In a town where odds are everything," Big John rumbled in a low voice. This drew quiet laughter around the table, and even Celeste smiled.

"We must focus," Celeste chided softly. "Tonight, we gather to seek guidance from the spirit world. We welcome any spirits who are near us to join our circle. Please make your presence known."

The large table rose straight up into the air several inches, and the guests released their hands to capture their drinks before they toppled to the floor. Jyanette grabbed her champagne flute, and Rosie grabbed Lombardo's drink and handed it to him.

Celeste opened her eyes and smiled. "Ah yes, you may wish to put your drinks on the floor. We're never sure what is going to happen."

Lombardo looked across the table at Wells and said, "You put your drink on the floor when you sat. I guess you knew this would happen."

Wells smiled, but said nothing.

Lombardo finished the drink and put the glass on the floor, as did many of the others.

"Let us join hands again," Celeste said. "From this point on, no matter what, we must not break the circle."

The group joined hands again as Celeste closed her eyes and leaned her head back. "We pray for protection. We only allow good spirits in our circle tonight."

"I almost spilled my good spirits," Big John said to Rosie.

The woman leaned forward and politely said, "Sh."

Everyone around the table gasped as the shuttle on the ouija board moved on its own with no one touching it.

Celeste's eyes blinked open. She fixed her gaze on the planchette as it glided slowly across the board. Various markings adorned the flat surface, such as letters from A to Z, numbers from 0 to 9, and phrases like 'yes,' 'no,' 'hello,' and 'goodbye.' Amidst the symbols and designs, the planchette encountered the word 'hello,' and came to an abrupt stop.

"We have made contact," Celeste said and gazed around the table. "Who has a question for the spirits?"

The flames on the pair of candles rose to almost a foot tall. Several people gasped a second time. After a moment, they receded to their original level.

Celeste smiled and observed the group. "Don't be shy. Who has questions for the spirits?"

Suddenly, the room shook, the dark chandelier tinkling as the hanging glass vibrated. Celeste and Wells both looked up at the ceiling in surprise, then exchanged a worried glance.

"Look out!" Bonnie Summers screamed, as the room shook again, her eyes focused on the wall behind Celeste. The display case that held the gun jiggled to the edge of the shelf, then crashed to the floor, the glass smashing, and the gun clattering across the room.

Sal Lombardo jumped to his feet.

"You must not break the circle," Celeste shouted.

Wells said, "That's not part of the show."

The room shook a third time, and Lombardo lost his balance and fell back into his chair. The overpowering smell of perfume made the air seem thick with its cloying scent.

"What's going on?" Jyanette asked me.

"I'm not sure," I said, but something in the room didn't feel right.

The gun clattered again, and with no one near, it rose from the floor and hovered, suspended in midair.

With my psychic abilities, I perceived colors surrounding the weapon, keeping it in the air. I focused harder and saw a form the size and shape of a human body, lifting the gun and holding it. It was unusual, as instead of a face, it was merely a silhouette,

Instead of being black, it consisted only of a multitude of layered colors, almost like a human aura.

Whatever it was, it aimed the barrel directly at Sal Lombardo.

Sal rose again, his complexion pale and his face drawn.

I focused my mind on the gun, attempting to reach out and block the weapon off from whatever entity was manipulating it.

The human-shaped spirit tried to hold on, but the pistol quivered for a moment, then fell to the floor with a loud metallic 'thunk' which made everyone jump.

Desiree screamed.

I watched the amorphous entity look at the weapon fallen from its grasp, then lift its head to observe me. I could almost sense it staring at me, assessing me. After a moment, it faded away.

Sal backed away from the table, his eyes wide. He took two steps and collapsed to the floor, which elicited another scream from Desiree.

Wells ran to the white-haired man. "Sal, are you all right?"

Connor leapt from his chair and got on one knee next to Sal, opening his tie and collar, as Lombardo lay on the floor gasping for breath.

Wells rushed to a wall phone, quickly tapping out a series of numbers before yelling into it. "There's a medical emergency in the séance room. I require immediate medical assistance."

"What is it? What are you trying to say?" Connor asked Sal as all of us looked on.

"Sarah," Sal said haltingly.

His eyes met Connor's and his head rolled back and he closed his eyes, releasing one last gasping breath.

At that moment, the door burst open and Kofi Johnson rushed in, followed by a tall, lean man in his mid-thirties, with jet black hair and a well-groomed beard.

Kofi got down on one knee next to Lombardo, feeling for a pulse as Connor stepped back.

"He's dead," Kofi announced somberly.

Celeste shook her head. "The spirits have taken him."

4. LEGAL FORMALITY

W e all remained in the room as EMTs arrived and carted out Mr. Lombardo. Soon, a female uniformed officer came into the room. Her name tag read Rodriguez, and she asked all of us to follow her downstairs to allow a forensic team to work.

We followed her down the one flight of stairs and into the closest meeting room, which was the Longhorn. She talked to all of us and took notes as we told the story of the floating gun and Mr. Lombardo collapsing.

"So this floating gun wasn't a part of the show?" she asked.

"No, no," Wells said. "We don't have an effect that could do that. But it couldn't do any damage because we didn't load it."

I had to agree. During the entire séance, up to the point of the room shaking and the gun falling had all been tricks. It was only when the gun was lifted that I had detected the entity holding it.

"Did Mister Lombardo know the gun was unloaded?" Rodriguez asked, making notes.

"I... don't know," Wells admitted. "It was a rusty old thing when we found it and we restored it. No one in their right mind would have a loaded gun on display as part of a show."

But I knew Lombardo recognized the gun.

The officer questioned all of us, and when she finished, she closed her notebook and told us we could go.

Ms, Summers and Mr. Johnson escorted us to the elevator, and I summoned an Uber.

"That certainly was unexpected," Jyanette said as we got into the vehicle.

"Completely. Most of the effects were fake, but the gun floating was real. Same with the shaking of the room."

"Wait, the planchette moved all by itself," Jyanette said. "You're telling me that wasn't a ghost?"

"No. That table was gimmicked. The legs were on pistons that use compressed air to raise and lower the table. Even the candles are not real, but use gas jets running through flexible pipes up the legs. The planchette on the ouija board contained a powerful magnet, probably Neodymium, with someone manipulating where it went by remote control."

"Someone at the table?" Jyanette asked.

"I'm sure there was a guy in a control room we never saw."

It annoyed Jyanette that I had figured out the trick when she didn't. "Okay, how did Ms. Summers open the wall? Did she cover an optic sensor in the poster with her hand?"

I shook my head. "No. Did you see that ring she was wearing? It's called a PK ring, and magicians use them for certain effects. It contains a magnet like the ouija board and the wall is closed with a magnetic lock. All she did was lift the ring to the lock, and the wall opened."

We were let off at the Majestic Odyssey, and we went up to our room. It surprised me to see it was well after midnight.

"A pity about Mr. Lombardo," Jyanette said, yawning. "Do you think it was a heart attack?"

"Probably," I said. "He knew that gun. It had meaning to him."

"How do you know that?" Jyanette said as she took off her blouse. "One of your buzzes?"

"Yes, also observing his reaction. Seeing it aimed at himself probably pushed him over the edge."

I finished undressing and pulled out a pair of pajamas.

"Put those away," Jyanette said. "I made it clear. I expect nudity."

I turned to see her completely undressed, smiling at me with lust in her eyes. "That might lead to trouble."

"I certainly hope so."

The next morning, I woke to knocking — make that pounding — on the door of our hotel room. Jyanette and I woke with a start, and I gazed blearily at the clock, which read eight AM.

"Dammit," she cursed as I grabbed the discarded pajamas and pulled them on. "I'm on vacation. Who in their right mind is bothering us at this time of the morning?"

I went to the door and yanked it open, only to be blinded as flashes went off and a group of people shouted my name.

"Doctor Wise, is it true there was a ghost in the haunted hotel?"

"Doctor Wise, are you investigating the gun that moved by itself?"

"Doctor Wise—"

"Doctor Wise—"

I unceremoniously slammed the door and fastened the security latch as well.

Jyanette stood in the living room of the suite wearing a robe. "What on earth was that?"

"Reporters," I grumbled. "Call the front desk and tell them to get security up here.."

Grace Matthews had been at the event the previous night. It was a publicity stunt! Why hadn't I realized there would be repercussions?

On my laptop, I went to the website for the Las Vegas Journal. On the home page was a large photo of the séance room with the gun floating in midair, pointed at Sal Lombardo. The headline proclaimed:

BIZARRE DEATH AT SÉANCE
RETIRED CASINO OWNER DEAD

Jyanette looked over my shoulder. "I guess this won't be going away soon."

I sighed. "Wells wanted to get some publicity out of the situation and promote the hotel."

"He certainly did that, but why are there reporters outside our room?"

She sat next to me on the sofa. Most of the article was factually correct with Grace's eyewitness account, stating that the moving table trick and the candle flame illusion were as much ghostly phenomenon as the levitating pistol. As the story continued, there was a photo of me from the Garden State University website with the caption:

Doctor Leonard Wise
The Super-Psychic of Scudder House

Somehow Grace, or a staff writer, had pulled up my history and retold the events at Scudder House and the treasure trove I found there. The writer mentioned I returned to the house on a research project and then the city demolished it afterwards.

All of that was true, but the sensationalized writing exaggerated both events.

The article mentioned I was a consultant for the Mountainview Police Department and that I had assisted the FBI in multiple cases.

Finally, the entire article ended with the supposition that the ghost of the Golden Era killed Lombardo.

I closed my computer and exhaled loudly. "This doesn't help."

"It also doesn't involve you or me at all. We are here for Thomas and Julia's wedding, and we are going to spend time with your family," Jyanette stated and rose.

There was a knocking at the door again.

Jyanette sighed. "Do you think it's more reporters?"

"I'll handle it," I said. By this time I was angry and I walked to the door, flung it open, and loudly proclaimed, "I have no comment at this time—"

The hallway was empty except for a robust African-American gentleman in a suit. He was tall, his toned physique emanating strength. He had a strikingly handsome, rough-edged countenance, adorned by a closely trimmed hairstyle and a hint of stubble.

"Doctor Wise?" he announced gruffly, sounding more like an accusation than a question.

"I'm Leonard Wise."

He held out a black billfold showing official identification and a gold shield. "I'm Detective Washington with the LVPD. May I speak to you for a minute?"

I was caught off-guard. "Uh, sure. What happened to the reporters?"

"I threatened to arrest them for obstructing an investigation if they didn't leave at once."

I smiled. "In that case, please come in."

As the man strode into the room, his mere presence demanded attention. With discerning brown eyes, he surveyed the space. He carried a large manilla envelope with him.

Jyanette placed a possessive hand on my shoulder.

"What's this about?" Jyanette demanded.

"Ma'am," he said with a nod to Jyanette and then focused on me. "I'm Detective Tyrone Washington with the Las Vegas Police Department. You were both witnesses last night in the death of Salvatore Lombardo, is that correct?"

"Yes, we were there. But I gave my statement to the officer last night."

"Yes, Officer Rodriguez. I'm sorry to call on you like this, but I saw that article about you in the paper, saying you worked with the Mountainview Police."

"A lot of that article was incorrect, but that part was true."

He nodded. "Bill McGee is an old friend of mine. I spoke with him this morning, and believe me, he didn't like me calling at five AM, east coast time, but he spoke to me. Anyway, he suggested you could help me."

I met the detective's piercing stare. "What can I do?"

"May I sit down?" he said, gesturing at the single padded chair. He pulled a long notebook from his jacket pocket.

"How do you know Bill?" I asked as Jyanette and I sat on the sofa.

"Bill and I used to work together in the FBI, still keep in touch when we can. They assigned me this case, and it's all pretty strange. Mr. Wells, the CEO of the Golden Era, is putting a lot of pressure on the LVPD to investigate Mr. Lombardo's death to make sure it was natural causes and nothing else."

"I thought it was a heart attack," I said.

"The Medical Examiner has yet to make a statement as to the cause of death. He said that Lombardo was in good shape for a man his age, and had a strong heart and no blockages. According to him, Lombardo should be up and walking around."

"Except for the fact that he's dead," I said. "Did the ME run a tox screen?"

"So far he has found no poison or illegal substance in his body," Washington said. "But none of it explains the floating gun or his last words."

"He spoke the name Sarah," I said. "But I don't know why, or who it is."

Washington handed me the manilla envelope. "I may have a theory about that."

I opened the envelope and pulled out an eight by ten photo — obviously a publicity shot — of a slender young woman with high cheekbones and a small nose. Long lashes framed her bright blue eyes, and her hair was a rich brown color that fell to her shoulders.

"Who is this?" Jyanette asked.

"Sarah Lewis, a local television reporter," Washington stated. "She went missing back about twelve years ago. I have the police reports, which my captain says I'm not allowed to share with anyone outside the department."

"That might limit my ability to help," I said.

"I thought so too," Washington said and indicated the envelope. "But no one said I couldn't print up her Wikipedia page. That'll give you the basic facts."

I pulled the paper out of the envelope and read it.

Sarah Jane Lewis: an American news anchor for KTNV in Las Vegas, NV. She disappeared in the early morning hours of June 24, 2012. Signs of a struggle outside her apartment led people to believe Lewis was abducted.

Early life

Sarah Lewis was born and raised in Boulder City, Nevada, the youngest daughter of Michael Nicholas Lewis and Eugenia L. "Jane" Lewis (née Silva). Lewis was a cheerleader in high school. She enrolled at the University of Nevada, Las Vegas (UNLV), where she studied mass communications and speech, graduating with a bachelor's degree.

Lewis began her broadcasting career with KTNV in Las Vegas, Nevada, doing events and gossip reporting, but worked her way up to become the morning news anchor for the station.

Disappearance:

The day before her disappearance, Lewis claimed to her producer, Amy Landy, that she had a breaking story about cheating at a Las Vegas casino and would reveal what she knew once she compiled all the evidence.

At about 4:00 a.m. on Friday, June 24, Ms. Landy noticed Lewis had failed to report for work as scheduled and called her apartment. She failed to answer her telephone, and at 7:00 AM Ms. Landy called the Las Vegas Police.

When police arrived at Lewis' apartment, they found evidence of a struggle near her car. Her personal items were strewn about the area.

Investigators interviewed at least three neighbors at Lewis' apartment complex who said they had heard nothing, though a nearby neighbor reported seeing a white Ford van in the parking lot at about the same time.

The Lewis family hired private investigators and made appearances on several national television shows, but they did not find any new leads.

Two years later, The Las Vegas Journalists Group created the website FindSarah.com for people with information or leads to use. Extensive investigations uncovered no clues to her disappearance, and her family had Lewis declared legally dead in 2019.

I raised my head and met his eyes. "You think this has something to do with Lombardo's death?"

"I talked with the detective who worked the Sarah Lewis case this morning. From his notes, her coworkers said she was working on a casino cheating scam, but they never found out which casino," he said. "Bill McGee told me you can see things other people can't, is that right?"

"Yes, I can detect nonphysical beings."

"I'll take your word for that," he said. "So, tell me, did you see anything last night?"

I glanced at the photo of the pretty woman. "I did witness an entity," I admitted, returning the photo and the printed page back into the envelope. "It was a human shaped collection of colors. It was as if I was seeing the aura and not the spirit."

"You can see auras as well?" the detective asked, narrowing his eyes.

"Yes, but I usually have to put myself in an altered state," I admitted. "I believe it was a spirit, and one powerful enough to move objects."

Washington nodded. "I see. McGee said you also get insights other people can't."

"Sometimes. I also get flashes of precognition."

He frowned. "Future events? That must come in handy."

"It's saved my life on more than one occasion."

"Let's say I believe you — I want to interview all the witnesses a second time. If you can do what you've said, I'd like you to come with me, see if you get anything I might miss."

I considered it. "I would need to have access to the crime scene as well."

"I can do that," he said. "Though we aren't calling it a crime scene yet."

"When would we start?" I asked.

"Right away, if you can."

Jyanette grabbed my hand and dug her nails in, making me wince. "Darling, may I speak to you in the bedroom for a moment?"

"Excuse us, Detective," I said, rising. "Help yourself to the fruit basket."

Jyanette all but dragged me into the bedroom and shut the door.

She turned to me, fire in her eyes, and hissed, "What the hell do you think you're doing?"

"Helping?" I whispered back.

"You are not — I repeat — you are not leaving me alone to deal with your family and people I don't know, while you go off to play policeman."

"Jyanette," I said. "You were there, you saw it. Admit it! This is an interesting case—"

She scowled. "Interesting case, my fine black ass!"

I smiled. "You do have a fine ass."

She shook her finger in my face. "You are to be at all the dinners, lunches, rehearsals, and whatever else we are supposed to be at. We're a couple, dammit, and I'm not showing up without you."

"What will you do if I can't make it?" I asked.

She folded her arms and glared at me. "I'll stay in the room naked and call a stud service."

"Seems extreme…"

"You are not ruining this week for me," she said through gritted teeth.

"Jyanette, this case requires someone with my abilities," I said. "A poltergeist that can move a heavy object like a handgun? I might learn something."

"You're gonna learn something you won't like if you leave me to deal with your family," she threatened.

"Okay, I get it. Will it be alright if I go with the detective now and talk to witnesses, examine the scene?"

"You have the wedding schedule on your phone. We have the welcoming dinner tonight. You be there or I will show you the dangers of life with a furious woman. And if you show up with a black eye or stitches, you're sleeping on the sofa."

"And if I show up late, you'll give me the black eye and stitches?" I joked.

Her lips were a tight line. "Don't tempt me."

Holding up my hands defensively, I said. "I get it. I promise I'll be there."

This finally soothed her, and she waved at me and said, "Go! Play with your detective. I'll go have breakfast and gamble."

I stepped out of the bedroom and found the detective looking over his notes.

"I can go with you right now if you drive," I said, grabbing my folded cane off the table.

I turned around and glimpsed Jyanette, standing with her arms tightly folded, clearly unhappy.

5. ON-SCENE OBSERVANCE

I was glad Detective Washington drove. Being used to driving the one and sometime two-lane roads in New Jersey, the multi-lane wide roads of Las Vegas were daunting. Also, from years of driving a van with hand-controls, using the foot pedals of a rental car might be difficult for me.

Washington turned toward downtown Vegas in the same route the Uber took the previous night. The casinos appeared different during the day, without the darkness and fanciful lighting to cover the flaws. It was like seeing a dowager who looks attractive at night wearing makeup. Now, in the harsh light of day, every wrinkle was obvious.

The detective spoke first. "So tell me, Doctor—"

"Please call me Len. If we're going to work together, it will make things easier."

"Call me Tyrone. How will seeing the scene again help you?"

"I was a spectator last night, and had my mental barriers in place," I said.

"Mental barriers?" he repeated.

"Sorry, McGee is used to my terminology. Psychic impressions bombard my mind all the time, unless I shut them off with alcohol. I trained for years to create mental barriers that protect my mind from the constant barrage."

"I get it."

"I only saw things like anyone else last night, except for that entity. But if I put myself into an altered state, I'll be aware of things I didn't notice last night."

"Hopefully something useful," the detective said as he pulled into the multi-level parking lot connected to the Golden Era Casino and Hotel.

Using my cane, I followed Washington to the hotel's entrance.

"I guess Mr. Wells doesn't want the adverse publicity of someone dying in the hotel," I suggested.

"It's more than that. After years of trying, the hotel has a high-stakes poker tournament coming in, with television coverage and the whole works. Mr. Wells is afraid this might keep away some of the big-name players. Those guys are a superstitious bunch."

"He should have considered that before he went with the haunted hotel theme."

Tyrone led me through a door marked Employees Only and headed down a dark and dirty hall.

"Where are we going?"

"Security office. I have to meet with Mr. Wells first."

As we approached the end of the hall, there was a sizable glass window to our right. I could see Kofi Johnson on the other side.

Tyrone said, "Kofi, you got a minute?"

"Sure," Kofi said and rose from the desk. "Ray, watch the desk for me." He joined us in the hall. "Any word on how Mr. Lombardo died?"

Tyrone shook his head. "The ME is still investigating."

Kofi's eyes widened. "It could be a curse. In Haiti we take curses seriously." He looked over at me. "You're the doctor fellow who was at the séance last night?"

I shook his hand. "Doctor Leonard Wise."

Kofi broke into a broad smile. He looked at Tyrone. "I think he can help."

"You think so?" Tyrone asked.

"He got the look of a bokor — that is a man who knows Voodoo."

"You holding out on me, Len?" Tyrone asked.

"Never, Detective," I said, smiling myself. "But Mr. Johnson is right, we might need a bokor to solve this case."

"What do you need, Detective?" Kofi asked.

"We have an appointment to see Mr. Wells."

"I will send you up in his private elevator."

Kofi led us through a series of dimly lit hallways. To my surprise, the decor wasn't as grand as in the areas the guests walked through. The lights were nothing more than bell-shaped frosted glass shades with a single bulb. They might have installed such fixtures during the hotel's original construction in the 1930s. Some areas remained shrouded in darkness, while pools of light illuminated others.

"Did you see anything unusual last night?" I asked.

"I brought guests up and stayed in the hall. I only came in after the floor shook and I heard something fall on the floor, and there was all the yelling. Mr. Lombardo was dead by the time I got to him."

"And you heard him say the name 'Sarah'?"

Kofi nodded. "That I did."

"Any idea who he may have been talking about?"

Kofi shook his head. "Not a one. Then again, I only started working here since the renovation."

"Thank you," I said.

We reached a solitary elevator in the hall, where Kofi used a magnetic card to open and then to activate the controls. He left us as the doors closed.

When the elevator doors opened, we looked out at a space decorated with warm and inviting colors, comfortable couches, and a well-stocked bar. Large windows looked out onto the casino floor several stories below, flooding the room with light, giving a sense of openness and grandeur.

Robert Wells rose as we came into the room. Sitting in a chair nearby, a notebook in her hand, was Bonnie Summers.

"Detective Washington, you're right on time," he said, and shook hands with Tyrone.

Ms. Summers rose as well. "Doctor Wise? I'm surprised to see you again."

"Detective Washington asked me to consult," I explained.

Wells shook my hand. "From the newspaper articles Bonnie told me about, we could've used you when we put the show together."

"You didn't need my help on *Mystic Shadows*," I said. "From the short amount I saw, your special effects team did a phenomenal job."

"Glad to hear it," he said, returning to his overlarge desk and gesturing at a pair of chairs facing it. "Come, ask me anything you need. I knew Sal Lombardo for almost a decade, and if there was any foul play involved, I want whoever did it to be caught."

Tyrone and I sat facing Wells, and Summers sat to the side watching all of us.

"I appreciate that, Mr. Wells," Tyrone said, and turned to me. "Is there anything you want to know before I start, Doctor?"

I nodded. "What made you decide to go with *Mystic Shadows* as a show?"

"It was all marketing," Bonnie said.

"Correct," Wells agreed. "There are so many casinos that offer Cirque Du Soleil, huge illusion shows, and musicals. We couldn't compete on that level. We don't have a vast arena or a thousand seat auditorium. In the renovation, we turned our one theatre into several restaurants. I got the idea for the show when we discovered that room. At first, we didn't know what to do with it, so it stayed empty. I finally put the séance idea together about six months ago. That way, we offer something unique that other properties can't."

"Every property needs a hook," Bonnie said. "We needed a reason for people to choose our hotel instead of the behemoths out on the strip."

Wells nodded. "There is tremendous competition for hotel rooms in this town, and we had to go a different route. Restore the rooms to better than when the place first opened and give the guests a nostalgic experience with dial phones and 1930s decor."

"How did you create the effects for the show?" I asked.

Wells looked over at Bonnie. "Bonnie put the team together."

"Jackson DeHart created most of the effects and runs them. I also knew Connor Maxwell and Rosie Graham for the lighting. I felt they could provide what we were after."

"I had a hand in the brainstorming phase," Wells bragged.

"When did you announce the show to the press and put tickets online?" I asked.

"Three months ago," Bonnie said. "We've been doing a slow burn on the publicity for months, leading up to the first séance. Getting Sal to show up for it was important, as he's a legend from the old Las Vegas."

Tyrone spoke up. "In your press releases, did you mention he would be there?"

"Repeatedly," Bonnie said, nodding. "As I said, it was a big deal. Nobody had seen much of Sal since he sold the hotel."

"How did you pick the group that was there for the show last night?" Tyrone asked.

"I kept it to specific people, like Desirée Longing," Bonnie said. "It was a publicity stunt, so we wanted someone who looked good in photos. I also invited Connor and Rosie, so if there was some lighting that needed to be changed, they would witness it. And, of course, Doctor Wise and his fiancée."

"Why didn't you pack the room?" Tyrone said.

Wells spoke up. "Bonnie wanted to keep it to a small group. She thought that the focus of the night should be Sal and his return to the hotel he used to run."

"You were both there for the room shaking and the floating gun. Did you notice anything else unplanned?" I asked.

Wells leaned back in his chair, thinking. "Until the tremors, things were going according to the script."

"You have a script?" I asked.

"Well, more of an outline than a word-for-word script," Bonnie said. "We start with specific effects, and then Celeste improvises, with Jackson backing her up with the special effects and answers he creates by manipulating the ouija board."

"The moving table effect is the start," Wells said. "We want everyone's drinks off the table. Later in the show, the table jumps like a bucking bronco, but we didn't get that far."

"Things went off the wires when the room shook," Bonnie said. "And how did that gun float in the air? That scared the shit out of me."

"It's a pity we can't recreate the whole thing," Tyrone suggested.

Wells glanced at Tyrone, then looked at me. "Wait. What if we could?"

"That's a great idea, Mr. Wells," Bonnie gushed.

Wells rose and spoke faster. "We get all the people, the same group — except Sal, of course."

Bonnie stood as well. "Yes, with famed parapsychologist Doctor Leonard Wise. I mean, the papers have headlines all about you—"

I felt my face turn red. "I'm certainly not famous, nor am I looking for any publicity—"

"Are you kidding?" Bonnie said. "You're some kind of super-psychic."

Tyrone said, "That's really not a bad idea."

I glared at Tyrone.

"Think about it," Tyrone said. "I can observe the group for their reactions, and you can be there if anything weird happens."

He had a point. Recreating the séance, I could pay closer attention to the guests during the event, and maybe sense if one of them did something.

"We've had to delay the show's opening until the investigation is over, anyway," Bonnie said.

"It would help us speed up the process," Wells said. "I'll call Celeste. She has staff at the museum, and it closes at six."

"When would you want to do this?" I finally asked.

"How about tomorrow evening, seven o'clock?" Bonnie said.

I pulled my phone and looked at the wedding schedule. My tuxedo fitting was tomorrow at noon, with dinner with my parents at eight. I'm sure Jyanette would be okay, as she would be with me at the séance.

"I guess so," I said, giving in. "But I don't want this to be about me. I'm just there to observe."

"Put it together, Bonnie," Wells said.

"I'll get right on it."

Tyrone glanced at his watch and rose. "We have a meeting with Jackson DeHart in the séance room."

Wells rose and escorted us to the elevator. "I appreciate your efforts, Detective."

The door opened immediately when he hit the call button. "I'll see you both tomorrow, unless you need me sooner."

We got into the elevator, and it started down.

"I hope I helped," I said.

"You asked good questions. It's obvious you've done this before."

"Glad to hear it."

The door opened, and we were in a hallway I didn't recognize, but Tyrone headed out and I followed. I glanced back and noted a sign over the elevator that read Private.

Passing through a door, we found ourselves in the casino area, which wasn't a surprise, as Wells had a view of the gambling floor from the windows in his office. In order to avoid being overwhelmed, I quickly erected my mental barriers. The glimmering lights and blaring music were so intense I wished I also had earplugs and sunglasses.

Tyrone led me directly to the elevator we used the previous night, and we headed up.

"About the séance room," I said. "Last night, Lombardo mentioned it used to be his office."

"Yeah, they found it during the renovations. Very few people knew it was there." Washington shrugged. "It was Lombardo's private office to take care of problem customers. Or a secondary counting room away from the legitimate one."

"Was Lombardo crooked?"

"Lombardo was a Chicago gangster who came here to become legit. How legit is anyone's guess."

The door whooshed open, and we stepped out into the well-appointed hallway. We walked to the doorway and the false wall was wide open.

Tyrone started up the stairs. "During the renovation, the workmen heard strange sounds and noises all focused in that room. That's when they started marketing the place as the haunted hotel. They even brought those ghost hunters from TV in to go over the place."

I made a grunt of disgust. "I'm surprised the LVPD didn't request them to investigate."

The detective glanced down at me over his shoulder. "Believe me, I had enough trouble getting the captain to okay bringing you in on this case. And you have credentials as a legitimate police consultant."

He started up again, and I did my best to keep up, finding I needed my cane to help me along.

We reached the top of the stairs. Washington opened the door, and we stepped into the good-sized room. Someone had opened the drapes that covered the window, allowing sunlight to filter into the room.

A young man was sitting at the table, shuffling a deck of large tarot cards. He was lean and in his mid-thirties, with jet black hair styled into a slick side-part, and a well-groomed beard, sharp jawline, cheekbones, and large bright eyes. He wore a stylish black suit, with a matte black collared shirt and a skinny black tie.

"I'm here," he said, then added, "not that I got anywhere else to be with the show closed. Though Bonnie Summers just called and said we're doing the show tomorrow?"

"That's right. I appreciate your time, Mr. DeHart," Tyrone said, and gestured at me. "This is Doctor Leonard Wise. He's a consultant working with me."

"I recognize you," I said. "You ran in with Kofi after Mr. Lombardo collapsed."

"That was me," DeHart said, rose, and walked over to the bar. "I'm going to have some water. Can I get you anything?" He opened a bottle of water and poured it in a glass.

"How do you run the effects for the show?" I asked.

Glass in hand, DeHart walked over to a mirror on the wall facing the séance table. "This is a one-way mirror and I watch from the next room." He pointed up at the chandelier. "Up there is a camera, so I can see where to move the planchette on the ouija board." He pointed at the corners of the room. "Cameras are also there, there, and there."

"So you can see everything that happens," I said.

"Yes. We equipped the cameras with night vision, so I can observe the room even during the blackout sections of the show."

"Blackout section?" Tyrone repeated and looked at me.

"Yes, it adds to the effects if you black all the lights out for short periods of time," I explained. "It's an old trick used in fake séances."

"That's right," DeHart said. "You know about ghost shows?"

"I do. But where do you run things for the show? The séance room was the only doorway on this floor."

DeHart smiled. "That doesn't mean there isn't another room. Come with me."

We followed him out to the hall, and he walked up to a piece of trim, turned it, and a hidden door opened inward.

I examined the doorframe. "That fits in almost invisibly. I would never have found it."

"I know," DeHart said, pleased with himself. "It's my solitary confinement."

I looked into the space behind the wall. It was a small room, and only one or two people could work in it. A maze of wires and cables snaked across the floor, connecting various control panels and computer equipment. There was a board housing a range of buttons, switches, and sliders, each of which controlled a different effect. Some had labels, while others did not. An operator could control the room's lighting, temperature, sound, and pyrotechnics all from this one location.

"I run the whole thing from there," DeHart explained. "I can used pre-programed effects, or do things on the fly to flow along with what Celeste says or does."

"Impressive," I said as I stepped out of the space, and the technician allowed the door to close, disappearing into the wall once again. "The hotel went to a lot of trouble to build all of this."

We walked back into the séance room.

"Did you see anything unusual when Mr. Lombardo died?" Tyrone asked.

"It was all going by the book until those earthquakes began. I did the table move, and Rosie grabbed Lombardo's drink at the same time he did."

"Rosie? The lighting person?"

"Yeah, she was sitting right next to him," Jackson explained. "She knew the table move was going to happen. She helped me run rehearsals."

"You rehearsed the show?" Tyrone said.

"We rehearsed with Celeste, but when we were working out the effects, we did dry runs without her. Rosie would sit in

Celeste's chair and just make stuff up, and I provided effects that went with what she said."

"I'm aware of the hydraulics built into the table legs to lift the table," I said. "You also use the gas jets to raise and lower the flames of the candles."

DeHart was enjoying talking about his creations. "I can also light them and put them out."

"We saw that. You have magnetic control of the planchette on the ouija board. Is there anything else?"

"Sure. Hidden speakers in the room, they can create the effect of something moving around the table." He pointed up at the chandelier. "During a blackout, I can lower a ghostly ball of light out of the chandelier on a reel. Before the lights come back on, I turn it off and reel it back up."

"Anything else?"

He walked over to one of the wall sconces and touched a hidden lever. The fixture opened on a hinge and I saw a bell connected to a black telescoping arm.

"This is what they call a spirit bell. When the lights are low, I extend it out and ring it. It looks like the bell is floating in midair. Then we use the speakers to make the bell sound like it's moving around the room."

I nodded my approval.

He went on. "Hidden in the ceiling are strobes for flash effects. In the control room with me is a dry ice fog machine with nozzles to release the fog at ankle level. That's very effective, because the fog is cold and it lowers the temperature in the room."

"Like at a haunting," I said. I recalled the haunted houses I'd worked in. The temperature was always low, and when there was a manifestation, the air would become downright frigid.

"Exactly. I even have a bubble machine for when the lights all go out."

"Wait, a bubble machine?" Tyrone asked. "How is that scary?"

"When all the lights and candles go out, the room is pitch black. It enhances people's tactile senses when they can't see anything. If a person feels the bubble touch their skin, they're convinced it's a spirit touching them with an icy finger."

"That's brilliant," I said, impressed.

"It's all about selling the effect," Jackson said, smiling. "And that's the part that Celeste does."

"Okay, I'm going to ask an odd question," I said. "Did anything happen when you put the show together? Have you witnessed any actual manifestations?"

Jackson rubbed his short beard. "I don't know. This is an old hotel, and buildings make noises, like any old place would. I heard a lot of creaks and strange sounds."

"That isn't what I asked," I said.

Jackson hesitated, looking from me to Tyrone before he finally spoke. "Look, I just try to do my job — but things happen in this room."

"Do you have an example?" Tyrone asked.

Jackson rubbed the back of his neck. "I want you to know I don't believe any of this stuff. But one night I was here late, checking out the equipment, getting it ready. I flicked on a strobe effect, and there was a woman standing in the corner." He pointed to an empty corner near the bar. "She was only in silhouette, but it freaked me out. I mean, she was just standing there. Then I brought the lights up, and she was gone."

"Anything else?" I asked.

"Sometimes there are sounds, like a woman whispering," he said. "Y'know, I thought all séances were bullshit when I first got here. Now, to be honest, I'm not so sure."

6. WITNESS PROCEDURE

Tyrone thanked Jackson, and he left as I peered around the room.

"McGee said you had your own way of working a scene, so give me the lowdown on what you need."

"Okay," I said with an exhale. "My technique is to put myself into an altered state."

"Like a trance."

"Exactly. Then I open myself up to what comes."

"So you're going to talk to ghosts or something?"

I smiled. "That's what people think, but it's more scientific than that. My mentor was a man named Doctor Kohl, and his theory was that traumatic events leave an energetic residue at a location. This is what you find in most places where there is a haunting. There is the imprint of an emotional event, and a sensitive can pick up on it. When I open myself to that energy, I interpret it as a vision."

"Like a movie in your head?"

"More than that, I see it like it's being acted out in front of me in the location. Sometimes, I get everything: sights, sounds, and colors. Many times, I see everything as a black-and-white silent movie."

"Why the difference?"

"To be honest, I'm not sure. My guess is that I get the black and white images from memories, and full color and sound from the mental energy of someone who is still thinking about a situation or taking action to resolve it."

"You think there are no ghosts? Only this energetic — what did you call it — residue?"

"There are indeed lingering entities, but it is far rarer than you would think."

"What do you need me to do?" Tyrone asked.

"Have your notebook ready. I'll speak aloud and describe anything I see. If I am silent for too long, say something, keep me talking."

"Sounds easy enough," he said, withdrawing his notebook from his jacket pocket.

"I also want to sit over here," I said, pointing at the spectator chairs. "That way, I can watch the scene from a different angle than I experienced last night."

"Go for it."

I walked to the first row of chairs and sat facing the big table. I nodded at Tyrone, closed my eyes, and focused on my breathing.

In… out, in… out.

I felt myself slip into an alpha state, and after a moment, opened my eyes.

The lighting was dimmer, and everything shifted to sepia tones. I could see the guests from the previous night seated around the table resembling semi-transparent phantoms, including myself — which is always an odd experience.

I saw Tyrone, and phantom images of Bonnie Summers and Grace Matthews. Grace was holding her camera and shooting photos.

The only source of light for the room were the two lit candles on the table.

Celeste was speaking, her mouth moving, but I heard nothing. This was one time my vision was a silent movie. The group all joined hands.

Celeste closed her eyes, and a phantom version of the table rose a few inches off the ground, while the actual table remained in place.

"The table just moved," I said aloud.

As I watched, a shadow version of the planchette on the ouija board slid by itself to the word HELLO and the flames of the candles shot up twice their height and lowered again.

I described everything aloud as it occurred.

Focusing on the vision, I watched as the room shook, startling the participants. I glanced around the room to see if there was anything else, anyone else there.

The room shook again, and I saw the display case on the shelf fall to the ground and smash. I saw Wells stand, his mouth moving silently.

That's when I saw her.

A figure stepped away from the corner of the room, bent down, and, using both hands, lifted the gun — or rather, the ethereal image of the gun.

The figure was female, I could tell that much now, but she was out of focus, the face and the body still a blur of different colors. She was clearer than the previous night, but I couldn't see her face. She aimed the weapon at Sal Lombardo, who stood, his expression a mask of fear.

I saw my shadow-self gesture at the weapon. That was when I had reached out and used my mental barriers to shield the gun.

The pistol fell out of the entity's hand, and it crashed to the floor as Sal Lombardo collapsed.

"Someone held the gun, a woman," I said.

"Can you see her face?" Tyrone asked. "Is it Sarah Lewis?"

I concentrated, but the ghostly figure only became more unfocused. "I can't tell. It could be."

In my vision, Wells and Connor rushed to Sal, and then Kofi burst into the room and rushed to the fallen man as well.

I looked down at Sal, and for that one moment, I heard him perfectly.

"Sarah," he said.

He closed his eyes. I looked over at the phantom.

The rest of her form was still out of focus and unstable, the colors shifting and changing.

Except for her eyes.

Now I could see her eyes, and I felt her staring directly at me.

An icy chill ran up my spine. This was only a vision, a memory of events. There was no way she could look at me.

I saw the anger in her eyes, and knew she was sensing me, right there, right at that moment. This wasn't a memory, but an entity, focused on me.

I reached out, sending my thoughts to her.

Who are you…?

Instead of a response, she fixed me with a piercing stare. A warmth spread through me, as if her acknowledgment carried a palpable heat.

Suddenly, what felt like a blast of wind struck me hard, as if I was in a wind-tunnel. I fell backward and hit the floor with a bone-shaking crash.

"Len!" Tyrone yelled and rushed to me, as I lay on the floor, seeing stars.

He helped me unsteadily to my feet.

The spirit was gone.

"Did you feel that blast of wind?" I asked.

"What are you talking about?" Tyrone said. "There was no wind."

Her mental energy had knocked me over. I rubbed the back of my head where I hit the floor.

"Any chance you got a look at this ghost?" Tyrone asked.

I sighed. "Sorry, I wasn't able to bring her into focus."

He glanced at his watch. "It's good you finished. We have to go interview our next witness, if you're still up to it."

I shook my head to clear it. "I don't think the spirit here wants me to see her. We might as well speak to the other witnesses."

"Our next one is at another casino, but it's only a block away. We can walk there."

Tyrone led me out of the hotel and out a different entrance. It was not a street with traffic, cars, and sidewalks but a crowded pedestrian mall, with people rushing about and kiosks where all the vendors were reaching out, trying to get sales.

There were multiple entrances to various casinos and hotels, as well as many bars and restaurants along our route. It resembled nothing more than a salute to capitalism in its basest form. This was the last thing I needed after my ghostly encounter and the noise and crowds made my head spin.

"What is all this?" I asked, unsure why Tyrone had brought me here.

"This is the Fremont Street Experience. It's a mall and tourist destination closed to automotive traffic," he explained. "I thought it would be the fastest route."

I looked up and saw that way overhead was a barrel vault canopy that was one incredibly long LED screen spanning the length of the pedestrian mall and was at least 90 feet above the walkway. It displayed a sparkling array of lights that were moving in waves of colors and images that made my vertigo worse.

I stopped and closed my eyes, and focused on my mental barriers as much as I could. In the crowded mall, I found it difficult. My head ached, and all the lights and sounds inundated my eyes and ears, and there were so many people overloading my mind. It's not just that I received the thoughts traveling through their minds, but it was the need to do things, see things, and be important. Everyone was pushing themselves and their thoughts into the world around them, and for me, it was maddening.

Tyrone took my arm and guided me. "You all right, Len?"

"Next time we should take a side street," I said, finally shielding my mind enough to open my eyes. "How far is it?"

"We're here, come on."

He turned us into the entrance for the Three Kings Casino Hotel, and I was happy to get away from the bustle of the pedestrian mall, the bright lights, and most important, all the minds.

Tyrone led me up to the second floor.

"You sure you can handle this, Len?" Tyrone said, and I could hear the concern in his voice. "You got really pale out there."

My mind was clearing, and my dizziness passed. "I'll be fine. It was just too overstimulating after what happened in the séance room."

"We're here," he said and pointed at a plaque on the wall that read: Royal Theater.

"Wait, this is the Three Kings Casino and they have a place called the Royal Theater?"

"Don't laugh," Tyrone said. "The smaller theater is called the Regal Room."

"Only in Vegas," I said with a sigh, feeling more like myself.

We went into the dark room, which only had work lights on. A large step ladder was center stage.

Two men, wearing black and holding the ladder, looked over as we came in.

"Rosie Graham, please," Tyrone said.

A man looked up and yelled, "Hey, Rosie the Rigger. A guy down here wants to talk to you."

Rosie descended and turned to the two men on the crew. "Give me a few minutes, guys."

Rosie Graham gestured for us to sit in a pair of the audience chairs facing the stage. I immediately noticed she was wearing the same pentagram earrings as the previous night.

"We're getting ready for the show tonight," she said. "I need to ensure the lights are all aimed right."

"Rosie the Rigger?" I asked.

She smiled. "It's meant as a sign of respect. I can move about the catwalks better than most of the guys, so I end up doing most of the rigging."

"We'll be brief," Tyrone said. "First, Mr. Wells has given us permission to do another séance with all the same people tomorrow evening. Can you be part of it?"

She thought for a moment. "Yeah, we're dark tomorrow."

"How long have you been in Las Vegas?" I asked.

"My whole life. My parents were involved in shows, and I enjoyed doing the backstage stuff. They died when I was sixteen, but the stagehands took me under their wing. Been rigging ever since."

"Besides the other night, have you ever been to a séance?"

"Sure," she said and touched her pentagram earrings. "I've also tried Tarot cards and stuff. The supernatural has fascinated me since I was a kid."

"You helped set the lights for *Mystic Shadows*. You're familiar with the room?" Tyrone asked. "When the table moved, did you grab Mr. Lombardo's drink?"

She frowned. "I... guess. I mean, I didn't want it to spill."

Tyrone continued. "Did you see where Mister Lombardo was looking when he fell?"

"Yeah, he was staring at the spot the gun was floating, like he saw a ghost or something."

"Did you see anything?" I inquired.

She shook her head. "Nothing. I'm sorry."

Tyrone interjected. "Does the name Sarah mean anything to you?"

She shrugged again. It seemed to be a nervous habit. "Afraid not."

I exhaled heavily. "Okay. Well, that's about it, Ms. Graham."

"I think doing the séance again is a good idea," she said, brightening. "I'll be there."

We returned to the Golden Era parking lot using East Ogden Street, where a few people were walking the sidewalk. This didn't affect me the same way as East Fremont Street and the pedestrian mall.

As we got into Tyrone's car, I asked, "Who are we seeing now?"

"Celeste Moon."

"She's the actress who played the medium?" I said.

Tyrone grinned. "That's the thing. She's no actress. Celeste says she can actually talk to spirits."

We were on the road for only about ten minutes and then pulled down a side street. Before us was an oversized mansion constructed in the Spanish Revival style, with wrought-iron balconies, terra-cotta roofs, and ornate tile work. A wrought iron post held an illuminated sign:

Celeste Moon's

CRYPTIC COLLECTION

Ghostly Encounters

Tyrone brought his car to a halt at the curb, and we made our way to the entrance. A cluster of individuals congregated in a line near the entryway, waiting patiently.

"What are they waiting for?" I asked.

"They're getting the tour," Tyrone explained. "Sometimes it gets backed up, and a group has to wait."

Tyrone approached the front of the line, where a slender gentleman held a clipboard and sported a devilish Van Dyke beard.

Tyrone flashed his detective shield and asked to see Ms. Moon.

The young man turned to the crowd. "It'll only be a few more minutes, folks."

A graying heavyset man complained, "Our tour was supposed to start a half-hour ago!"

We entered the ticket room. It was a dark space with large flickering faux candles everywhere and the walls decorated with old photographs of Victorian-era families, dusty antique dolls with missing limbs, and aged oil paintings of long-dead people staring with unblinking eyes.

The air felt heavy and a damp odor lingered. The artifacts scattered about the room included a rusty iron maiden standing in the corner, a mummified hand in a jar, and a bat with spread wings hanging from the ceiling.

The ticket booth had an old-fashioned cage on the front of it, and the young man went inside. I looked up to see a sign hanging over the booth.

WARNING

This edifice harbors apparitions and paranormal relics. By stepping inside, you acknowledge the management is not accountable for any potential encounters with these intangible entities.

This got my attention, so I carefully concentrated on my mental barriers. I already had an encounter with an 'intangible entity' and didn't want to repeat the experience.

In a short time, a solid young woman sporting multiple piercings came out to guide us. The hallway was lit by dim spotlights and flickering electric candles. An artificial mist added to the effect, which was the source of the strange damp odor.

The decor exuded a dark 1930s splendor, featuring classic woodwork and ornate gilded accents. As I followed Tyrone and the woman, we passed groups being led through the various exhibits in a maze of narrow corridor-like rooms, which added to the unsettling atmosphere. In several of these rooms, video monitors played. In each video, Celeste Moon explained the stories behind the strange artifacts which filled each chilling display.

I glanced into several of the dimly lit rooms with glass cases of various curiosities and stared at a dollhouse and a collection of antique dolls. Ms. Moon was proclaiming in a video that a dead young girl haunted the dollhouse. Her voice followed me down the hall. "Visitors claim to have heard unexplained giggling and have seen the dolls move on their own…"

It was clear to me that the number one thing promoted by this entire exhibit was Celeste Moon..

Soon we reached a door marked Employees Only, and after a brief knock, Ms. Moon opened the door.

She looked the same as at the séance, but she was wearing a black caftan covered in hundreds of white stars sparkling in the dim light of the hall.

She smiled at us. "I didn't know I was so dangerous. You need two big men to ask me a few questions?"

Tyrone became quite charming, as this lady inspired deference. "No ma'am. This is Doctor Leonard Wise—"

"The super psychic of Scudder House? Oh my! I didn't recognize you last night. I must say, you look quite different without the long hair and beard you sported when the Scudder House story broke."

I didn't want to tell her it was one reason I shaved and got a haircut. Scudder House was a tremendous success for me. Acting as a medium, I found a hidden vault with a treasure trove of money and valuables. I returned years later to help my mentor, Doctor Kohl, confront the entity tormenting the house and the poor souls who died there. Our involvement led to the destruction of that famed haunted house.

It was the last time I faced a spirit with the strength to move heavy objects and it almost cost me my life.

"I'm surprised you've heard of me," I said modestly.

"Oh, there is a lot of talk about you in the community," Ms. Moon said. "I believe you are teaching these days? Whatever are you doing here in Vegas?"

"My brother's getting married," I said. I glanced at my watch to check the time.

"Well, do come in," she beckoned, stepping into the office. The walls displayed a warm, muted color, with ornate moldings and decorative motifs. There was a pair of large windows that allowed natural light to enter the space.

Bookcases lined the walls. Some housed leather-bound books, but mostly there was spiritual paraphernalia. Large unusual crystals, rolled parchments, multiple decks of Tarot cards, and curiosities. Several shelves held bottles marked with fanciful names, like 'Love Potion,' 'Money and Success', and 'Drive Out Evil.'

On her office desk sat a crystal ball on a brass stand and a multi-line phone.

Ms. Moon gestured to two straight-back chairs facing her on the opposite side of the desk.

Tyrone asked, "I have your statement, but we have a few more questions for you."

Giving us her complete focus and twinkling with enthusiasm, it was clear why she excelled as a medium. Her gaze conveyed a sense of significance, making you feel like you were the most important person in the room.

"The effects at the séance are fake," I said. "Why are you part of it?"

She appeared not to be offended by my question and merely smiled. "Robert Wells asked me to be part of the team and run Mystic Shadows. I thought the show would be a good cross promotion for the Cryptic Collection. Since the collection is open during the day and they wanted the show at night, I didn't see a conflict. But you're mistaken, Doctor. The séance isn't fake. They merely add special effects to make it more exciting."

"You're saying that the séance is real?" I said.

Ms. Moon sighed daintily. "Every séance I take part in, I attempt to contact the spirit world, sometimes with startling results." She looked away. "What happened last night was truly unexpected."

"You offer a supernatural experience?" I said.

"I try to, and there is a genuine interest. But for tourists and people paying for a show, we have to make sure they get their money's worth, or the hotel will suffer. So, to make sure there are spectacular effects, I have Jackson DeHart, and the man is a veritable miracle worker."

Tyrone asked. "Can you give us any insight into the death of Mr. Lombardo? Anything in retrospect that you felt was odd."

"I felt... off... last night." She gazed at me. "I'm sure Doctor Wise knows what I'm speaking about. A feeling of not being in sync with the spirits."

"I'm sorry, Ms. Moon," I said. "But I've only ever acted as a medium one time and I have no recollection of the experience."

"Really?" she said, surprised. "Yes, to allow yourself to truly be a medium, to allow another to take control of your body, can be an off-putting experience."

"You've had that happen to you?" Tyrone asked.

She smiled. "Oh yes. The first time it happened, I felt a sudden and potent energy rush through my body. It was as if an unstoppable force took over, leaving me helpless to resist. My thoughts, feelings, and my very movements controlled by a presence. I heard whispers in my ear, urging me to speak, to move, to act in ways not my own."

"But you learned to control it?" I asked.

"I realized the power of surrender. I discovered a sense of peace and clarity. The entity that had taken over my being wasn't evil or ill-intentioned. Rather, it was a wanderer seeking connection with the living. Through that experience, I learned to connect with the spiritual world. After that, I devoted my life to becoming a medium and bridging the gap between the physical and metaphysical."

"I understand you used to be a showgirl," Tyrone said.

With a smile on her face, she reminisced, "Oh, that was great fun! I used to perform in one of those infamous topless shows when my bosom was nothing short of awe-inspiring. However, that line of work has an expiration date. You can do it till you hit thirty-five, maybe forty. Fortunately, I was lucky enough to have the spirits guide me to Doctor Jameson."

I shifted in my seat. "Doctor Jameson?"

"He was a physician and a collector of haunted artifacts long before I ever met him. He served as my guide and confidant for a decade and taught me about making potions and learning how to use herbs." She gestured with one graceful hand at the shelves lined with the bottles of various potions.

"You make these potions here?" Tyrone asked.

"Yes, I have a kitchen converted to a laboratory. I do them in batches, depending on the demand." She gestured to the surrounding room. "When I told Jameson we should open a museum for the public, he loved the idea. It took years to find this building, and he supplied the funding and bought a significant number of the artifacts." She glanced upward, adding, "He passed away four years ago, but I sense his lingering presence, offering counsel to me on running this place." She met my gaze. "We still have conversations."

"I'm sure you do," I said. "But back to Detective Washington's question. Can you think of anything that was different last night? Did you sense a presence in the séance room?"

Proudly holding her chin up, she declared, "I sensed a presence in that room the first time I went there, though she does not reach out to me."

"Does the presence seem female to you?" Tyrone asked.

"Very much so. But she will not communicate with me. I often have spiritual visitors in my séances. Loved ones ignored for a long time, seeking desperately to connect. Last night was different. I couldn't perceive anyone or anything attempting to reach out to me, even though we saw the manifestation."

"Did you expect it?" I asked.

"Oh no. Since it was the first show, I stuck to the rehearsed routine to test the special effects and get the feel of the whole thing. Imagine my surprise when those tremors began and the display case smashed to the floor."

"And you saw the gun rise into the air?" I asked.

"Yes. I thought Jackson had added a special effect he didn't tell me about, because I could not sense an entity."

"Did you detect any kind of manifestation when Mister Lombardo died?" Tyrone said.

"Only his spirit leaving his body," she said.

We all sat in silence, staring at each other.

Tyrone stood up and said, "Well, thank you for seeing us, Ms. Moon."

Celeste also rose to her feet and faced me. "Doctor, you really should come and take our tour. I think you might find our artifacts quite interesting on several levels."

"Thank you for your time, Ms. Moon," Tyrone said. "I'll be in touch."

We went back into the hallway, and I decided I wanted to understand this place better, so I allowed myself to lower my mental shields a little as we walked down the hallway.

A stabbing pain struck me, directly over my right eye.

I tried to retreat from the onslaught, but it was too late. There were bad things there. I sensed entities attempting to invade my mind, trying to feed on my mental energy. It was a mental attack, one that left me reeling. I seldom experienced situations like it before, and for a moment, I was terrified.

"Len, are you feeling all right?"

I pushed my mental protections back into place, the way I'd repeatedly trained, shutting off anything attempting to invade.

After a moment, I was aware of my surroundings. I was in the hallway of the Cryptic Collection, and I had doubled over from the onslaught of powerful mental energy. I took a deep breath and forced myself upright.

"I'm fine," I reported. "But I really need to get the hell out of here."

We quickly left the building and headed for Tyrone's car.

7. PRESCRIBED RENDEZVOUS

A s the afternoon sun beat down, we drove through town, casinos and strip malls transitioning to gated communities, and then to individual homes.

"That's twice you looked like death today," Tyrone said. "Does doing what you do always affect you like this?"

"No," I assured him. "I usually just deal with murder and mayhem. There are a lot of things with this case that hit me on a psychic level — between the ghost and the haunted artifacts."

"You can see why McGee advised me to bring you in on it."

Finally, we turned down a side street and came to a stop in front of an unpretentious stucco home on the city's outskirts.

"Whose house is this?" I asked.

"Big John Rossi," Tyrone said as we walked up the sidewalk to the front door. "So, no ghosts or possessed objects."

"That's good. I met him at the séance. He used to work for Lombardo, right?"

"Some say he was his enforcer. He did prison time about twenty years ago. No one's been able to pin a serious crime on him since."

Tyrone pushed the doorbell, and a moment later, the door opened and the large man stood before us. Unlike the suit he wore the previous night, he was wearing gray sweats and sneakers.

Tyrone flashed his shield. "Mr. Rossi? I'm Detective Tyrone. We'd like to speak to you about the event last night."

"Hey, Detective," Rossi said, his eyes moving to check the street and me before he let us in. "You wanna ask some questions?"

"If you don't mind, Mr. Rossi," Tyrone said amiably. "This is Doctor Leonard Wise. I've asked him to sit in on our interview."

Rossi engulfed my hand with his and shook it. "Yeah, we met. What are you? A shrink?"

"No, I'm a parapsychologist. Since Mr. Lombardo died at a séance, they asked me to look into it."

He led us through the house; the walls adorned with pictures of his family and friends. When we reached the kitchen, he said, "A ghost chaser, huh? That fits my theory."

"What theory is that, sir?" I asked, as he gestured for us to sit at a breakfast table.

"I think it was a curse that killed him," Rossi said.

"You're the second person to suggest that," I said.

"A lotta people think it's bunk, but I've seen curses take people out like that!" He snapped his fingers.

He lowered his large body into a chair, slowly and painfully. "It's a damn shame. Sal did good for me and my family. He even hired my cousin, Joe to work as a dealer at the Sphinx. I kept Sal safe for over twenty years. Then he drops dead like that."

Joe Rossi…

The buzz flashed through my mind.

"Would it be all right for us to talk to your cousin, Mr. Rossi?" I said.

The big man frowned. "Why do you want to talk to him? He wasn't there."

I said the first thing that came to mind. "Background information, nothing important."

This answer seemed to satisfy Big John.

"You think Lombardo died because of a curse?" Tyrone said. "Who would want to put a curse on him?"

Rossi shrugged his massive shoulders. "I dunno. I mean, there were people who wanted to take him out, back in his heyday. You know he got the tournaments into the Sphinx when he was running the joint?"

"The poker tournaments?" I asked.

"That's right. He brought in the Poker World Series at the Sphinx right after he opened the place. There were seven players that first year. It only got started because Sal was a big-time player himself. One year, he came in seventh and won pretty big. But Sal was a mover and shaker and sometimes he stepped on toes."

"Any one stand out?" Tyrone asked.

Rossi shook his head. "That's still around? Not that I can think of."

"You went to the séance last night," I said. "Was that the first time you'd been there?"

"First time at the Golden Era." Rossi nodded. "I know Celeste Moon. She's done some one-on-one seances for me. I gotta tell you, she's the real deal. My Isabella, she passed about two years ago. She was the strongest woman I ever knew, raised our four kids even when I did a two-year stretch at HD."

"HD?" I repeated.

"High Desert State Prison," Tyrone said. "I've read your file. You were in for Aggravated Assault."

"When I got out, Isabella put me in touch with Sal and I spent the next twenty years working for him."

"How did you meet Ms. Moon?" I asked.

"To be honest, I've been kinda lonely, what with the kids all grown and livin' their own lives. But, I go to that museum she's got, and I talked to her. She agreed to a private session. I get there expecting the usual crap, a bunch of tricks. To my surprise, Celeste gets in touch with Isabella. I mean, I could feel her in the room, and Celeste told me things only Isabella would know."

"Do you see her regularly?" I asked.

"I go for private sessions every coupla months. But then I get a call from Bob Wells to invite me to go to the séance show, and he says Sal's already said yes. I figured I'd get to see Sal, and it might be fun."

Tyrone took over. "Last night, did you notice anything?"

Rossi considered it for a minute. "I dunno, it was all pretty strange, the table shaking and the candles burning bright. Also, the thing on the ouija board moving by itself. Then those freakin' earthquakes."

"What did you do when the gun rose into the air?" I asked.

"I froze. It was weird. I used to be Sal's bodyguard, protected him for all those years, but I couldn't move. It was like someone put a curse on me." He looked at the floor and shook his head.

"Y'know, when I was younger, big as I am, if I saw someone pull a gun on Sal, I'd be up and blocking it before he could get a shot off. Last night, I was stuck in that chair."

"Sal's last words were 'Sarah'," Tyrone said. "You worked for Lombardo. Can you give me any insights into a woman with that name?"

Rossi didn't meet my eyes but kept looking at the floor. I could tell he was holding back. Finally, he exhaled heavily and spoke. "Sal knew a lot of ladies over the years. He liked 'em young, the younger the better. He used to say a girlfriend always looks good, but a wife just gets fat."

"Charming," Tyrone said.

I said, "Any idea why Sal spoke the name Sarah?"

He avoided my eyes. "Maybe she was the one that got away."

I couldn't fight the feeling he knew more than he was telling.

As we drove to our next witness' home, Tyrone asked, "Why did you want to know about Rossi's cousin?"

"I don't know. I just had a feeling," I said. "Can you track him down?"

"Do you think it will help?"

"I do."

Tyrone pulled into a driveway with a closed metal gate. He input a number on a call box, and a feminine voice spoke up. "Who's there?"

"It's Detective Washington, Ms. Longing. I called and asked to talk to you?"

Without another word, the gate before us opened. We drove through winding trails past lookalike two-story buildings until we reached the tallest structure in the development.

We got out, and I looked up at the light brown stucco structure. "Are all the houses done in tan and brown in Vegas?"

"Pretty much," Tyrone said, and we headed to the entrance. "We're meeting Desirée Longing and her boyfriend, Connor Maxwell."

"I remember them."

"So you know, Ms. Longing's real name is Samantha Smith. Now, if you get anything useful—"

"Which so far I haven't," I muttered.

"If you do, we can separate them and work on them. Let me know."

We entered the lobby, got into one of a pair of elevators, and Tyrone hit the button for the sixth floor.

"All the way to the top?" I asked.

"Yeah, I hear she has a spectacular view of the city."

The doors opened, and we walked down the hall, finally stopping at the last door, where Tyrone rang the bell.

"Coming!" yelled a voice. The door opened, and before us was the striking woman I'd seen the previous night. She wrapped her long, dark hair in a bun, and wore workout clothes that showed off her bare stomach. She stepped aside and invited us in.

"I've only got a little time, Detective. I've got to get to the gym," Ms. Longing said, using that breathy little girl's voice again. If I lived with a woman who sounded that way all the time, I'd lose my mind.

"Is Mr. Maxwell here as well?" Tyrone asked.

"Yeah, he's just getting out of bed. We work nights, you know."

"I'm aware of that, Ms. Longing," Tyrone said. "I appreciate you fitting us in."

My eyes had to adjust as heavy closed curtains covered the windows, shutting out a good deal of the light.

Off to my right was the door to the bedroom, and it surprised me to see a life-sized portrait near the door. It was obviously Ms. Longing, but she was completely nude.

She noticed my gaze. "That's something, isn't it? I had that done because I won't look this good forever. I have something to show people when I'm old and gray. It's cool. In the painting, my eyes follow you… and my nipples."

"Impressive," I remarked as I shifted my stance. She was right — the artist used a technique that made the eyes and the tips of her bosom track the viewer, creating an unsettling effect.

"Yeah. Nudity doesn't bother me at all. I'm in a show called *X-tacy*, where I strip down to a G-string while spinning plates on sticks. I can balance those sticks on my fingers, my head, and even on one leg, which I can hold up pretty high." She grinned. "That show is how I bought this place."

Tyrone and I gazed around the condo.

"It's nice," Tyrone said.

Skipping to a nearby curtain, she whisked it aside to welcome a deluge of bright sunlight into the room. As she gazed out of the window, Tyrone's assertion proved true; the panoramic view of the city was absolutely breathtaking.

"This place is a short drive from the Strip, easy to commute, but far enough away to avoid the crap. There's a gym and a swimming pool."

"We need to ask some follow-up questions," Tyrone said, trying to get her to focus. "Can we sit down and have Mr. Maxwell join us?"

"Sure," she said, and traipsed into the bedroom.

My ears caught the muffled voices of Desirée and Connor coming from the bedroom. Despite their attempts to keep their argument subdued, it was clear they were in a heated dispute. As Tyrone and I settled into a pair of chairs, Desirée finally emerged from the room with Connor in reluctant tow.

Connor's eyes were barely open, and he wore a white T-shirt and pajama bottoms. He didn't look pleased to talk to us.

"Mind if I grab coffee?" Connor mumbled, pulling away from Desirée and heading for the kitchen's one-cup coffee maker.

Desirée promptly seated herself on the sofa, sitting with her back straight, which emphasized her bosom. She flashed a polite smile in our direction.

We waited patiently, enduring the machine's hisses and gurgles. Once Connor obtained a brimming mug of coffee, he joined Desirée on the sofa.

Tyrone said, "You both met Doctor Leonard Wise. He's acting as a consultant on the case."

They nodded almost in unison.

"I read your interviews with Officer Rodriguez," Tyrone said. "Any new impressions from last night?"

"It was all so strange!" Desirée gushed. "I mean, the table moved by itself, and that ouija board! I could feel the spirits there, like they were right around me."

I focused on Desirée. "Have you experienced psychic episodes before?"

"I dunno. I've always been kinda intuitive." She met my eyes, but quickly looked away.

Mustn't tell...

I received a buzz from her at that moment, and wondered what she mustn't tell me.

"As I reported to the lady officer," Connor said between sips of coffee. "I'm the one who rushed to Lombardo and opened his tie and shirt."

Tyrone said, "You also heard his last words, correct?"

"Yeah, he said, 'Sarah'."

"Does that name mean anything to you?" I asked.

Connor shrugged, but I felt his nonchalance seemed forced.

"Does the name Sarah Lewis mean anything to either of you?" Tyrone asked.

"Sure!" Desirée said. "I used to see Sarah Lewis on the television when I was a kid. She, like, disappeared years ago, right?"

"Are you a local?" I said.

"I grew up in Boulder City, and my folks worked at the casinos. My dad was a dealer at The Sphinx—"

"Which is now the Golden Era?" I asked.

"That's right. I even met Mr. Lombardo once. My daddy took me to a party one summer at his house."

Mustn't tell…

There it was again, something touching my mind coming from Desirée.

I pressed it. "Do you have any bad feelings about Mr. Lombardo?"

Desirée wouldn't meet my eyes. "I felt bad he died. But it's not like I knew him. I just met him that one time."

Mustn't tell…

She was definitely holding something back, and I wasn't sure how to get her to open up. I needed to get Desirée alone.

I turned to Tyrone. "I think it would help if you saw the clothes they wore last night."

The detective instantly got the hint. "Yeah, I get that." He turned to Connor. "Connor, can you show me the outfits you two had on?"

"Why does that matter?" Connor complained. "There was no blood or anything."

Tyrone rose. "Are they in the bedroom? It'll only take a minute."

Connor rose, annoyed. "I'll get them for you."

"No need, I'll come with you," Tyrone said and followed the young man into the bedroom.

I let down my mental barriers, turned to Desirée, and lowered my voice. "Is there anything about Lombardo that you don't want to talk about in front of Connor?"

"What do you mean?"

"Something happened to you that you're afraid to tell," I said, and she met my eyes. Images flashed through my mind: a dark room, a leering face, pain and fear.

"No," she said and forced her eyes shut, breaking contact before I could get any more. She glanced at me as tears filled her eyes and leaked out of one, smearing her mascara.

"What are you doing?" she demanded, standing up, her voice no longer having that little girl's sound to it.

"If someone hurt you, did something to you, I can help."

"By getting into my head?" she yelled. "Connor!"

Connor burst back into the room, surprised by the shift in Desirée's tone. "Yeah, babe?"

Her demeanor shifted from playful to fierce. "No more talking. The police need to leave now." Her gaze was unwavering, devoid of any traces of innocence or flirtation. She was all business. "And if you intend to speak to me further, it will be through my attorney."

"What happened?" Connor said.

She pointed an accusing finger at me. "Him! He's like a witch or something."

I spoke directly to Tyrone. "We should go."

Washington nodded. "Sorry about any inconvenience. I'll be in touch."

"Only if my fuckin' lawyer is present," she shrieked.

Washington and I headed for the door as Connor tried to calm her down. Glancing back, I saw two black streaks of mascara on her reddened, blotchy face. The poise she previously exhibited, complete with the childish voice, was gone.

We headed for the elevator. "What the Hell happened? We weren't out of there for two minutes."

"She was hiding something," I explained. "I asked her about it and got a peek into her mind."

"You can do that?" Tyrone said.

"I didn't force myself into her head, it just came out, and I saw images. Something happened to her, something bad. And I think it was with Sal Lombardo."

---

8. FAMILY CUSTOMS

I planned to get an Uber, but Detective Washington offered me a ride to the location of the family dinner.

"Len, I almost feel embarrassed I took you away from your family, because I thought there was an actual case," Tyrone said. "But it looks like it may have been a heart attack."

"Trust your instincts, Detective," I said as I pulled up my brother's address on my phone. "We'll do the séance tomorrow night and see if we get any insights."

When I told Tyrone where we were going, he whistled in appreciation. "That's one neighborhood I couldn't pull off on a cop's salary."

"I couldn't afford his house on a professor's salary either," I said.

The traffic was slow, which made me anxious about being late.

We traveled down a road that ended with an open gate and pulled into a courtyard with a fountain in the middle.

I got out and waved as he drove away, then entered the lavish high-ceilinged foyer, with a grand staircase leading to the second floor. The main living area was expansive, with a modern and elegant design. There were floor-to-ceiling windows offering a stunning view of the city and the mountains.

It was certainly a step up from the one-bedroom apartment he lived in when he moved out here. I was proud my brother achieved all of this by pursuing what he loved.

A petite woman approached me. She had a lean frame, her back straight with shoulder-length straight blonde hair pulled back in a ponytail without a strand out of place. The stern expression on her face didn't seem to fit. She looked me up and down with blue-gray eyes, as if scanning for any signs of disarray.

"Excuse me, are you Leonard Wise?"

This surprised me and I felt a bit put-off. "Yes, I am. Can I help you?"

"You can help me by showing up on time," the woman chided. "I'm Emily Patterson, the event planner, and I'm in charge of every event this week. Tell me, is showing up late going to be a habit?"

"I was called in on a police matter."

"Really?" she stated, as if what I told her was a lie. "I thought you were a university professor on summer vacation."

"I also do consulting work for the police," I said, my jaw set. "By the way, it's Doctor Wise."

"Oh, you're a physician?"

"I have a PhD."

"Of course you do," she snapped, unimpressed. "Don't you have a copy of the event schedule? I was told everyone received the schedule—"

"I have it on my phone, it's just that I—"

"As the best man, I expect you to be at events when they begin from now on!" She stepped to the door and pulled it open. "Now, if you'll follow me?"

She strode down the hall, faster than I could, even though she was almost a foot shorter than me. She stopped at a closed curtain., "Can you let me know the plans for the bachelor party as soon as possible?"

"The what?" I said.

"The bach-e-lor par-ty?" she said, over-enunciating the words. "The night before the wedding? The ladies have made reservations for a show that showcases male dancers. You could do something similar for the men. There are several shows with scantily clad women here in Vegas." She looked me over again, which made me feel intimidated. "I take it you've never been the best man before?"

I paused, not wanting to give an inch to this unpleasant woman, but I had to admit the truth. "I've never even been a guest at a wedding."

She nodded. "I see. Please go on in, they're still only on cocktails."

I entered a cement patio made with delicate tile work. My parents and the other guests were there, including my nephews.

"Uncle Len!" Ben, my seven-year-old nephew, raced over with Judah, his five-year-old sibling, right behind him.

They grabbed my legs in a ferocious pair of hugs.

"Easy guys," Mark said. He was my brother-in-law and the boys' father.

My brother Thomas moved away from the bar where the adults were standing. "Len's a little late, but if you kill him, I can't give him a hard time about it."

The small people released me and went back to running around the manicured hedges.

"Nice to see you, Len," Mark said, and followed the boys.

"Likewise," I said and turned to Thomas. "Sorry I'm late."

"Don't worry," he said, walking with me away from the others. "Jyanette said you might be." He lowered his voice. "How did you end up working a case with the police?"

"It just happened," I said. "I don't want to upstage you and Julia."

He beamed. "Bro, there is no way you can ever upstage me."

We soon moved into an enormous dining room, which was also grand. The atmosphere was further enhanced by live music from a grand piano at the far end of the room, played by a pianist in a tuxedo.

"Wow," I said as I escorted Jyanette.

"This whole place is something," she said. "You would have had the tour if you'd gotten here on time."

As we sat at the large table, a voice asked, "So, Lenny, how are you?"

The bride's parents sat across from us.

"Mr. and Mrs. Tannenbaum," I smiled.

"Please, Lenny, call us Aaron and Leah," Mrs. Tannenbaum said.

Aaron spoke up. "We've known you for about fifteen years, right?"

"And now we're going to be family," Leah said, with a glance over at Thomas and Julia, who were sitting next to each other and chatting with my sister, Rayna.

I knew them from when I dated Julia in the past. Mr. Tannenbaum was a high school art teacher and had aged like fine wine. Mrs. Tannenbaum, a successful artist, was a vibrant and self-assured woman. Her hazel eyes conveyed her creative nature, and a cascade of brown hair accentuated her delicate features.

Jyanette spoke up, an amused look on her face, "Tell me Aaron, what was Lenny like in high school."

"He was always doing something," Aaron explained. "Him and Tommy were coming up with magic tricks, Len would head off to watch his father perform surgery at the hospital, or his nose would be in a book. Lenny was always late."

Jyanette glanced at me sidelong. "You would think Lenny would work on that."

"All Lenny talked about in high school was being a surgeon like his father," Leah said to Jyanette.

Aaron looked at me. "It surprised us you didn't pursue it."

I held up my walking stick. "I lost the ability to stand for hours and that changed my priorities."

Disassembling the sections, I carefully folded the sleek black cane.

"I noticed you using it when you came in," Jyanette said quietly in my ear, her face awash with concern. "Are you all right?"

"It was a long day, with a lot of difficulties," I said quietly, then returned my attention to the Tannenbaum's. "It's nice to see you both again."

"When Julia told us she was dating your brother, you could've knocked us over with a feather," Leah said. "Then she said she was getting a job in Las Vegas to be near him, after they dated for what — a week?"

"Her first husband was a bum," Aaron said, seriously. "And we were nervous when she just dropped everything to be with Tommy."

"But I've never seen her so happy," Leah added.

We finally had time to speak to Julia. She was in her early thirties, with long, chestnut-colored hair and hazel eyes like her mother. Her complexion was flawless, with a sprinkle of freckles on her nose and cheeks that I remembered so well from when we dated. She wore a feminine pink outfit that looked dressy, yet casual.

"How are you holding up, Jules?" I asked the bride, with Jyanette at my side.

"Pretty well," Julia said, smiling. "I wanted to plan everything myself, but Tom insisted we hire people to make the arrangements."

"Like Ms. Patterson?" I asked. "I met her on the way in. She seems high-strung."

"She's a perfectionist and expects nothing but the best from those around her. Then again, because she is, I don't have to be."

"She's the dragon lady, while you get to be the sweet, blushing bride," I said.

"Exactly. Don't annoy her, Lenny."

"I want to thank you for asking me to be your maid of honor," Jyanette said.

"It was my pleasure. When Tom told me you two were engaged, I decided it was the thing to do right then and there." She pulled Jyanette into a hug, which Jyanette happily returned.

"I just hope I didn't make you feel obligated," I said.

"Not at all. It takes a special person to deal with one of the Wise boys," Julia said.

"No argument there," Jyanette agreed.

"Now I should let you know, the press will be all over the wedding. Tom said it will be good for his show."

"And you're okay with that?" Jyanette asked. "We had the press at our door this morning, and I didn't like it."

Julia glanced over at Thomas, who was speaking with her parents. "I am. Since I've moved out here, and seen everything his show requires, I've learned that any publicity that keeps his name in the papers is good for business."

"Has my brother made good on his threat to get you up on stage?"

Julia laughed. "He's tried. So far, I've been able to remain a humble museum curator."

"You're still at the Las Vegas Museum of Art?" Jyanette asked.

"Yes. After the dress fittings tomorrow, all the girls are going for a tour of the museum."

"I hope to be there, Julia," Jyanette said, with an annoyed glance at me. "I need something to keep me busy while my man is otherwise engaged."

As the evening progressed, Jyanette and I mingled. We saw my sister Rayna, who sat with Mark and my nephews. We also spoke briefly to my parents, catching up and making all the polite chitchat.

"Tomorrow we're having dinner with the Tannenbaum's, just the four of us," my mother said. "It's so wonderful. We've been friends for years, and now our children are getting married."

"They seem very nice," Jyanette said.

"Yes. Jyanette, darling, do you think your parents would like Vegas?"

"Miriam, who doesn't like Vegas?" my father said, not letting Jyanette answer. He turned to me. "So, this policeman takes you away from your family. Is he paying you for your time?"

"Dad, you know I don't get paid for my work with the police."

"Son, when I consult on a surgery, I get paid. It's bad enough they don't pay you back home, but now you're out here and they still stiff you."

"Len has received several large rewards for cases he's solved," Jyanette said, ever my defender.

"Sam, it's a big deal that the police want his help," my mother said. "I mean, he could become one of those profiler people."

"A nice fee wouldn't hurt either," my father grumbled.

The rest of the meal went better, and we all parted a few hours later, a hug from my dad and mother, as well as my nephews and my sister, and finally a big hug from Tom.

I asked Jyanette about attending the second séance, and she checked the schedule on her phone. "You think we can make dinner with your parents at eight?"

"I don't see why not."

"I'll let them know that we might be late."

She drove our rental car back to the hotel. "You think it was murder?"

"I don't know what to think."

"You sound annoyed."

"I am," I admitted. "I mean, all the pomp and circumstance and rehearsals and dinners and then that dragon lady giving me a hard time when I got here."

"You agreed to be best man," Jyanette said

"I know," I said. "It's just — I didn't expect to have a case here in Vegas and I… I…"

"You're enjoying it," she said, and shook her head.

"What?"

She kept her eyes on the road. "Leonard Wise, I love you, but if there is a case and they ask you to work on it, you simply can't resist. I never worry about you cheating on me, because you're not the type. But if there is an unsolved mystery, I'm the last thing on your mind."

"That's not true," I grumbled, as an idea struck me. "I can prove it— let's get married tomorrow."

Her head snapped back in my direction so suddenly I was afraid she'd given herself whiplash. She faced the windshield and murmured. "What?"

"I mean it. They don't need a blood test like in New Jersey. We can get a license online and be husband and wife by tomorrow, without all the dinners, family drama, and bullshit."

She glanced at me like I'd lost my mind. "You mean it, don't you?"

"Jyanette, I love you with all my heart, and I'm glad we got a vacation here in Vegas that my brother is paying for. But I don't want to go through all of this stuff when we get married. Also, I don't want to wait anymore. I want us to stop being roomies — let's be husband and wife."

She was silent as we pulled into the mammoth parking lot for our hotel. "I never expected this coming from you."

"Seeing all the hoops Julia and Thomas are jumping through makes me want to streamline the process."

"But my sisters, my parents—"

"We'll have a party in Virginia later to celebrate. Then they don't have to drive up to New Jersey. Let's do this and get it out of the way."

"You make it sound like a chore. You want to do it and get it over with."

I said nothing, but she hit the nail on the head. All of this socializing was not what I enjoyed. I wanted to marry the woman I loved and be done with it.

"I guess I'm not blessed with a sense of romance," I muttered.

"True, but you have your uses," Jyanette said breezily as we got out of the car. "Let's get back to the room and I'll show you how useful you can be."

As we walked to the elevators, I said, "What's gotten into you? I've never seen you this lusty."

"It must be the pageantry," Jyanette said, then murmured in my ear. "Weddings make chicks horny."

9. QUESTIONING OCCASION

I woke up the same way I'd slept, with Jyanette in my arms. Carefully, I extracted my arm, which had fallen asleep, got out of bed, and used the bathroom. I found my phone and a text from Detective Washington:

Have located Joe Rossi

We can see him today.

Are you still interested?

I texted back I was, and that I had a tuxedo fitting at noon. It was already almost ten.

Tyrone let me know he could pick me up in a half hour.

As I was putting on pants, Jyanette spoke up from the bed in a voice filled with sleep. "Good morning, darling."

"And a good morning it is," I said, and bent to kiss her. "I have to get ready to meet Tyrone. We slept almost ten hours."

"Jet lag and good sex," Jyanette said. "And if you're going to perform like you did last night, you can ask me to marry you anytime."

"I wanted to make it up to you for being late," I said.

"Apology accepted," she said and stretched languidly. "I wouldn't mind another apology this morning."

"No time. Tyrone's coming by in ten minutes."

She blew out her breath in a hiss. "Just like when you get a case at home. Will you be on time for your fitting?"

"Yes, I'll be fine."

I headed out front as Tyrone pulled up, and I got into his car. "Where are we going?"

"A retirement community in Henderson," Tyrone said. "It only took a couple of phone calls to track him down. People knew him from when he was a dealer at the Sphinx."

"There's that connection with Lombardo again," I said.

"I brought the ME's preliminary report about Lombardo," he said and pointed to a large envelope. The paperwork was brief and technical, but with my medical training, I understood the terminology.

"I couldn't make heads or tails of it," Tyrone confessed. "Do you understand it?"

"Yes, the ME thinks he died from acute organ failure," I said, and frowned. "That's unusual, as is his notation of pleural effusion in the lungs."

"What's that?"

"It is when fluid builds up in the space between the lungs and the chest wall. It could suggest pneumonia, heart disease, or complications from kidney disease."

"So he might have died from natural causes," Tyrone said and sighed.

We veered from the road and pulled into a driveway.

We drove the winding paths of the retirement community with a sign that announced it was Blissful Acres. Although each house was a standalone unit, they were all one-story high with the same light brown color and white trim around the windows and doors.

We reached the clubhouse in the center of the community. Tyrone parked the car, and we headed into the building.

The main lobby was comfortable, with cozy armchairs and decorative plants.

The woman at the reception desk was middle-aged, with a warm smile and kind eyes.

"We're here to see Mr. Joe Rossi," Tyrone said as we drew near.

"He's playing cards in the dining hall," she said, smiling the entire time. "The group meets three days a week and Mr. Rossi is always here."

"Thank you," Tyrone said, and we headed down the hall.

The dining hall had a spacious interior and was adorned with comfortable furnishings and décor, creating an inviting space.

"How are we going to find him in here?" I asked, overwhelmed by the amount of people in the room.

"I think I see him." Tyrone moved between the different groups until we reached a table where five men sat, with cards in front of them, and dollar bills piled in the center.

The dealer looked up as we approached. He was a sturdy man in his late sixties bearing a rugged, weathered face with deep wrinkles and a strong jawline. His hair was gray, but it was still thick and well-groomed. He wore a black suit with a white shirt and a silver Rolex watch.

Tyrone asked, "Mr. Rossi?"

The man smiled and said, "Okay, boys, it looks like the cops are here to shut us down."

The men at the table groaned. One man said, "Hey, gambling is legal in this state."

"We just need to talk to Mr. Rossi," Tyrone said.

"But he's winning," the man complained.

Tyrone focused on Rossi. "Sir, can we go to one of the meeting rooms? I have a few questions about Mr. Lombardo."

"God rest his soul," one man said.

Rossi became serious. "Yeah, Sal. What a tragedy." He rose. "Look, guys, I gotta talk to them."

The three of us went to the closest meeting room, closing the door as we went in.

"You're playing cards?" Tyrone asked. "I thought you'd been a dealer. Aren't you tired of cards?"

"Nah, I love 'em," Rossi explained. "I got one of those photographic memories — but only for cards."

"A unique skill for a dealer," I said.

"Yeah, well, y'know," Rossi said as he took a seat at the large table. "I don't know what help I can be. I haven't seen Sal Lombardo in years."

"Do you know anyone who might have a reason to want Lombardo dead?" Tyrone asked.

Rossi shrugged. "Nowadays? No one I can think of. I mean, when Sal was younger, he was a mover and shaker."

"Could there be something from years ago?" I said. "Something he wanted to keep secret?"

For a moment, I got a glimpse into his mind and saw him in the séance room, but now there was a desk and filing cabinets, and a phone. He stood looking at a much younger Big John and dark-haired Sal Lombardo.

Sitting in a chair — slouching would be a better description — was a fourth man. He appeared to be tall, with short hair and a performer's presence. He finished talking and now was tapping his foot.

They were talking, but what I heard sounded like mumbling. It was an animated conversation with the good-looking man explaining things, but unfortunately, I heard it as mumbling from a distance. The one clear thing I heard was Joe Rossi saying, "When can you fix me up?"

Everyone smiled, and the scene faded.

I turned away, breaking free and putting my mental barriers in place. Joe Rossi was one of those rare people I sometimes ran into. His mind was an open book. I didn't even have to reach in. Unfortunately, I didn't know what the entire thing was about.

I'd apparently zoned out because Tyrone looked at me and said, "You okay, Len?"

"You better not be sick or anything," Rossi warned. "You got anything around us seniors and it could be fatal."

What went through my head had been a memory of Joe Rossi's. It seemed like Sal Lombardo and Big John asked him to do something. But when did this happen?

"I'm sorry." I took a deep breath. "Where were we?"

"You were asking if I knew anyone who wanted Sal Lombardo dead," Rossi said.

"Did you and Sal Lombardo ever work together on some special project?"

Rossi went pale but put on a stern face. "I was a dealer in Vegas for thirty years. Sal asked me to do a lot of things."

"I understand," I said, feeling him out. "If Sal pressured you to do anything illegal, I'm sure the statute of limitations has expired —"

Rossi stood up. "I don't have to listen to this crap. You come here, saying I was a crooked dealer?"

"I never said that," I replied, but I was sure I'd hit the mark.

He shook his fist at me. "If I was a younger man, I'd knock your block off."

Tyrone stood, speaking in a soothing tone. "Mr. Rossi, we're just trying to find a reason for Sal Lombardo's death."

He glared at Tyrone. "Look, Sal was an old guy, and I figure his heart gave out." He started around the table, heading for the door. "Now, if you don't mind, I'm going back to my card game."

Bottom deal…

The buzz came to me, and I remained in my seat and spoke without thinking. "Where you can do your trick of dealing from the bottom?" I said, the image of him doing it so clearly in my mind. "It's small wonder you always win."

For an older man, Rossi moved fast. He punched me in my chest, knocking me and my chair over as I sprawled to the floor.

Tyrone pulled Rossi back. "Calm down, Rossi, just calm down!"

Rossi let his arms drop and said, "I'm calm. You gonna charge me?"

I slowly rose from the floor.

"Len, you want to charge him with assault?" Tyrone asked.

"No," I said, using my cane for support. "But I will talk to you again, Mr. Rossi."

Tyrone let him go, and Rossi stalked out of the room. I leaned against the table for support. I felt the back of my head. After being knocked on my ass two days in a row, I had a nice-sized lump forming.

"You sure got a way with people," Tyrone said.

"It's part of my charm." I was just glad he didn't give me a black eye. That would be all I needed for Jyanette to be angry. "He's holding back, hiding something."

"Yeah, I know, it was all over his face," he said, and glanced at me. "Was what you said true? Is he really cheating his friends out there in a penny-ante game like that?"

"He likes to win," I said, as I thought about the memory I received from the man. "And I think we may be close to something."

We headed out to the car and Tyrone said, "We should have the ME's full report before the séance tonight."

"That should help," I said. "Can you take me to my tux fitting? I'll try to figure out what Rossi was up to."

"Do you think you can?"

"It had to be something that happened when Lombardo was still running the casino that would require the help of a dealer."

"Could be anything."

"That's the problem."

In a few minutes, he pulled the car into a strip mall, and I saw the store with the sign announcing, 'Friar Tux'.

I headed inside with low expectations. However, a pleasant surprise awaited me upon entering a lavish, upscale boutique. All the men were there: Thomas, Aaron Tannenbaum, Mark, and my father.

The salesperson quickly handed us our tuxedos.

Thomas opted for a white jacket with black formal pants and a black half-vest.

When I opened my bag, I found my tuxedo jacket was white as well. I turned to Thomas. "Why does my jacket match yours?"

"Because you're the best man, remember?"

I shrugged and tried it on. The pants fit like a glove. The inseam was perfect, which was uncommon for me since I have long legs and struggle to find suitable clothing. I knew I'd sent my measurements, but it pleased me they were spot on.

Everything in order, we departed, each of us carrying our own black vinyl bag.

Thomas drove me back to the casino in his sports car. As he drove, he said, "Tomorrow, for the rehearsal, we may have you and Jyanette stand in a couple of different places. Are you okay if we need to experiment a little?"

"Tom, I'm here for you and I'll do whatever you want."

"Good to hear, bro. Also, there is going to be a hotel photographer during the ceremony. The Majestic Odyssey wants to use our photos to promote weddings at the hotel. We're combining several meeting rooms for the ceremony and the main ballroom for the reception."

Leave it to my brother to do things in a big way.

"And the Rabbi?" I asked.

"You'll meet him at the rehearsal. Great guy, Rabbi Goldstein. He even arranged for the chuppah."

Thomas was talking about the cloth canopy upheld by four posts that shelters a Jewish couple during their ceremony.

"Getting anywhere on your murder case?" he asked.

I sighed. "We're not even sure it is a murder. The preliminary ME report suggested organ failure. The only thing I can think that would cause that is sepsis shock, but there would be symptoms leading up to it. Of course, the ME could mean refractory shock or respiratory failure as a cause."

"Ease up, Len. Dad would know what you're talking about, but I have no idea."

"Actually, I should ask Dad. That's a brilliant suggestion. Thanks, Thomas."

He shrugged. "Glad I could help."

Despite finishing medical school, I never pursued my residency as intended. My father, a renowned neurosurgeon, had far more medical expertise than anyone I knew.

As we pulled into the lot and Tom waved goodbye to me, I called my father.

"What's up, Len?" he said. "Your mother and I are on our way for the tour at the museum with Julia."

"Technical question, Dad," I said. "The ME for my current case gave COD as acute organ failure. I thought the only way that could happen was sepsis shock."

"Not necessarily," he said. "Multiple Organ Dysfunction Syndrome is often fatal. Sepsis could be the culprit, but an extreme response like an infection could cause it. Another cause could be anaphylaxis."

"An extreme allergic reaction?" I said. "Wouldn't that be rare?"

"Not as rare as you might think. Other factors might be hypoxia, intestinal permeability, bacterial translocation and endotoxemia. I would need to see the autopsy to get a better grasp of what killed the man."

"I'll keep that in mind."

"Alright, son. See you later."

I ended the call and went into my room, and heard Jyanette on the phone as I came in. I listened as I hung my clothing bag in the closet.

"Yes, I think that will be fine, but it will have to be this afternoon. I just have to get away from Len."

"Hello?" I said as I walked into the sitting room.

"Gotta go," Jyanette said, and as I walked into the bedroom, she was putting her phone on the nightstand.

"I thought you were kidding about calling for a stud service," I said, smiling.

Jyanette paused, then stretched out seductively on the bed and purred, "Not if you take care of things first."

This was a grand strategy because I almost forgot about the phone call. I focused on the issue. "What are you doing? I thought you were going to take the museum tour with the family?"

"Thomas, Julia, and I are going sightseeing later this afternoon." A sultry smile appeared on her face, her hands going to the buttons on the front of her blouse. "I wanted to be here to have some time alone with you. After all, you ran off this morning."

"Is everything okay?" I asked, unable to fight the feeling something was going on.

"You are the most suspicious man I ever met. Len, all I've done is find things to do, so you are free to investigate your murder."

"Well, technically, it's not my murder…" I said as she opened her blouse, which shut me up.

"You have some time now, right?" she said as her bra followed suit and fell to the floor.

I completely forgot about any further conversation.

10. PHANTASM PROTOCOL

I lay in bed dozing. The afternoon lovemaking left me totally drained, but seemed to invigorate my fiancée. She was up and about, showering and getting ready to go sightseeing. She organized my clothes, putting them on a chair, as I lay there semi-conscious.

With a kiss on my cheek, she headed out.

I slept for about an hour and my cell phone finally woke me up as the sun was heading toward the horizon.

"Wise," I answered.

"It's Tyrone, Len. All the witnesses agreed to be part of the séance tonight."

"Good to know. Jyanette and I will be there."

"I did some digging into all our witnesses, especially Connor Maxwell. It took some time and some help from friends in the FBI."

"Sounds serious," I said.

"Turns out he did two years in prison on drug charges when he was twenty-two in Idaho. That's where he's from. He was on the lighting crew in high school, but then decided drugs were easier than working. I had a little trouble tracking him down because, after prison, he legally changed his name from Connor Lewis."

"Wait, Lewis?" I said. "Like Sarah Lewis?"

"Connor is her nephew."

"Do you think he might have sought revenge for his aunt?" I said.

"We still have no connection between Sarah Lewis and Sal Lombardo. I just thought you should know about it before the séance tonight. I'm going to keep an eye on him."

"Got it."

I ended the call and headed for the shower. It was a good thing I took a nap, as I needed to be at my best for the evening's investigation.

As I put on underwear, I heard the door open and Jyanette come in.

I glanced up to see her carrying a huge dress bag.

"You're here?" she said, looking guilty.

"Yeah, I slept after you left," I said. "Is that your dress? It looks huge."

"Yeah… um… it's bigger than I planned. But, you know, I have to match the other bridesmaids."

"Can I see it?" I asked.

"See it?" she repeated.

"The dress?" I said. Why was she acting weird?

"Oh, you'll see it at the wedding, when I'm wearing makeup and looking good. Besides, isn't it bad luck to see the maid of honor's dress before the ceremony?"

"I believe that's only the bride."

"No point taking chances," she said and hung the bag in the closet.

"Why are you acting so strange?" I asked.

She smiled. "I'm not acting strange. I'm just surprised you're here."

As I stepped closer, she put up her hands to stop me, staring at my bare chest. "Are those bruises?"

I attempted a grin. "Only a little one."

"Goddamn it, Len," she complained. "Are there any other major wounds I need to be concerned about? You know we're taking photos in two days! What am I going to do with you?"

"Jyanette—"

"Seeing you bruised and battered is not a turn on for me, Doctor."

"We have to get going. The séance is in an hour."

"Get dressed. I can yell at you in the car."

I quickly put on the rest of my clothes, which Jyanette handed to me. She bent to pick up something off the floor.

"Here's your wallet. It must have fallen from your pocket."

Jyanette did not yell at me on the drive over as threatened. Instead, she didn't speak at all, and the ride was silent as we pulled into the lot for the Golden Era and headed to the elevator that would take us to the top floor again.

As we came to the stairway, Tyrone waited next to the open false wall. He nodded to Jyanette and drew close to us. "If we get nothing tonight, this case is going to be moved to the cold case file. We just don't have anything we can run with."

"But you still think it was a suspicious death?" Jyanette asked.

"My gut tells me it was, but without evidence and a vague ME's report, I have nothing to go on." He turned to me. "Maybe you can have the ghost testify?"

"I can try," I said.

We walked up the steps and down the hall to the séance room. As we opened the door, there was the flash of a camera, and I looked up to see Grace Matthews had joined us again.

Bonnie Summers stood next to her. "Detective, Doctor Wise, and Ms. Emery. Glad you could all be here. Help yourself to a drink."

I stepped forward and stopped. Jyanette and Tyrone stopped with me.

On the shelf behind the séance table, in a new display case, was the revolver from the previous séance.

I faced Bonnie. "Why did you put that back?"

Bonnie brightened and walked around the large table to get to it. "We thought it added to the decor. But don't worry, this time we bolted the display case to the shelf. And this case isn't glass, it's bulletproof polycarbonate, locked to the base. You can't open it without a key."

The three of us stared.

"How did you get a bulletproof plastic cover so fast?" I asked.

"There's a place here in Vegas that does the work," Bonnie said and looked at the weapon standing upright in the display. "We wanted to make sure it wasn't going anywhere this time. Now, how about that drink?"

We headed over to the bar where Will Anderson was working. Will was the one witness in the room Tyrone and I hadn't questioned.

Will placed a glass of water out for me and poured a flute of champagne for Jyanette.

"You remembered," Jyanette said.

Will smiled. "Certainly Ms. Emery. It was easy enough."

"And you remembered my name as well," Jyanette said. "I'm impressed."

The door opened, and Celeste Moon, Jackson DeHart, and Robert Wells came into the room. Wells immediately came over and shook Tyrone's hand.

"I noticed that Grace Matthews is here again," I said.

Wells grinned. "She's here to document the séance. Think about it, gentlemen. I mean, I'm sorry Sal Lombardo died, but a séance to find out how he died? Photos of that will sell out this show for years."

This annoyed me, and I saw Tyrone was not pleased either.

"Mr. Wells, this is not a publicity stunt. This is an attempt to find the truth," Tyrone said.

"And the Golden Era Casino supports that effort. Don't worry, I've instructed Ms. Matthews to focus on Celeste, and keep everyone else in a soft focus. Unless Sal Lombardo's ghost shows up, at which point the camera should be on him."

"Does she use film or a memory card?" I asked.

"She's old school and so she tells me she's using a high-speed, high-resolution film," Wells explained.

"You should have consulted me," Tyrone said, and looked at me. "Will this affect you, Doctor?"

"No, Detective," I said. "Sometimes a camera at a séance is a good thing, especially if it uses film."

Wells frowned. "Why is film a better choice for a séance?"

"I can answer that," Celeste said, getting her glass of water from Will. "Paranormal activity can affect digital devices, while film is unaffected."

I smiled. "That's the reason."

Wells' smile widened. "Good, then it's settled. Jackson is going to get into the control booth now, just like he would during a regular show."

Wells nodded to Jackson, and he went out into the hall, touched the correct piece of trim, and the door opened inward. In a moment, he concealed himself in the control booth.

Desirée Longing and Connor Maxwell were the next arrivals, and Desirée made it a point to approach the detective and quietly said, "I'm only here because my lawyer advised me to cooperate."

As she headed for the bar, I whispered, "Nice of her to show up."

Tyrone leaned in close to murmur back, "Yes, and Wells using this for publicity never entered her mind."

"Do you want to talk to Connor about his aunt before we start?"

"No, after the séance would be the better time. Also, if Desirée wants to demand her lawyer again, I can take the pair of them downtown and they can wait there until he arrives."

"Effective," I agreed.

I looked to the doorway as Rosie Graham came in, wearing her black stage-hand outfit, but she seemed unconcerned she was underdressed. She wore the pentagram earrings again, and I also noticed the large ring on her middle finger. She wasn't wearing it the last time I saw her at Three Kings. Noticing its size, she probably couldn't wear it while working with lighting equipment.

Finally, lumbering up the steps, was Big John Rossi, the final participant. He was panting and sweating. He approached Tyrone. "I hope this is it, Detective," he wheezed. "Those steps are murder."

"Let's hope so," Tyrone said.

"Yeah," Rossi said and pulled a cloth handkerchief from a back pocket to mop his brow. "I'm thinking maybe those private sessions with Celeste are a better choice."

He moved to the bar and saw Celeste holding a glass of water. "Could I get water, too?"

Smiling, Will poured water into another glass, added several ice cubes, and handed it to Big John, who smiled and took a large swallow.

"Anyone else?" Will asked, gesturing at the bar.

Desirée and Connor each got champagne, and Rose asked for water as people went to their seats.

I spoke up, "Please be in the seats you were during the last séance."

"Who will be in Lombardo's seat?" Connor asked.

"I'll be taking that one," Tyrone said as he moved to the table.

I walked with Jyanette, pulled her seat out for her. Then I walked past Celeste's empty seat and sat, quickly folding up my cane to put it in my lap.

With glances at each other, the attendees moved to their seats.

Celeste took her place at the head of the table, strategically positioned to command attention with the special lighting focused on her.

"Let us all unite our thoughts and energies," Celeste said. As she spoke, the lights dimmed as before. She gestured and the candles lit by themselves.

"It's déjà vu all over again," quipped Connor.

Desirée moved her and Connor's empty champagne flutes to the floor, as did Jyanette, though hers was still half-full.

Rosie picked up her water glass and Big John's and said to him, "Should we move these?"

This startled Big John, but he said, "Oh, yeah." He drained the glass before putting it on the floor.

"Now we must join hands," Celeste said, holding out her hands. "All of us tonight must focus on the same goal. This intensifies our energy and increases our chances of success."

I held hands with Celeste on one side of me, and Big John on the other.

Celeste went on with the script. "Each of you are here for a reason. If there is someone you wish to contact, let your thoughts go to them." She closed her eyes dramatically. "Tonight we gather to seek guidance from the spirit world. We welcome any spirits who are near us to join our circle. Please make your presence known."

On cue, the table rose a few inches, and carefully returned to the floor. This time, it surprised no one.

"From this point on, no matter what, we must not break the circle," Celeste said. "We reach out to make contact. Is there anyone with us this night?"

Danger...

I received the buzz and glanced around as pain stabbed through my brain, forcing me to wince. I refocused and concentrated on my mental barriers and forced my eyes open to watch the planchette as it moved over to the word HELLO, and the flames on the pair of candles rose and fell back.

I looked over at Celeste and noticed her face suddenly contorted in agony, with sweat collecting on her brow. She was experiencing the same thing I felt, but didn't have the training to push it away.

I shut my eyes and held onto the hands next to me, focusing on expanding my mental barrier.

The surrounding air seemed to crackle with an unseen force as I felt a dark, cold shadow descend upon us. I had Celeste's hand in a tight grip. I relaxed a bit, not wanting to hurt her.

A sound like a rushing wind went through the room, and quickly changed into whispers all around us, climbing in volume. Around the table, everyone exchanged frightened glances.

Celeste looked better, but I saw the panic in her eyes as she made her best efforts to regain control of the session.

The planchette vibrated, at first a little and then more dramatically.

"That's impossible," Wells hissed, looking at the shuddering, heart-shaped wooden board.

As we watched, the planchette rose — a mere inch at first, but soon rose higher and higher, defying gravity.

I felt a wave of cold energy pass through my body and fought to block myself from the force trying to use me.

The planchette hovered in mid-air, and then rotated, slowly at first and then spinning faster and faster.

DANGER...

I yelled out. "Everyone, shut your eyes and cover your head!"

I released both Celeste's and Big John's hands. The others were stunned by my words, but everyone put their heads down and covered them with their hands.

With a sudden violent jerk, the spinning planchette exploded with a powerful force into countless fragments, sending shards of the board flying everywhere. There was the sound of breaking glass as pieces of wood struck the overhead chandelier and glass rained down upon us, along with the wood debris.

One of them screamed as the shards of the planchette embedded themselves into the table.

Following the explosion, the energy in the room abruptly shifted — a tangible weight lifted from the air, and the chaos dissipated as quickly as it had arrived.

I turned to face the corner where I'd seen the shadow of a woman in my earlier vision. There stood a full-body manifestation which I could plainly see was Sarah Lewis. She appeared like a real person in the room with us.

She knew I could see her.

I glanced at Celeste, who raised her head and was staring at Sarah as well. Stumbling to my feet, the spirit raised its hand, and I fell back into my chair as if propelled.

At that moment, the lights came up full, and Jackson burst through the door and into the room, out from his hidden compartment.

When I looked back at the corner, Sarah was gone.

Grace had hit the floor when I yelled out and now she slowly rose to her feet, and as if she couldn't help herself, snapped off several photos.

I got up and slid past Celeste to get to Jyanette. She only had a few cuts on her hands, all of them minor. She raised her head, and I was relieved to see she was unhurt. Her lovely face didn't even have a scratch.

She looked a little dazed, but murmured, "I'm fine. Check on the others."

I moved to Celeste. Drained of strength, she slumped in her chair, shaken but looking grateful the worst was over.

Everyone around the table looked like they were in a state of shock. People were bleeding from small wounds caused by the exploding planchette and the falling glass.

Wells rose unsteadily to his feet and grabbed the phone on the wall, and did the same thing as last time, calling for medical personnel.

Rossi...

I felt the buzz and shifted my eyes to Big John, who had leaned forward and put his hands over his head when I yelled the warning.

He had not moved.

"Detective," I said, and pointed at Rossi.

Tyrone was examining the cuts on his own hands, but now swiftly moved around the table to Rossi. The large man elicited no response.

Tyrone put his hand to Rossi's neck, then pulled one of his limp hands free and checked the pulse on his wrist.

I met Tyrone's eyes, and he shook his head.

Big John Rossi was dead.

11. SOLEMN STUDY

Will Anderson raised his head from behind the bar, where he had ducked from my shouted warning.

Mr. Wells got up and plodded unsteadily for the door, and Bonnie Summers walked over to him.

Tyrone spoke up. "Nobody leaves. You're all witnesses."

"I was just going to go to my office," Wells said.

"Sorry. We have to look you over. Your hands are bleeding," the detective told him. "You called the medical team?"

Wells looked at his hands. Thin streams of blood trickled down his fingers. "Yes, they'll be here soon."

He collapsed into a chair near the door and Bonnie sat next to him.

I looked at Jyanette. "Are you sure you're alright?"

"A bit shaken up," she said. At this point, there were tiny droplets of blood on her hands from the wounds. She glanced over at Celeste. "She needs your help more than I do."

I went to Celeste Moon. Celeste clung to me as I helped her get out from behind the séance table to sit in one of the spectator chairs.

"It — it consumed my mind like a shadow," she said, her voice dry and cracked. "It's all my fault."

"How?" I asked.

"I didn't ask for protection when we started. I always ask for protection and for only good spirits to enter our circle." She shook her head and looked over at Big John, still slumped on the table. "I forgot to do that tonight."

"This isn't your fault. An entity forced its way in."

"Did you sense it?"

"The entity, yes."

"No," she said. "The portal. We opened a portal."

I felt it during the séance. The spirit was using our minds to supply herself with the energy she needed to destroy the planchette, as well as push me into my chair.

She stared at the empty corner where Sarah had appeared. "The spirit killed Mr. Rossi."

"We don't know that," I replied.

A team of four EMTs arrived quickly, followed by Kofi Johnson. Two of them eased Rossi's body onto the floor, while the others cared for the minor injuries of the guests.

"You're bleeding, sir," an EMT said and touched a gauze pad to my head. I hadn't noticed my own wounds. The back of my hands had multiple cuts and abrasions. I held the gauze pad the female EMT placed on my head, and I felt it was wet with blood. Blood dripped down one side of my face.

The leader of the medical team spoke up from where he sat treating Wells. "What happened here?"

"A piece of wood exploded in the center of the table," I explained, and holding the gauze pad on my head, pushed myself up to go to Tyrone, who had his cell phone to his ear. "Is LVPD coming?"

"They're on their way," Tyrone assured me. "We were lucky the hotel has EMTs on staff."

"We need to get forensics and the medical examiner attendants in here to remove the body."

Tyrone nodded. "We need to move the witnesses to a meeting room and get statements." He turned to Wells. "Mr. Wells, is there someplace we can move people to hold them for a while?"

"We'll use the Longhorn room, like last time," Bonnie said, and she went to the wall phone to call someone.

The photographer slipped between Tyrone and me. "What the Hell happened?"

I looked down at Big John Rossi laid out on the floor. "Hell happened."

We headed to the large meeting room one floor below the séance room. Two of the EMTs went with us, and Tyrone stayed up in the séance room to navigate between the LVPD, the forensic team, and the morgue attendants.

I held Jyanette's hand, carefully, as we both had cuts, and we walked down together.

"Great," she whispered. "Bad enough you get hurt. Now I can't show my hands in the wedding photos."

We arrived at the meeting room, and each of us collapsed into seats like a group that survived a battle.

Maybe we had.

The female EMT moved to Jyanette and quickly cleaned and put several small Band-Aids on her hands. She moved to me and wiped the blood off my face and put a fresh gauze bandage on the scalp wound.

"Will I need stitches?" I asked as she dressed the wound.

"No, it's not that deep. Head wounds bleed a lot. Once it scabs over, you can cover it with your hair."

Jyanette was removing debris from her own hair, being careful not to cut herself as she found shards of glass and wood.

"I'm lucky," Jyanette said, pulling a brush from her purse. "I've got this thick, curly hair, not straight like yours. It protected my head."

"I'm glad."

"I guess we're not going to make that dinner with your parents tonight," she said and sighed.

"I forgot," I said. "I'd better text my dad and let him know."

"I already did," Jyanette said.

I smiled. "You're the best."

"That's the right thing to say."

"Be careful with my hands," Desirée yelled to the woman EMT, not with her little girl voice but as a full-throated bitch. "I have a show tomorrow." She glanced over at Wells. "If my face is scarred, I'm going to sue!"

Connor attempted to calm Desirée and keep her still so the female EMT could treat her minor scratches.

One of the male EMTs was treating Rosie, taping closed a shallow cut on her forehead, and bandaging several cuts on her hands.

It was fortuitous that I yelled the warning in time and that everyone paid heed, or it could've been a lot worse.

The leader of the medical team spoke up from where he sat treating Wells. "What happened here?"

"A planchette exploded," Jyanette said.

"A what?" the man asked, confused.

"A piece of wood exploded in the center of the table," I explained. "It contained a large magnet inside. I don't know where it ended up, but it could've given someone a concussion."

I pushed myself up with my cane and felt my leg complaining. I went over to Grace Matthews, the photographer, who was sitting off by herself looking at her camera, as stunned as the rest of us.

"Ms. Matthews, is it possible to get your film developed? It would be a help to the police."

"Hm?" She gazed up at me. "Um... I normally develop the film myself... and I can't leave..."

"I see."

Her eyes became clear, and she snapped her head up. "I could call my assistant. He knows his way around my darkroom, and he's a photographer himself. You'd want prints, right?"

"Of everything you have. And from the last séance as well."

"I shot two roles of thirty-six tonight, and three rolls last time."

"That will help. How long would it take to develop the film and make prints?"

She considered it. "A few hours, if Henry is even available. Do I need permission from the police?"

"Call your assistant and I'll see what can be done."

She pulled out her phone and stepped away from the group into an unoccupied corner of the room.

Tyrone came through the door with a uniformed officer by his side and once again, it was Officer Rodriguez. She peered around the room as I noticed the Band-Aids on Tyrone's hands. One of the EMTs had taken care of him upstairs.

"Ladies and gentlemen," Tyrone announced. "You all have met LVPD Officer Michelle Rodriguez. She's going to bring each one of you, one by one, into the meeting room next door. There, she will take your statement and your contact information. After that, you may leave. Thank you for your cooperation."

I approached Tyrone and murmured, "I asked the photographer to call her assistant. He's going to collect the film and develop it. I wanted to make sure that was okay with the police."

Tyrone nodded. "Good call. I'll run the request by my captain and make sure it's all right. At least one of us is thinking clearly. I'm still trying to process what I saw."

"I would define it as poltergeist activity, but it was at a level I've seldom seen before."

Tyrone frowned. "You've seen shit like that before?"

"Things moving on their own, a spirit controlling a person, and worse," I said. "But this case was unusual."

Tyrone shook his head. "Suddenly, I'm sorry I got involved in this at all."

"But forensics is here, right? Are they upstairs?'

"They just got here. They're going over everything in that room. Why?"

I took Tyrone's arm and stepped back. "Because I don't think the ghost killed Rossi."

Tyrone glanced around the room. "You think it was someone here?"

"There are several possibilities. Can you tell the team to make sure they bag and check every glass in that room? Even the ones on the bar?"

He looked at me, his cop sense kicking in "You think that in the commotion someone could have switched a clean glass for the one that Rossi drank from, is that it?"

"That's what I was thinking."

Tyrone grinned. "McGee said you were good."

"Only because I had excellent teachers. Bill was one of them," I said.

Tyrone slipped out of the room, and Officer Rodriguez asked Connor Maxwell, aka Lewis, to join her in the next room. I would have preferred to be in on the questioning so I could ask him about his aunt, Sarah Lewis. But I knew Rodriguez was only taking statements, and any serious interrogation would have to take place later.

"You! Doctor guy!" Desirée called out from across the room.

I looked up to see the showgirl stomping over in my direction. All pretense of the seductress was gone; her once warm smile twisted into a malicious sneer, contempt filled her glittering eyes.

Jyanette got up to intercept the woman as she stomped toward me, and I gestured to her not to. With an annoyed look, Jyanette returned to her seat.

"You're the big expert the police called in," Desirée said as she drew near. "Tell me, what happened up there?"

"We experienced poltergeist activity," I said. "At an extremely high level."

She folded her arms and continued to glare at me. "If you didn't yell out, I could have lost an eye."

"We're lucky all that happened were some scratches and bruises."

"Was it a ghost? Is that what you're saying?" she challenged.

I felt compelled to tell her what I saw. "Yes, it was a ghost."

"Really?" she said, unimpressed.

"Yes. The ghost of a woman, a reporter named Sarah Lewis, who disappeared years ago. I don't know how she ended up in this hotel, but I think there's a connection between her and Sal Lombardo."

I'd often heard the expression "folded like a cheap camera", yet seeing someone actually collapse was something entirely new for me. Abruptly, Desirée's sneer melted, and she fell in a heap.

I pulled her into one of the nearby chairs against the wall. We were at the far end of the room from the others, and I was lucky I could seat her without falling myself.

I was unprepared for the wracking sobs shaking her body.

Everyone was looking at the two of us, and I spoke up. "She's all right, just a little upset, that's all."

The others seemed to accept this and went back to their own conversations as I comforted the crying Ms. Longing.

"Disappeared," she groaned. "God, it could've been me that ended up that way."

I handed her a tissue. "Something happened to you, something bad. Did Lombardo molest you?"

She took the tissue and nodded, and I knew this was hard for her. "Y-Years ago."

I took her free hand. "You can tell me."

"My f-father worked for Lombardo as a dealer, and Lombardo met me at the company picnic. He t-talked to me, and the way he looked at me creeped me out. My father took me to see him when I was fourteen."

"Your father?" I said, shocked.

"Y-yes. He told my mom that we were going camping, but he actually took me to the Sphinx, and up to Sal's special office."

"The room that is now the séance room?" I said.

"Yes. My f-father left me there. Sal started off being nice, offered me a drink, but I said no."

"Could you get out of the room?"

"I didn't think so. I just kept asking when my father was coming back. Lombardo told me he wasn't and tried to kiss me. I backed away, told him to leave me alone, and he — he slapped me. He tore my clothes, threw me on his desk and he — held me down and raped me."

She sobbed again, and I handed her another tissue.

"After he was done, he just left me there. Finally, my dad came back, and he acted all concerned and took me to one of the hotel rooms. My clothes were all torn. He went out and got me new ones.. The next day he takes me home, but he says I mustn't tell mom, that it's our secret. He owed money and the mob would've killed him if he hadn't given me to Lombardo."

"And all these years you've told no one," I said.

She shook her head. "A few days later, I got real sick, with a temperature and everything. I found out later from my gynecologist that I had vaginal tearing, and that caused an infection. It meant I couldn't have kids."

I gritted my teeth, pushing back the anger I felt. "I'm so sorry. How could he have done this to you in a hotel office? Wouldn't someone hear?"

She looked at me in pure misery. "You've seen that room, hidden away like it is. I realized it when I went up for the séance that it was the room where that bastard raped me."

"Why did you stay for the séance if that room had terrible memories for you? Sal was right there."

Her jaw tightened, and her eyes were full of fury. "I wanted to see him, to see that he was a pathetic old man who could no longer hurt me. But it was better than that. I got to watch him die."

Connor and Officer Rodriguez returned, and Rodriguez asked Rosie to join her.

Connor saw Desirée and I, huddled close together talking, and he didn't like it. He stormed over, glaring at me. "What the hell do you think you're doing?"

Desirée put her hands on Connor's forearms. "It's okay. I had things I wanted to tell him."

Connor was undeterred and pointed at my face. "You keep away from my girl."

As soon as we locked eyes with each other, something inside of me shifted. "Why didn't you tell us that Sarah Lewis was your aunt?"

He looked at me like I'd grown a second head. "My aunt? She died years ago, when I was a kid. What does that have to do with anything?"

I realized this was true. What I thought was a clue was nothing.

As I stood staring at him, I glimpsed directly into his mind and I saw the way he treated women. He had been involved with many over the years. Each time, he was a user, taking advantage anyway he could. I glimpsed the way he treated them and used them for his own benefit.

I looked away from him, breaking the connection as I rose to my feet, anger filling me. "So Desirée is your girl. More like your convenience."

Connor looked at me, shock on his face. "What?"

"You only spend time with her when one of your other women isn't available, or you need some money," I spat, wondering why this made me so angry. "She doesn't mean a damn thing to you. She's just a warm place for you to stick it."

Desirée stared at me, shocked by my words. I can't say I blamed her.

"If you had any consideration, you'd treat this woman with respect and not be 'doing a gig' when you're really out banging a woman you met online."

Desirée now looked at Connor. "Is that true? That gig you had that took you all night? That wasn't real?"

Connor turned bright red and stepped back. "He's crazy. You watch your step, buddy."

Connor turned away and headed back to the group.

Desirée gazed at me. "How did you know he did a gig last week?"

"I just saw it in his mind," I said. "Like with you the other day. I'm sorry. I had no right to peek into your mind the way I did. You were correct to be mad at me."

"But it didn't work with me. How did you look into his mind so easily?"

"It's easy with some people," I explained. "After what happened to you with Sal, I can see why you didn't want people to do anything that invaded your mind."

She glanced at Connor and then back at me. "Thanks for the apology, and for listening to me now."

"You didn't deserve what happened to you." I peered over at Connor. "And to be honest, you deserve better now."

She followed my glance. "I think you're right, but I don't know if I'm up to it."

I returned to Jyanette. Out of the corner of my eye, I glimpsed Sarah in the room. She was not glaring at me, but watched me with an odd expression on her face. It surprised me so much I turned in her direction.

She was gone.

I had a feeling I would see her again soon.

12. INVESTIGATING INSTITUTION

I t took several more hours, as Rodriguez interviewed each of us in turn.

At one point, Bonnie Summers took me aside from the others. She handed me a business card with her name and number on it. "Here, take this. You can call me day or night."

I took the card and looked at her, confused.

"You're working with the police. I want to be kept in the loop. I mean, what you're allowed to tell me."

I frowned, but she went on. "Mr. Wells isn't thinking clearly, but two people dying puts the hotel under a terrible burden. What if a relative wants to sue?"

"I don't think—" I attempted.

"Doctor, I've been in the casino industry since I left college. People file lawsuits over anything these days. These deaths will get the show a lot of publicity, but it opens us up to litigation. If you can let me know anything you find out, I would appreciate it."

I nodded. It was good to have her contact information in case I needed to get into the séance room again.

The crowd dwindled as each person gave their statement, and Rodriguez released them. She saved me for last and questioned me in the Longhorn room with Tyrone and Jyanette there.

She asked me to tell my observations and impressions, and I kept it as normal as I could. I didn't mention the painful mental attack or the appearance of Sarah. I stuck to the observable facts, the strange sounds, the lights, and the exploding planchette.

"What exactly is your profession, Doctor?" she asked at one point.

"I am a university professor. I teach classes on parapsychology."

"And Detective Washington called you in as a consultant?" she asked, taking notes.

"I have experience with the paranormal."

"Would you call what happened tonight paranormal?"

"I sure as shit would," muttered Tyrone, sitting a few feet away.

"As I told Detective Washington, what we experienced is called poltergeist activity. It happens when an entity lashes out in an uncontrolled environment."

"That's what you believe this to be?" she asked, her eyebrows raised. "A ghost that got loose?"

From the corner of my eye, I caught Sarah standing at the other end of the room. Her image was clearer now. She was wearing a full blouse and a dark skirt. I turned to look at her straight on, but once again, there was nothing there.

"Are you all right, Doctor?" she asked.

Shutting my eyes, I turned back to Rodriguez and rubbed the bridge of my nose. "I'm tired."

"I think we have everything we need right now," Rodriguez said and closed her notebook.

I walked over to Tyrone. "Can you put me in contact with the medical examiner? I want to sit in on the autopsy."

"Len, I have to tell you the ME is very possessive of his morgue. I doubt he'll allow it."

"I'll try to convince him."

Tyrone exhaled heavily. "I'll text you his number in the morning. If you convince him, I'll owe you a drink."

As Jyanette and I headed for the car, I needed my cane more than ever. Once on the road, I told her of my talk with Desirée and her rape at the hands of Sal Lombardo.

"You realize that gives her motive," Jyanette said. "And Rossi was Lombardo's enforcer. It gives her a reason for killing him as well."

"Who's playing detective now?" I asked. "I don't think she ever met Rossi. Her father was the one who gave her to Lombardo to pay off a mob debt."

Jyanette shook her head. "I feel bad for her."

"You looked like you were ready to punch her when she approached me."

"Damn straight," she said. "No one pushes my man around."

"Down, tiger. She became hard because she needed to. And she still involves herself with men like Connor who take advantage of her."

We parked and made our way through the casino. The lights on the machines seemed to pulse, and the bells rang as the pair of us hobbled through luxurious hotel corridors. Once again I was overwhelmed by all of the input, and I was grateful when I reached the suite door. I fiddled with my key card to gain entrance, finding my hands trembled under the strain of the day's events.

"Len?" Jyanette said, looking at my hand.

"I'm okay," I said as I finally got the door open. "Long day."

I went into the sitting room and collapsed onto the small sofa, grabbing an orange from the fruit basket. Jyanette headed directly into the bedroom.

I finished the orange, and Jyanette appeared in the doorway. She was wearing only an airy and delicate nightgown draping her lithe form like an elegant dream. As she moved to me, the sheer fabric billowed around her body as it skimmed her skin, revealing each curve on her hips and breasts. Silk cascaded down her back, creating a sensual silhouette which bewitched me from across the room.

She quickly closed any remaining distance between us, wrapping herself tightly around me as her diaphanous gown whispered secrets against my skin. Our lips met in a tender kiss; for a moment in this hectic day in the city of lights and noise, I found peace.

I pulled back. "Sorry tonight was so—"

"Sh!" She ran her hands through my hair and touched the bandage on my head. As she pulled my lips to her, all worries and exhaustion vanished quickly into an exciting, passionate embrace. Her hands slid gently around my waist. Our gazes locked with such intensity we seemed capable of setting fire to everything around us.

As passion overtook us, we stumbled backward toward the bed as our instincts took over. Acting without rational thought or consideration, we slid clothing away and off; touching, tasting, whispering, and moaning. We surrendered ourselves to love's spellbinding dance, as we had only each other to consider.

In the afterglow, we lay snuggled, tangled under soft cotton sheets.

"That was unexpected," I gasped.

"We needed it — I needed it." She caressed my face and stared into my eyes. "What happened up there? It scared the hell out of me. I needed to do something that celebrated life."

"Consider me well-celebrated."

"Me, too," she sighed.

"I have to figure out how two men could die like that."

"This ghost you saw, this poltergeist? She could move objects. Could she have reached inside their bodies? Given them a heart attack?"

I shook my head. "Poltergeists throw things, anything from a rock to a knife, but actually reaching into a body? Doctor Kohl suggested the energy field around our bodies we call the aura acts as a shield against supernatural attacks. It stops a spirit from reaching into our body. That's why a poltergeist manifests objects in a room."

"What do you think killed them?"

"I'm not sure. The séance was strange, and Ms. Moon claims we opened a portal."

"A portal? A portal to what?"

"I don't know."

She put her head against my chest. "You know that tomorrow is the rehearsal and the rehearsal dinner. We have to be there, case or no case."

"I know. I'm sorry I've been away as much as I have."

"I've found things to do, like shopping. Do you like my new nightgown?"

"Very much," I said and kissed her head. "You are a vision."

"It's late, and now that I've had my wicked way with you, we need to sleep." With a kiss, she pulled herself free and moved to her side of the bed.

I closed my eyes and felt myself falling asleep almost instantly.

Suddenly I sat up, wide awake. I felt like I'd only just lay down, but the clock on the nearby end table read 4:10.

I turned over and saw a dim form in the room's corner where shadows were deepest.

I rolled from the bed, grabbed a hotel robe from a hook on the wall, and threw it on. The shape in the corner gradually grew clearer as an outline formed. As I watched, it became distinct until the figure of a woman appeared. Her body looked almost solid, with a faint blue light emanating from her.

Sarah looked at me, a puzzled expression on her face. She walked through the open door to the sitting room.

Not knowing what else to do, I followed.

I silently closed the door between the rooms. She sat primly in the chair opposite the small sofa, like someone waiting for a job interview.

Pulling a bottle of water from the small refrigerator, I took a sip. I stared at her solid-looking shape as I put the cap back on and put the bottle on the table between us. I pulled the robe closer to my body, as the room had grown colder.

"Are you really here? Or is this just a dream or a nightmare?"

The spirit looked at me, opened her mouth as if to speak, and closed it again.

"You're Sarah, aren't you?" I asked. "Sarah Lewis?"

She looked surprised, but nodded.

"Can you talk? You only have to project your thoughts, and I'll understand."

Her hand went to her mouth, and she shook her head.

I had to keep it to "yes" and "no" questions. Now I wished I'd brought the ouija board with me.

"Did you die in that office? Is that why you're in that room?"

She nodded.

"Did Sal Lombardo kill you?"

She raised her head, her eyes aflame, and the bottle on the table flew off and fell to the floor.

"Stay calm," I said, retrieving the fallen bottle and putting it back on the table. "I only want to help you."

She gathered herself and sat back in the chair.

"How can you be here?" I asked.

She met my eyes and pointed at me.

"Me? You followed me?"

She nodded.

I considered it. "Celeste said we opened some kind of doorway tonight. Did that give you the freedom to manifest wherever you want?"

She glanced up at the ceiling and then pointed at me a second time.

"You need me? Is it my energy, my psychic ability?"

She nodded.

I sat back on the sofa. "Why are you still here, Sarah? Why haven't you moved on?"

An angry expression appeared on her face.

"Were you trapped in that office?"

She nodded vigorously.

"I have to ask you this. Did you kill Sal Lombardo and Big John Rossi?"

She glared at me, and the water bottle fell off the table a second time and I heard a noise as the fruit fell from the large fruit basket behind me.

I held up my hands in a pose of surrender. "Stay calm. I am sure you hated them."

The basket stopped shedding fruit, and Sarah drew a deep breath, calming herself.

It is rare to see a full body manifestation of a spirit and it fascinated me that she did things such as drawing in a breath. Obviously, she didn't need to breathe. It was a habit from when she was alive.

I thought back to Doctor Kohl's lectures about the concept of lingering entities. It would thrill him to sit across from this disembodied spirit.

Of course, maybe only I could see her.

Plus, it was taking a toll on me. The room was growing steadily colder, and I was growing more and more exhausted. She was using the heat from the room, and my personal energy to manifest, and it was wearing me out.

"Were Sal and Big John murdered?" I said.

She smiled. She nodded.

"Do you know what killed them?"

She pointed at my bottle of water.

"Something they drank?" My breath came out in a fog. The room was freezing. "Who did it?"

She shook her head with a smug smile — and was gone.

A wave of dizziness washed over me. I fell back onto the sofa. Memories of my conversations with Doctor Kohl flooded my mind. Psychics tap into the residual energy of an event and often rely on their own mental energy to sustain contact with entities.

The reason cold temperatures characterize hauntings is the entity draws energy, like heat, from the atmosphere and the sensitive who detects it. Sarah had been feeding on my mental energy to manifest, and because of my exhaustion, she'd drained me and could no longer remain in a visible state.

I rose in the frigid room and stumbled back into the much warmer bedroom. I pulled a blanket from the closet and wrapped it around myself as I shivered.

I carefully got into bed, not wanting to wake Jyanette.

Sarah suggested it was something Sal and Big John drank. If she was correct, I needed to be there for the autopsy.

I woke to Jyanette shaking me. She wore the same silken nightgown but had pulled the terry cloth hotel robe over herself. "Len, there are a bunch of reporters outside our hotel room — again."

I sat up slowly, feeling groggy. The tiny cuts I received from the exploding planchette were aching, especially my head wound. "What?"

"I ordered breakfast and when the waiter arrived, a group of reporters were out there, shoving cameras and microphones in my face, yelling questions and taking photos. Len, they asked if I had any comment on the article that claimed you're a fraud!"

This brought me fully conscious. "Are you serious?"

"As a toothache. Len, they've started knocking on the door again. What do we do?"

I got out of bed and realized I couldn't confront whoever it was in only a bathrobe. I threw on socks, pants, and a shirt. "Did you call security?"

"I did."

"What were the reporters asking about?"

"They were all yelling. I only heard the fraud thing," she said. "What's happened since last night?"

"Let me get to my laptop."

"What about the people outside our room?" Jyanette demanded, as she poured us both a cup of coffee from a breakfast tray set out on a table.

"Just give me a minute," I said. "If they're camping outside our room, they're not going anywhere."

As we ate breakfast, I went to the website for the Las Vegas Journal. On the home page, once again, was a large photo of the séance room, this time with the planchette floating above the table, and the headline:

SECOND MAN DIES AT SÉANCE

I sighed. "Mr. Wells wanted publicity. I'm not sure this is what he was after."

Jyanette sat next to me on the sofa and we went through the article. Most of it was factually correct about what happened, but a box in the article shocked me. It showed a photo of me with the headline:

Leonard Wise, Parapsychologist or Pretender?

Psychic Faces Accusations of Deception

This differed from the article of only a few short days ago. Instead of praising my work with the police and my finding the treasure at Scudder House, it painted me in a negative light.

I read the article.

When the line between reality and illusion blurs, the extraordinary claims of self-proclaimed psychic, Leonard Wise, have sparked a wave of skepticism in the Las Vegas community. After the death of two people at a séance show, the question arises: is Dr. Wise a legitimate psychic or merely a skilled fraudster preying on the vulnerable?

Leonard Wise possesses a PhD and an unused medical degree. Though he has no medical license, he maintains the title of doctor as a sign of his own self-importance. Wise has gained a following in recent years, assisting the police and the FBI. He has claimed large rewards for his efforts. Supporters commend him for his supposed accuracy. However, whispers of doubt have echoed through the corridors of his once-loyal following.

Critics argue Wise's abilities are nothing more than smoke and mirrors, carefully cultivated tricks allowing him to dupe unsuspecting individuals and the police. They assert his predictions rely on vague generalizations and cold reading techniques, often employed by charlatans and tricksters throughout history.

Added to this, his brother is a well-known magician who makes his living fooling the public. Las Vegas Journal contacted investigator Doctor Henry Janis, an esteemed fellow at San Francisco University, who worked with Wise in the past.

"I investigated Leonard Wise after my work with him at Scudder House left me suspicious. What I discovered was a web of plausible deniability and a lack of concrete evidence to support his supposed psychic abilities."

Wise staunchly claims he is a scientist and denies all allegations of deceit. However, after the deaths of Sal Lombardo and John Rossi, Wise may have suggested a ghost killed them.

While the truth may remain elusive, it is undeniable the allure of the supernatural continues to captivate the public's imagination. Whether Leonard Wise is truly a scientific parapsychologist or an expert trickster perpetuating a ruse, only time will tell.

I closed my computer and exhaled loudly. "This doesn't help."

The article incensed Jyanette. "Who did they quote, Doctor Janis? Wasn't he the guy who was a pain in the ass when you were in California? The time you almost got killed saving his entire team?"

"The very one. I made him look bad, and he's never gotten over it."

"The article also claims you said a ghost killed those men?" Jyanette said and looked at me. "Is there any way that's true?"

I frowned. "No. Celeste made that suggestion. I didn't. There was an intense manifestation both times, but the spirit didn't kill them."

"How do you know?"

"I asked her last night. We had a chat in the sitting room."

She narrowed her eyes. "You talked to a ghost? Here?"

"Sarah Lewis. She's the ghost of the haunted hotel. I think Sal Lombardo killed her with Big John's help."

She looked at the door for our room as another knock came. "What do we do about them?"

"There's nothing we can do. I just hope Detective Washington doesn't regret asking me to be on the case."

"Do you think he will?"

"I don't know. As for the reporters, security will clear them eventually," I said. "Let me contact the detective and see if I'm still on the case."

I retrieved my phone and saw Tyrone texted me that morning with the name of Doctor Martin Peters and a cell phone number. I quickly texted him:

I saw the article today in the paper claiming I'm a fraud

Would you prefer to take me off the case?

After a moment, he responded.

Is that what you want?

I quickly responded I didn't want to be off the case, but I understood if he needed to let me go. He shot back:

Hell no

I don't care what they said.

Tell me what you need.

That was a relief. I quickly asked him to contact Grace Matthews about the photos from the two séances.

Jyanette came back into the room and I noticed she had dressed. I asked, "Where are you going?"

"I have things to do for the wedding," she explained. "Maid of honor, remember? With you on this case, I made plans." She glared at the door. "If I can get out of here."

"Not hiring a stud service, I hope."

She grinned. "No, you took care of that nicely, thank you."

"No, thank you. I promise you'll have the same service anytime you wear that transparent nightgown."

"Then it was an excellent investment. Do you know where the rehearsal is and what time?"

"Yes, I'll be there." I said, rising. "Let me run interference for you."

"That would be helpful."

We walked to the door, and I opened it as the reporters swarmed around me, shoving microphones in my face and firing off questions relentlessly.

"Doctor Wise—"

"Doctor Wise—"

Jyanette started down the hall.

"Who are you?" one reporter asked.

"Just a hooker he hired," Jyanette said, waved at me, and made a beeline for the elevator.

The scene was chaotic but electric, as the reporters struggled to capture any word and gesture I made.

It was time to take charge.

"Ladies and gentleman of the press," I bellowed, and even though I wasn't a trained stage performer like my brother, I got their attention. "The deaths at the Golden Era Casino are an open and ongoing case. I am aware of a scurrilous article claiming that I am a fraud. My only comment is that I am here to celebrate my brother's wedding. That is all."

I slammed the door and retreated into my room.

Retrieving my phone, I dialed the number Tyrone gave me for Doctor Peters.

"Coroner," was the response.

"Doctor Peters, I'm sorry to bother you. I'm calling about the large man brought to the morgue last night, John Rossi."

"Haven't gotten to him yet," Peters said in a world-weary tone. "How did you get this number, anyway?"

"I am working on a case with Detective Washington of the LVPD. My name is Doctor Wise—"

"Is this Sam Wise, the neurosurgeon?" Peters said, immediately perking up. "I've always wanted to meet you! I read your paper on deep brain stimulation—"

"I'm sorry Doctor," I said, "I'm Leonard Wise, his son."

"Oh," he responded, disappointed.

I sensed an opening. "However, my father is here in town. We'd like to sit in on your autopsy of Mr. Rossi."

"Both of you?" he said, considering it. "My autopsy bay is pretty small. If you don't mind tight quarters, I can arrange it."

"We'd be delighted to help if we can, Doctor. I also have a medical degree," I said, not mentioning I hadn't practiced medicine in nine years.

"Sam Wise assisting me? That would be something to tell the missus. I'll text you the address. Be here in an hour," he said and ended the call.

I looked at my phone. I promised my father would be there with no idea if I could deliver. Calling my father's cell phone, I waited nervously for him to pick up.

He answered on the first ring. "Morning, son. What's up?"

"Dad, can I ask a favor?"

"As long as it doesn't interfere with the rehearsal. Your mother would give me hell if I was late."

"I'd like to ask you to sit in on an autopsy. The ME is a fan of yours."

"I have fans?" he said, surprised. "That's a new one for me."

"I also need you to drive. Umm… Jyanette took our car."

"No problem, son. Give me ten minutes to get ready and I'll come to your room."

I glanced at the door. "Let's meet in the lobby. My room is being watched by reporters."

"Oh? Okay then, meet me near the elevators in the parking garage."

Taking advantage of the time I had, I hopped into the shower and dressed in fresh jeans, a shirt, and a sports coat.

I grabbed my cane and headed out, glad to see security had cleared the hall. Reaching the parking garage elevator, I found my father dressed in a full set of medical scrubs. I stopped and stared. "You brought scrubs with you? To Las Vegas?"

He smiled. "Never know when you're going to need them, son. Shall we go?"

"Yes, sir, Doctor Wise," I said, shaking my head.

We headed for the parking lot, and my father said, "Have you sat in on any procedures since medical school?"

"Not recently," I admitted. "Though I've sat in on autopsies at the Essex County morgue a few times."

"This'll be fun," he said as we got into his rental car.

Only my father would think going to an autopsy could be fun.

13. MEDICAL METHOD

"Wow, Samuel Wise," Peters said and took my father's hand in a hearty handshake when we arrived at the Clark County Coroner's Office. "After I got off the phone, I thought I was being scammed, but here you are! What are you doing in Las Vegas?"

"My other son's wedding. He's a headliner at the Majestic Odyssey Casino."

"I'm honored to have you here. Follow me. We've got your man on my table. It took several of us to do it."

We stopped in a small room where I changed into scrubs and all of us put on gowns, goggles, and masks before entering the autopsy bay.

The space was a good sized room filled with modern equipment and technology. Dr. Peters had neatly organized stainless steel tables and gleaming instruments on trays lining the walls, with powerful overhead lights illuminating the workspace. Strategic locations had high-resolution cameras and monitors mounted to provide clear visuals of the work.

A series of well-ventilated cabinets and storage units held a vast array of chemicals, tools, saws, and protective gear, including

heavy rubber gloves and face shields. Several high-tech devices —
advanced microscopes and imaging equipment — were nearby to
further aid in his analysis of each body.

Big John Rossi lay on a large table covered with a white sheet.

Peters reached up and started recording. "Doctor Martin
Peters, Coroner of Clark County, in the autopsy of John Rossi. I
have neurosurgeon, Doctor Samuel Wise, and Doctor Leonard
Wise assisting."

He quickly rattled off the overall appearance and the condition
of rigor mortis, then pulled out a measuring tape and took
measurements of height and weight, as well as arm span and foot
length. Finally, he described the eyes, ears, nose, mouth, and
palpation of the bones of the face.

Peters picked up the scalpel and offered it to my father.
"Would you like to make the Y-cut?"

My father chuckled under his mask. "He's a pretty solid fellow,
and I do a lot of delicate work. Would you mind if my son made
the cut?"

Peters turned and held out the scalpel to me. "Doctor."

Although medical school was a long time ago, I easily
remembered how to do a Y-cut. It was the first thing I'd learned
when we worked on cadavers, and it was as fresh in my memory
as the first day.

I took the scalpel and with the instrument in my hand, I felt a
sense of familiarity and ease, memories of my medical training
running through my mind. There was a rush of adrenaline, and I
experienced a sense of confidence in my ability to use it
effectively.

Dad was right, because of extra layers of fat, I had to cut deep, yet carefully enough that I didn't damage the underlying tissue. In a few brief minutes, I made the cut and peeled back the flesh from the underlying bones. It truly was like riding a bike. My hands did the work effortlessly.

I stepped back and turned to Peters. "You should be the one to remove the chest plate, Doctor."

"Agreed," Peters said, but his eyes were bright over his mask. "Though I am sure you're more than competent. That was some fine cutting, Doctor. Sam, where did you say he studied?"

"Johns Hopkins," my father said proudly. "Graduated first in his class and one year early."

"I don't doubt it," Peters said.

Soon Peters had the chest cavity open, and we were examining the internal organs. Since he was an expert on the procedure, he removed the stomach and prepared the stomach contents for analysis.

"This was the one who died at the séance, right?" Peters was saying as he removed the organs one at a time. "Like the other death, it was all over the papers."

"That's right," I told him.

Peters shook his head. "It looks very similar to the other man. There's nothing I can see that is a direct cause. What do you think, Sam?"

My father was looking at the heart and lungs. "There are small, straw-colored pleural effusions, bilateral diffuse pulmonary congestion, and acute pulmonary hemorrhaging within the right lung."

Peters nodded. "I saw the pleural effusions on that other man, Lombardo? I ventured it resulted from battling pneumonia at some point."

"But if both of them have it, what else could it be?" my father asked.

I glanced over to the corner of the room, and an image came to me. It was Sarah, pointing at a water bottle.

Muscarine...

The buzz went through my mind, and I turned to my father. "Could muscarine poisoning cause those symptoms?"

"Muscarine?" my father repeated and gazed at me, frowning. "You think he ate a poisoned mushroom?"

"I doubt it," Doctor Peters said. "The other man didn't have mushrooms in his stomach contents. Besides, he would have had other symptoms and been sick for hours beforehand."

I remembered both Lombardo and Big John Rossi each finished their drinks after the table moved. "Is it possible to mix it in a drink?"

Peters and my father exchanged a glance.

"How could a poison mushroom get into a drink?" Peters asked.

I paused. That was an excellent question, and I didn't have an answer other than I'd received a buzz.

"Is it possible for it to be in a liquid form?" I asked.

Peters looked up at the ceiling and exhaled heavily. "In theory, if you had the right equipment, you could synthesize the muscarine directly from the mushrooms. That would even make it more potent."

My father looked down at the body. "Muscarine poisoning would match the damage to the organs."

"It's also a substance we don't test for," Peters admitted. "I can put a rush on stomach contents and specifically ask them to screen for muscarine." He met my eyes. "Do you think someone murdered this man?"

All three of us looked down at the dead man on the table.

"Dad, I have to get this information to my police liaison," I said.

"I can finish up," Peters said jovially. "I'm just glad I met you, Sam."

"Tell you what, Martin, we got little chance to talk. How about we have lunch on Sunday, after my boy is married?"

"That would be great, Sam. My wife and I would love to have you and your wife over."

Dad and I headed back to the changing room, and soon I was back in my clothes. I gave him Peter's cell number, and we headed to the car.

As he drove us back to the hotel, I texted Tyrone the information about the possible poisoning.

As I returned my phone to my pocket, my father said, "Martin was right, son. That was some fine cutting. You always were a natural."

"Thanks," I said, not knowing where this was going.

"Have you considered going back to it?" he said.

"Surgery? Me?"

"You graduated with honors, and quit right before you started your residency. If you took some time, caught up a bit, you could be ready for a residency in six months."

I shook my head. "I don't think so."

"Len, I mean it. You gave it up because of your leg, and your inability to stand without the cane. Look how much better you are! You didn't need the cane during the autopsy. I'm telling you with some more physical therapy—"

"Dad," I said firmly. "I know you mean well, but it wasn't my path."

"Son, you just gave a reason that man died, which stumped a coroner and a surgeon. That was amazing."

"I... didn't do it, Dad. It just came to me. It was one of my glimpses of precognition."

"From the spirit world?" he said snidely.

"I don't know where it comes from."

"My point is you're a college professor, just getting by, living in a rented house. Len, in five years, you could be one of the top surgeons in the country. You could save lives. And these weird abilities of yours could only help you."

I felt my jaw grow tight. "I already save lives, Dad."

"At what cost to you? Constantly exposing yourself to danger, getting beaten up and injured? I can't think of a family dinner we've had where you didn't show up with stitches or a black eye because of your exploits. You think I didn't notice the cut on your head and those scratches on your hands today?"

I sighed. I'd forgotten about my injuries, and of course, my father would notice.

He went on. "And what about Jyanette? As a surgeon you could give her the life she deserves. Think about that or any children you want to have."

I clamped my jaw tight. This was not the time or the place to admit to my father Jyanette couldn't have children. And frankly, it was none of his business.

We pulled in front of the hotel, heading for the parking lot.

"Dad, let me off here. I have to meet the detective."

"Think about it, son. You have a talent for surgery."

I nodded, and using my cane, exited the car. As Dad pulled away, I thought about what he'd said. He was correct. The few quick minutes in the autopsy bay with the scalpel in my hand felt like I'd come home.

My father and mother lived simply, but I knew hospitals paid him a great deal of money over the years that he carefully invested. I knew he had no debt. He could easily afford elaborate trips with my mother and family vacations in faraway locales. Jyanette and I were struggling just to pay off our college debt.

It would mean more debt if I went back to medical school. But even if I got a scholarship, I wouldn't have any income. Also, what would happen to my parapsychology program at Garden State University? Without me, it would no longer exist.

As I thought about this, Tyrone pulled up, and I got into his car and tried to put my mind back to the case.

He glanced over at me. "From your text, I assume you saw the morning paper?"

I sighed. "I had another bunch of reporters knocking on my door this morning. Fortunately, security cleared them pretty quickly."

"I got a call from my captain. He complained about the paper printing that a ghost killed the two men and demanded to know if you were the one who suggested that. Fortunately, I talked him down, and explained that I said nothing to the press, and that it was Wells who brought in the photographer."

"I understand that," I said.

"I sent the information you texted me about that muscarine poison to the forensic team and told them to screen for it. Where does that stuff come from?"

"It's found in poisonous mushrooms. It's pretty nasty stuff. That genus of mushrooms have names like *destroying angel* and *death cap*. Weird thing is that symptoms usually take eight to twelve hours before it's fatal."

"Which means if that's what killed them, someone dosed them both earlier."

"No, they'd be too sick to attend the séance. When ingested as a mushroom, muscarine attacks the receptors of nerves and muscles, and it takes hours to build to a crisis and cause respiratory failure. But if someone gave Lombardo or Rossi a concentrated dose in their drinks, it would be a massive shock to the body and would take a much shorter time period. I'm leaning on the idea that someone could have distilled it and made it into a much more virulent form."

"Who do you think did it?"

I sighed. "It would need to be someone with equipment to make a distillation. Celeste Moon makes potions. If she has a laboratory distiller to make flower essences, it could accomplish what I'm talking about."

"Then we should visit her again," he said. "But it seems odd to me. First, why would she want to kill Sal or Big John? Second, if she did, why do it at the séance? It only makes her look bad."

"My other choice would be Will, the bartender. He handled the drinks," I said. "That certainly gives him the opportunity to poison both men. But I don't have a motive for him either."

"He worked under Lombardi when it was the Sphinx. Maybe there's some bad blood?"

"It's possible."

"I have his address from his interview with Rodriguez last night. Why don't we stop by and talk to him?"

We headed off, traversing the streets of Las Vegas in the bright sunlight.

We soon arrived at another community of condos. It seemed like everyone lived in a condo out here.

We parked, and Tyrone pointed. "That's his unit. He doesn't work until night, so he should be home."

We rang the bell on the first-floor apartment. Will opened it, saw us, and I saw the briefest flash of panic in his eyes.

He quickly smiled, apparently delighted we stopped by. "Detective, Doctor. This is a surprise."

"Sorry to arrive unannounced," Tyrone said. "May we come in? We want to get your impressions from last night."

"Sure," he said, and stepped aside.

The condo was an open-concept design that brought together the living room, dining area, and kitchen. Everything was immaculate, nothing out of place and everything so clean you could perform surgery.

"Very nice," I said.

"Yeah, I love this place," he said. "I like things simple."

"And clean," I noted.

"Let's just say I don't like messy situations," he chuckled. "Probably explains why I don't have kids — or a wife. Please sit down."

He led us to a sofa, and we sat. In a corner of the room, I noticed a card table and on top was a dealer's shoe, a clear plastic apparatus that holds multiple decks of playing cards. Three folding chairs were against the wall behind it.

I pointed at the table. "You have a dealer's shoe set up."

"Yeah, I… uh… use it to practice," Will said, and for a moment he sounded annoyed that I pointed it out. "With the tournament coming up, I want to make sure my skills are at their best."

Tournament…

I felt the buzz and decided I should press the matter. "The upcoming poker tournament at the Golden Era? Will you be dealing cards?"

I saw that nervous look a second time, quickly covered by his affable smile. "Probably. I mean, I know how to handle myself in that kind of setting. That's why I have to make sure my skills are up to par."

Tyrone pulled out his notebook. "You've been in the casino industry a long time, correct?"

"Twenty-five years. I started as a dealer after I turned twenty-one. Then, I went to bartender school, and that got me a lot of work. I could cover either a bartender or a dealer shift if someone didn't show up or was sick."

"I imagine that made you valuable," I said.

"Kept me working all these years."

"And you were familiar with Mr. Lombardo?" Tyrone asked.

"Sure, I was a bartender at some of his parties."

"About your impression of last night—"

"I told everything I saw to that officer."

I said, "Was there anything off about what anyone was drinking?"

"Off?" He looked perplexed. "What do you mean?"

"At either of the séances, did anyone have a specific drink that no one else ordered?"

He considered it for a moment. "Well, Sal had a scotch, but he wasn't the only one. Mr. Wells had scotch and so did that short woman in black."

"Rosie?" I suggested.

"Yeah, that was her name. Big John had water, Ms. Emery had champagne, which is what Desirée had as well."

"You know Desirée?" Tyrone asked.

"Who doesn't? They have billboards of her all over town." He looked upward, thinking. "Connor had a beer, and Celeste had water. Now, at the second séance, most people had water, except I poured champagne for Desirée, Connor, and your friend Jyanette."

"You have a remarkable ability to remember names," Tyrone said.

Except Rosie...

The buzz flashed through my mind. He remembered Jyanette's name and what she wanted to drink. Why didn't he remember Rosie? "Did you add anything to any of the drinks other than ice cubes?"

He frowned, and there was that flash of panic again. "Add anything to the drinks? What are you talking about?"

Tyrone's face was a mask. "We believe that someone poisoned the two victims."

"Poisoned?" Will said, and the affability was gone. "You think I poisoned Sal and Big John?"

"We're not sure where the poison came from," Tyrone said. "But you are the logical person to ask."

"Are you familiar with a substance called muscarine?" I added.

He glanced from Tyrone to me and back again. I saw that what I asked scared him. "Do I need a lawyer?"

"We're not accusing you of anything," Tyrone said. "However, forensics is going over everything at the bar. If you know anything, now would be the time to tell us."

He got up, his nervousness pushing him to move. "I didn't poison anyone."

"You seem agitated, Mr. Anderson," Tyrone said.

"You would be too, if you were me," Will said, pacing. "I mean, I got this tournament coming up and all. The last thing I need is to be accused of a crime. I could get thrown off and lose my big chance."

"Your big chance?" I repeated.

"Yeah," he said, and weighed his words. "I mean, to be a tournament dealer. They only pick the best guys, and you have to have a clean record."

"Calm down, Mr. Anderson," Tyrone said. "We just have to look into all the possibilities."

He glanced at his watch. "Look, I gotta get ready to go to work."

Tyrone rose. "That's fine, Mr. Anderson. We'll let you know if forensics finds anything."

I rose as well, and we headed for the door.

Once in the car, I said, "He knows something he's not telling."

"You don't need to tell me that, Len," Tyrone said. "I know when a witness is holding back."

"Sorry," I said.

"What about the setup on the card table?" he asked. "Are you buying the excuse that he needs to practice?"

"It's possible, or the poker tournament rules mean he has to deal in a way he isn't used to. I think we need to look into that."

"Do you have anything concrete, or is it just a hunch?"

"Actually, it was what I call a buzz."

"A buzz?" he repeated. "Oh yeah, those brief flashes you get. I'll get the tournament player list, see if any names pop."

"Good," I said and looked at my watch. "I have to head back for the wedding rehearsal. If I figure out what he's hiding, I'll let you know. Fortunately, I have help."

Tyrone glanced at me. "Besides me? Who's helping you?"

"The ghost of the Golden Era Hotel," I said.

Tyrone's eyes widened, and he broke into a belly laugh. "You got me, Len. I almost believed you for a second. I'll take another look into the background of our group, delve into any priors and see if I can find any other aliases they use." He glanced into the back seat. "Oh, I nearly forgot, I got those photos from Grace Matthews from the two séances." He reached into the back and handed me a thick envelope. "They're all eight by tens and pretty high quality even though the lighting went crazy."

"Do you need them?"

He shook his head. "No, Grace sent me copies through my email and brought me these prints. I went through them, but they just showed what we already knew and already saw."

"Can I review them?" I said.

"Knock yourself out, Len," Tyrone said as we headed down the wide roads.

Something else occurred to me. "Lombardo ran poker tournaments at the Sphinx, right?"

"Yeah, the Poker World Series started soon after he put the two hotels together," Tyrone said. "But the tournaments are all at the big casinos these days. They haven't held one downtown for years."

"I'll look into the history of the tournaments."

"I'm stuck until we get the final ME's report. Did he really let you sit in on the autopsy?"

"Yes."

Tyrone's eyes narrowed. "I guess I owe you a drink."

"A soda will be fine. It turns out Doctor Peters is a fan of my father."

"Your father?" Tyrone asked. "What does he do?"

I sighed. "He's a world-famous neurosurgeon."

"Damn. You got a father who's famous for surgery and a brother who's famous for magic. You ever get feelings of inadequacy?"

"Every day of my life," I said.

14. REHEARSING THE PROTOCOL

Tyrone dropped me back at the Majestic Odyssey with the envelope of photos in my hand. I didn't change my clothes and went in wearing the jeans and the sports jacket. Who needs to be dressed up for a rehearsal?

As I went up in the elevator, I silenced my phone so I wouldn't disturb the events with a call or a text.

The room was brightly lit, with chandeliers casting a warm glow over the entire space. The room was arranged with a wide aisle, flanked by dozens of chairs, each one adorned with a white sash for an elegant look.

At the end of the room was a raised dais, and upon it they set up the canopy. White cloth draped it and fresh flowers adorned it, which I thought gave it a romantic touch. The flowers filled the room with a sweet aroma.

Standing under the canopy were Thomas and Julia, the bride and groom, Jyanette, the maid of honor, and a man I didn't know. He had salt-and-pepper hair, a short beard and warm, expressive eyes. He was wearing a kippah, the traditional Jewish head covering. I assumed he was the Rabbi.

"The prodigal son returns," Thomas bellowed from the front of the room.

"I'm sorry, am I late?" I said as I rushed toward the stage. Waiting in the audience, a large group of men and women were milling around and I saw my mother and father and the Tannenbaum's.

The ever-present Emily Patterson, stopped instructing a photographer and videographer to approach me and grab the envelope from my hands.

"Hey, that's evidence," I snapped.

"You need your hands free," Emily said and pointed at the back of the room. "I'll just put it over there."

I didn't feel I could argue, so I rushed to the dais.

"Slow down. It won't help if you hurt yourself," Jyanette said. "We were just going over the ceremony with Rabbi Goldstein."

Slowing to a normal pace, I felt grateful when Jyanette spoke up because my right leg was aching from standing for the autopsy and rushing into this room.

I came up the steps and onto the dais. "Excuse me for being tardy, Rabbi. I'm Len Wise, Thomas's brother."

Rabbi Goldstein smiled warmly at me. "No need to apologize. We were just about to begin the rehearsal. You're the best man, correct?"

"Yes."

"Good." The Rabbi cleared his throat. "Everyone, please go to the back of the room in the order I gave you at the beginning."

The people nodded, and I realized there were about ten men and ten women. The men were an unusual group, and I recognized several of them from television appearances. One was wearing a top hat with a medallion in the center and wings coming off it. The man had long hair, a short beard, and dressed in a theatrical style.

"Who's the guy with the top hat?" I whispered to Thomas.

"That's Jeff McBride, one of the best sleight-of-hand manipulators and magic teachers in the world. He's been my mentor for years. If you hadn't been available, I would've asked him to be the best man."

The bridesmaids and groomsmen shuffled to the back of the room.

"I'll ask you to enter with your brother," Goldstein said. "I'll signal your time to enter."

Quickly, the Rabbi started the rehearsal, getting everyone comfortable with their roles and guiding us through the steps of the ceremony.

Since it was a Jewish ceremony, the Rabbi entered first. He signaled the groomsmen to come next, one at a time. Unlike a Christian ceremony, the groomsmen and bridesmaids come down the aisle separately, instead of in pairs.

I expected to go down the aisle before Thomas, but he put a hand on my shoulder and said, "Walk down with me, bro."

"That isn't traditional," I said.

"Rabbi Goldstein made some changes for me," he said. "Just go with it."

I shrugged and did as he told me. My mind was still reeling from the morning of activity.

We entered, escorted by our parents, as was the tradition. The group of us four made me understand why Thomas made the corridor so wide. Our parents moved to the first row on the groom's side and I stood next to him on the platform.

At the Rabbi's signal, the bridesmaids all came down the aisle, one at a time. I now understood why the rehearsal was so necessary. Getting the large group of people organized needed a rehearsal. This was more complex than one of Thomas' illusion shows.

Julia came down the aisle, with her parents on both sides of her and a veil covering her face. She was only wearing a simple cocktail dress for the rehearsal but wore the veil and carried a fake bouquet for practice.

What was completely odd was Jyanette entered after Julia separately. I frowned, because this was definitely wrong. The bride is the star of the show.

I leaned close to Thomas and murmured, "Isn't the maid of honor supposed to come down the aisle before the bride?"

Thomas sighed and whispered back. "Honestly, Len, do you have to control everything?"

Properly chastised, I stayed quiet and did what I was told.

As the rehearsal progressed, the Rabbi seemed to deviate from the traditional Jewish wedding ceremony. He changed the order of the service and I wondered if my parents and the Tannenbaum's were fine with the changes as they were conservative in following the traditions.

I could tell Rabbi Goldstein took his role seriously and that he cared deeply about making sure the wedding was a meaningful and memorable experience for everyone involved.

At the end, Rabbi Goldstein nodded as a small smile played at the corners of his lips. "Very good. Now enjoy the rest of the evening. You all have a big day tomorrow!"

It was still only the middle of the afternoon.

I broke away from Jyanette and walked over to Emily Patterson. "Where's the envelope?"

"Right there on the table," she said, and pointed, her eyes on an iPad in her hand..

I walked over, but the table was empty. "There's nothing here."

She strode over and said, "Oh, come on, I put it right—"

She halted and looked at the empty table. "That's odd. I put the envelope there."

Jyanette stood next to me. "What happened, Len?"

I raised my voice to the people still meandering around. "Did anyone take an envelope from this table?"

I saw a bunch of shaking heads, and one man spoke up. "I saw a woman at that table during the rehearsal."

"Can you describe her?" I asked.

He opened his arms in a gesture of helplessness. "I didn't get a good look at her. She was only there for a minute. I thought she worked here."

I stood there, stunned. Who could have taken them?

"Were those important?" Jyanette asked.

"They were photos from both of the séances," I said. "I hadn't looked at them yet."

"Can you get copies?"

I faced Jyanette. "I'll go back to our room and contact Tyrone, see if he can email me the photos."

She glanced over at Julia, who was talking with a bridesmaid. "I have things to do with Julia. I wasn't expecting you to be available."

"It's fine. I need to focus on this."

She gave me a quick peck and I headed for the hotel elevators.

Back in the room a few minutes later, I texted Tyrone and asked him to send me the photos. He questioned it, and I explained they went missing. A few minutes later, I received an email that let me go on a Dropbox account and download the photos, which I quickly did.

It was going to take a while for the photos to appear on my desktop. While I was waiting, I went on to the site for the Poker World Series, which featured a history of high stakes poker competitions that required a sizable buy in and offered large payouts.

I searched for Sal Lombardo, and his name came up as a listed player for four of the competitions over the years. Of the different tournaments, one he ended up bowing out and forfeiting his buy-in. Another two, Sal was a listed player, but not a finalist. But in one, he achieved his highest ranking, which was seventh place.

There, he won a prize of three million dollars.

Not a bad payout.

I thought it odd that back in the day, the Poker World Series had allowed Sal Lombardo, the owner of the casino, to play in tournaments. I decided that back then, things were looser.

A new thought ran through my mind. What if Lombardo cheated to win the money?

I thought of Joe Rossi — he had been a dealer for years at the Sphinx. Could Sal have used him to set up a way to cheat? But how could you cheat at games under such heavy scrutiny?

A chime sounded on my phone, a text from Tyrone:

The ME found muscarine in the stomach contents

Call me ASAP

Who could make a concentrated dose of poisoned mushroom? Only one name came to mind.

We need to question Celeste Moon.

Can you pick me up?

I left my computer running so it could finish the download and headed out of my room.

I stood out front of the hotel, and Tyrone drove up a few minutes later, and I got into the vehicle. As we pulled away from the curb, I said, "The ME found muscarine poisoning?"

"Yes, and Doctor Peters is re-examining Lombardo's stomach contents as well. He said that it would be easy to miss, even though it was a concentrated dosage."

"It's not part of a standard screening process, and to all appearances, Lombardo looked like he had a heart attack."

"He said you suggested it was muscarine. How did you know?"

"Lucky guess," I attempted.

"I'm sure," he said, obviously not believing me. "I did some digging, and I found some things about Ms. Moon that I thought would interest you."

This got my attention. "Do tell."

"Before meeting her benefactor and creating the Cryptic Collection, the police busted her under the name Madame Luna for pulling a fortune telling scam. Got some people convinced they were under a curse, and the only way to break the curse was to give her money that she burned as an offering to the spirits."

"That's an old one. You give the mark an envelope to put the cash in, then switch it out for one with maybe five one-dollar bills in it before you burn it."

"You know those scams as well?"

"There are a lot of them, but criminals have overused that one. How did she get caught?"

Tyrone smiled. "The mark took the ashes home to put in a bath, as instructed. Turns out a corner of a dollar bill was unburned. Since he'd given her only hundred-dollar bills, he put two and two together."

"Did she do any time?" I wondered.

Tyrone shook his head. "No, she made restitution and did community service. Then she hooked up with this Doctor Theodore Jameson."

"And that was the start of the Cryptic Collection," I said.

"Exactly. Jameson had the money to buy the building and the exhibits. Ms. Moon worked with him and they shared everything."

"I'm sure that included her, as she called it, awe-inspiring bosom as well."

Tyrone smiled. "From everything I've been able to find out, I would say so."

He pulled the car into a side street, and we headed for the entrance to the Cryptic Collection. There was no line out front, as we'd arrived on the day the museum was closed before the weekend tours.

As we drew closer, I saw a figure standing in the doorway wearing the same outfit I had seen her wearing in my hotel room.

Sarah Lewis.

I paused. "Detective, why don't you go ahead? I have to prepare myself before I go in there."

Tyrone seemed surprised at this, but opened the door. "I'll meet you in her office."

I waited until the door closed, then stepped next to Sarah. She appeared solid even in the sunlight. "What are you doing here?"

She looked up at me and shook her head.

"Someone murdered Big John. We found the proof."

Her expression grew hard, but she nodded.

"You knew it was murder, didn't you?"

She nodded slowly.

"If you focus, you should be able to talk to me," I said. "Try just sending your thoughts."

She shook her head.

"Do you know why someone killed Big John and Sal?"

She gazed up at me, and I saw Joe Rossi's memory, the scene in Sal's office with the other men. The man in the chair tapping his foot. Then it was gone.

And so was Sarah.

I sighed in exasperation. "Ghosts are the worst. Freaking enigmatic."

I had to admit I preferred tapping into the energy of a location and getting a vision rather than dealing with entities. I was grateful I didn't do it very often.

I focused on my mental barriers and stepped into the building. It was odd going in without the ticket-takers or the staff at the door. The darkened hallway was more eerie without people.

I continued down the hall, remembering my way from our previous visit, keeping my barriers strong, and not allowing the items in the rooms to break my concentration. I believed most of the displays were perfectly harmless, but there were a few that were surrounded by a potent energy — and not a good one.

I finally reached the office, where I heard an upraised voice. "How dare you accuse me! I'll have you know I am a clairvoyant, not some charlatan."

I stepped through the door and into the room, where the fiery Ms. Moon was standing behind her desk, her eyes aflame.

She looked at me. "Doctor Wise! Tell this man that I am not a fraud! You were at the séance, and you know what we manifested."

"To be honest, I'm not sure what happened," I said calmly. "Like you said, I think we opened a portal that a spirit came through."

"There, see! It was the spirit that killed Mr. Rossi, like the newspaper said," Celeste declared. "It was not anything I did."

"I didn't say that," I pointed out. "It was muscarine that killed Rossi."

"Muscarine?" she repeated, frowning. "What's that?"

"It's the substance in a certain variety of toxic mushrooms and someone used a concentrated dose," I explained.

Tyrone spoke up. "Doctor Wise and I recalled how you claimed to make your own potions. Do any of them contain any kind of mushroom?"

Celeste looked stricken, and she slowly returned to her chair. "Actually, several of my potions use different varieties of psilocybin mushroom. I am sure you know that they have psychedelic effects, but I dilute the amount a great deal. It certainly couldn't give anyone hallucinations."

"Ms. Moon, those mushrooms are illegal in this state," Tyrone said.

"Not in the quantities I use," she said, looking upset. "We make a Mother Tincture from the plant and mix one part with nine parts of ethanol in a new vial. The result is a one-one-hundredth dilution of the plant. Then I blend those tinctures to make the potions I sell."

"Have you ever used poisoned mushrooms in this process?" I asked.

She looked down, trying to focus. "Some of those mushrooms are part of ancient Native-American healing potions. I may have used them in one recipe as an experiment, but I followed the strictest care, diluted them two hundred times to make sure it is far too weak to be of harm."

Tyrone pointed a finger. "You're telling me that if I brought forensics into your shop and tested your equipment, it might come up positive for muscarine?"

She looked around in a panic. "I don't know. There might be traces, but certainly not enough to harm anyone."

"Ms. Moon, where do you make these potions?" Tyrone said, taking charge.

"I have a small room down the hall," she said with a glance at me.

She led us back into the hallway. We went into another side hall that ended in a bookcase with more of the strange curios on it. Upon reaching the bookcase, she hit a lever, and the bookcase swung out, revealing a room behind.

We stepped in. The space may have been a kitchen when this was a house, as I saw a stove, a stainless-steel sink, and an ancient refrigerator. Now, it more resembled a laboratory with bunsen burners, beakers, pots, a mortar and pestle for grinding herbs, a small industrial distiller, and various scales and measuring tools for precise measurement of ingredients. I saw a collection of iron and copper pots, some resembling small cauldrons. She lined the walls with shelves filled with jars of dried herbs, powders, and ingredients from all over the world.

The room appeared unused with dust and cobwebs collecting. Someone had spilled substances on the floor and did not clean them up. Large pots were soaking in a stainless-steel sink and looked like they had been there for a month. Clutter covered the counters.

Celeste ran her fingers nervously through her hair. "Oh dear! The room is a mess. I don't understand it. I haven't made potions for months. How could it be in such a state?"

"And people drink things you make here?" Tyrone said, gazing around the room. "You're lucky you haven't already poisoned somebody."

"I cleaned the room when I last used it," she said.

Tyrone pulled out his phone and input a number. "Ms. Moon, I am shutting you down."

"What?" she said. "But I have tours—"

"Consider them canceled for now. I am getting the forensic team in here and going over everything." He scrutinized the room again. "And that might take some time." He faced Celeste, who seemed to have become smaller. "I'm bringing you downtown for questioning."

Tyrone stepped away and spoke into his phone to arrange uniformed officers and forensics to come to the address.

"Is he serious?" Celeste said to me.

"I'm afraid so. Ms. Moon, the ME found proof that someone murdered Big John and possibly Sal Lombardo as well. The police are going to need to examine this room."

She backed up a step. "You should look to the spirits, Doctor. They'll tell you I didn't do it."

"Ms. Moon. If you've done nothing, then you have nothing to fear—"

All at once, the temperature dropped in the room, and Celeste noticed it as well.

I saw Sarah appear, once again looking quite solid. She was pointing to a rectangular metal box. I recognized it as a laboratory distiller.

Celeste saw where I looked and turned, her eyes growing wide. "Oh, my."

I glanced at Celeste. "Can you see her, too?"

"Of course," Celeste said. "How is she manifesting here?"

"She's using our mental energy," I said and raised my voice. "Why are you here?"

Sarah pointed at Celeste.

"What do you want with me?" Celeste said, her breath coming out in a fog as the temperature dropped so much.

Sarah walked right through a table heading towards Celeste. Out of instinct, I moved in front of her, blocking her path. "Talk to me. What do you want?"

Sarah gestured. I was flung aside like a rag doll and I fell to the messy floor, hitting the floor with the back of my head.

Stars flashed in my vision as I blacked out.

15. COMPETITION CONVENTION

I returned to consciousness slowly and saw Tyrone standing at a door that opened to the outside I had not noticed before. Next to him was Celeste, her hands handcuffed behind her back. She raised her eyes to me in despair.

Tyrone came to me, helping me to my feet, and I felt the back of my head.

"You okay, Len?" Tyrone asked.

"How long was I out?" I muttered.

"Only a minute or two," Tyrone said, his face lined with concern. "What happened? Did she knock you down, try to escape?"

"I did no such thing," Celeste said defensively.

Tyrone glared at Celeste. "I heard a noise and came back into the room. Len, you were on the floor unconscious and she was trying to do something to that metal box on the counter." Tyrone turned to me. "I had to handcuff her to make sure she didn't tamper with the evidence."

"She didn't knock me down. It was the ghost from the séance room," I said and glanced over at Celeste. "Celeste, you saw her. Did she tell you anything?"

"She kept pointing at the distilling machine. I went over to see what she was trying to show me," Celeste said. "Doctor, there was a piece of a mushroom under the distiller. I recognized it."

"You didn't touch it, did you?" I said, worried.

"Of course not! It was a piece of an Ivory Funnel mushroom," Celeste said. "It's still there, but you should only touch it with gloves."

"Forensics is on the way. I'll have them go over the place," Tyrone said.

At that moment, we all turned to see an LVPD police car pull up outside the open door, its lights flashing. Officer Rodriguez got out of the car and walked over to join us.

"What's up, Detective?" Rodriguez said.

"Rodriguez, please escort Ms. Moon to the station and put her in an interview room."

"Are you arresting me?" Celeste cried, indignant.

"You are a material witness," Tyrone said. "We're taking you into protective custody."

Rodriguez nodded and said, "If she gets rowdy, I'm putting her in holding."

"Talk to the spirits, Doctor," Celeste said as they headed out a side door, Rodriguez leading her to the car. "They'll tell you I didn't do it."

Tyrone and I followed them out to the parking lot. I looked at the outside of the door, which was painted to match the siding, and from a few feet away, it blended in with the stucco finish. There was a small sign on it stating: No Entrance.

What if someone came into this room through that outer door? No one would have seen them, even if the Cryptic Collection was full of people.

Tyrone noticed I stopped walking. "What's up?"

"I'll be a minute. I need to do something."

"Knock yourself out, Len," he said and went inside.

I was concerned about lowering my defenses so close to all those odd artifacts, but I tried.

I put my hand on the doorknob, closed my eyes, and shifted into an alpha state, allowing myself to sense any other person who may have been here. I stood for several minutes, but nothing came.

I stepped back into the dirty laboratory, where Tyrone was leaning against the old refrigerator.

"Any luck?" he said casually.

I shook my head. "Nothing. If anyone touched that doorknob, they weren't emotional."

"Emotional?"

"If you were intending to murder someone — or more than one person — wouldn't you be emotional?"

"Is that what leaves this energetic residue you keep talking about?"

I nodded. "Yes, a strong emotional situation creates an imprint. There is none here."

As I spoke, a van drove into the parking lot.

The team leader, a tall woman with light brown hair, walked over as the other two men pulled on disposable polypropylene coveralls. She glanced into the room without going in, and said, "Someone's a lousy cook?"

"It looks that way," Tyrone said. "I'm Detective Washington and this is Doctor Leonard Wise. Officer Rodriguez is escorting a witness to lock up."

I spoke up. "We're searching for any traces of muscarine."

"Mushrooms?" she said with a frown. She peered in the door and appraised the room a second time. "Looks like that's the least of your worries."

She headed back to the van to get suited up herself. By now, the other two were in the suits with gloves and booties. She yelled out, "We have a hazmat situation. Full PPE on this."

The two men groaned in annoyance, but pulled out the extra coverings they needed as another LVPD police car pulled into the lot. I turned to Tyrone. "If an officer can supervise, I'd like to get back to the hotel."

Two uniformed officers got out of the police car and Tyrone talked to them as I headed to his car.

He came over, opened the trunk, and handed me a couple of folded up trash bags.

"What's that for?"

"Your jacket got dirty with whatever was on the floor when you fell. Since we are looking into a poison, I don't want it in my car. Take off those clothes as soon as you get back to the hotel and bag them. I want to have the forensics team analyze them. Take a hot shower and wash thoroughly."

"Nice to know you care."

"Are you kidding? If anything happens to you, Bill McGee would never let me hear the end of it."

It took ten minutes to get me back to the hotel, and after seeing the forensic team in the full Personal Protective Equipment, I took Tyrone's concerns seriously. I sped through the casino as quickly as I could.

Jyanette had not returned. It was good she was out enjoying herself while I worked the case.

I stripped my clothes and put everything in the trash bag. I cleaned the outside of my shoes, my wallet, and my phone with some alcohol wipes I had in my laptop bag.

I had a shower and dressed in fresh clothing.

I checked my laptop to see it had finished downloading the photos.

Considering Grace Matthews took both sets of photos in little or no light, they were very good.

I started with the first séance, reviewing the photos one by one. There was a photo of Sal holding his glass of scotch with ice, prepared for him by Will Anderson.

The glass...

The buzz gave me pause. If Sal died from muscarine, the drink would have to be the way he'd received it.

Yet, when I mentioned poison, Will seemed surprised at the suggestion and his reaction rang true.

Could the ice cubes have contained the poison? That seemed a far too risky idea, as the guests could easily grab a cube without asking and poison themselves. Also, if Will knew the cubes contained poison, it seemed risky he used his bare hands to add them.

I continued through the photos. Desirée got champagne, and Rosie got a scotch as well, but nothing seemed important in that first séance.

There were photos of the group around the table, and the table moving, which, frozen in a photo, looked amazing.

Grace captured a great shot of the display case with the gun as it fell. The next photo showed the gun floating in the air and pointing at Sal Lombardo. This was the photo the Associated Press picked up, and it ended up in newspapers and all over the internet.

I moved to the photos of the second séance.

These shots started with the group around the table, with Rosie putting her glass of water on the floor as Big John drained his.

The glass...

I received the buzz a second time, and looked closely at the photo as Big John held it to his lips, but I couldn't see anything out of the ordinary.

The collection of photos ended with the explosion of the planchette. It had all of us around the table with our heads down. This was the photo the Las Vegas Journal used on its front page.

I closed the folder of photos and stared at my computer, trying to think of other avenues I could explore. We now knew it was murder, and the killer used muscarine, but I didn't have the delivery method.

I did research about the possible cheating situation I glimpsed in Joe Rossi's mind.

First, I texted Tyrone and asked if he'd been able to get the list of players for the upcoming tournament. He told me he would email it to me.

Since Sal was the first victim, I needed to know a bit more about him, and I found a puff piece written about him when he was retiring, titled "The Last Great Casino Mogul."

Lombardo had a reputation for being a shrewd businessman and an expert in the casino industry as he built the Sphinx. He not only created a successful hotel, but had an eye for talent. He brought the magicians, the Amazing Coles, to Las Vegas, adding a successful magic show to his hotel.

Known to be a skilled poker player, he played several poker tournaments himself, up against some of the best players in the world…

It went on and on about his different accomplishments, putting him in the best light.

I went to my email and found the list Tyrone had sent. I went through the players. One name caught my eye:

Victoria Cole.

I went back to my web browser to reread the article about Lombardo.

The article mentioned the Amazing Coles. It said Lombardo discovered and brought them to Vegas. I had never heard of them. I wondered what happened to them.

Doing another web search, I quickly found multiple hits on the Amazing Coles. This husband and wife pair, who specialized in both magic and mentalism, had graced the main stage of The

Sphinx for years. This was before the renovation into the Golden Era, when the hotel still had a theater.

One article specifically highlighted their family business, including how they incorporated their young daughter, Vicky, into the act.

Victoria Cole.

I looked at the photos on my web search. I found one of Jack Cole, who was tall and slender with an infectious grin — and familiar. This was the man I saw in Joe Rossi's mind in the office with Big John and Sal Lombardo.

In the photo, Jack had his arm around his spouse, Olivia, a diminutive lady who exuded a powerful presence. It made sense she was small, as getting in and out of large illusions used in magic shows requires someone small and quick.

Nestled between them was twelve-year-old Vicky Cole, wearing a huge smile. Looking at the young girl, I thought she appeared familiar, but I couldn't place her.

According to the interviewer, the Coles had a long-term contract at the Egyptian Showroom at The Sphinx. It was in the showroom where they took this photograph.

Researching further, I uncovered a tragic twist in the narrative. Three years after the article, Olivia Cole died in a severe car accident near their Las Vegas home.

The incident shattered Jack's spirit, rendering him unable to perform. Consumed with grief, he eventually succumbed to an overdose of pills months later, bringing a premature end to the act and his life.

I wondered what happened to Vicky? She'd be in her late twenties by now.

My phone rang, and it was Tyrone.

"Did you take off those clothes and bag them like I asked?" His tone was intense.

"Yes. I also took a hot shower."

"A preliminary report says that there were traces of muscarine all over that room. Forensics brought in that distilling unit and the plant found under it was indeed an Ivory Funnel mushroom."

"What should I do with my clothes?"

"I'll come by and pick them up. I think your assessment was right. The laboratory distiller was used to make the concentrated version of muscarine that killed both Lombardo and Rossi."

"What are you doing with Celeste?"

"Ms. Moon has called in a lawyer and we are officially charging her with murder."

If the case was closed, I could move on, focus only on my brother's wedding and serving as his best man. The rehearsal dinner was only a few hours away, and I didn't have time to play detective.

But I didn't think Celeste did it, even though the evidence pointed to her. Considering this case went from natural causes to murder, we'd come a long way.

I'd done my part.

But I couldn't let them charge an innocent person when I knew they were not guilty. "She didn't do it."

"Look, Len," Tyrone said. "I appreciate your help in this case. Hell, we wouldn't have known to look for muscarine if it weren't for you. But we have evidence from the place she owned and worked. She even admitted to making potions with mushrooms."

I exhaled sharply. "I understand. But it doesn't clear up the ghost in the séance room. I think something happened years ago, and reporter Sarah Lewis was looking into it. I think it involved cheating at a poker tournament."

"Len, I'm a homicide cop. It's not my job to find out about ghosts or cheating from years ago."

"Tyrone, could we take one more run at Joe Rossi? I think there's something there."

"We've just solved two murders. It's not up to us to uncover a scam no one cares about."

"Please, I think it will help the current case as well."

Tyrone sighed. "All right. I'll be by to pick up the clothes — and you — in thirty minutes."

He ended the call.

I said out loud, "Sarah, if you're going to tell me the story of the murder, now would be the time."

Nothing.

I need to figure out a technique to work with ghosts in a more effective way.

It looked like I had no other cards to play, but then I recalled the flash I had of Joe Rossi's memory. I couldn't hear what anyone was saying in that brief encounter, but if I moved into an alpha state, maybe I could understand what the people said to Rossi.

I only had a half-hour, so I quickly set a twenty-five-minute alarm on my phone, closed my eyes, and focused on my breath.

In… out, in… out.

As I moved into an alpha state, I thought back to when I made eye contact with Joe Rossi, and the images slipped from his mind into mine.

I focused as the images flowed, and I was in Sal's private office. I glanced around as Big John Rossi and Jack Cole faced Sal behind the enormous desk.

The desk where he raped Desirée, back when she was an underage Samantha Smith.

Sal and Big John were both younger. Sal, his hair black instead of white, and Big John looking formidable but not nearly as large as he would become later in life. There was also Jack Cole, looking polished and full of energy.

Sal spoke first, and this time I could hear him. "Joe, how did the shoe we gave you work out?"

"Great. I get a peek at each card as I deal and no one can see me do it," the voice coming from me said. I was watching from inside Joe Rossi's head, and from his point of view.

I assumed Joe was speaking of a dealer's shoe used to lay out playing cards during the game. If I understood what he said correctly, it suggested Sal had a special one made that would allow Joe to peek at the cards as he dealt them.

With cards, Joe Rossi had admitted he had a photographic memory.

Sal looked over at Jack Cole. "How does it work?"

"We keep it simple," Cole said, smiling as he went. "You both have the device in your footwear. Joe deals the cards, and he knows who has what. If he thinks you should bet, he'll tap his big toe twice for 'yes', and once for 'no'. You'll receive the vibrations on your foot and know what to do."

"If it's twice, I should bet," Sal repeated.

"Exactly. And if you're not sure you read the signal right, you scratch the back of your head as a sign and he'll repeat the signal."

"I got that," Joe said.

Cole smiled. "And if he sees you can win big, he taps his toe four times, and you go all in."

"How long will the batteries last?" Sal asked.

"Six to ten hours."

"Boss," Big John spoke up, "we gotta make sure no one knows about this."

"You kidding? Of course not!" Sal said. "I could lose my casino license. It took years for Joey to be selected to be a dealer for the tournament. I'm not trying to take the big prize, just get as high as I can. We'll all make out good."

Joe turned to Jack Cole. "When can you fix me up?"

The beeping of my phone pulled me out of the memory, and I gently rose out of the alpha state to shut it off.

The article I read online stated the Coles were mentalists and magicians. A way to tap a code from one partner to another using a radio-signaled vibrating device was not a new technique. I never heard of one hidden in footwear, but I could see why it would work.

Sal Lombardo had cheated at cards with Joe Rossi's and Jack Cole's help.

Now I needed to learn what that had to do with the two murders.

16. FERVENT LITURGY

T yrone was sitting in his car out front..

"We'll take the clothes to the forensic unit," he said, taking the bag from me and putting it in the back. "Hopefully, they'll get it back to you before you leave. Then we can go see Joe Rossi."

"I know for a fact that Sal Lombardo cheated in a tournament fifteen years ago, and Joe Rossi helped him," I said.

"Great," Tyrone said without enthusiasm. "Now tell me why I should care."

"It's the motive behind this case. Somehow it's related, and Joe Rossi knows the truth. If we talk to him again, I can get him to tell us what happened."

Tyrone grinned. "Or he'll punch you out. You want to go to your brother's wedding with a black eye?"

I frowned. "You haven't been speaking to my fiancée, have you? She said the same thing."

He chuckled. "Maybe she and I are the psychics."

"Please, Tyrone. I know what to say to Joe Rossi this time."

Tyrone sighed. "We'll drop off these clothes at the lab and stop by his retirement home. He should be playing cards again."

I glanced at my watch. "Really? Today as well?"

"That's what they do. Play cards all day. Then they go to the casinos a couple of days a week."

"Not my idea of retirement," I said.

"Me neither. When I retire, I'm moving far away from Sin City," he said, and opened his door. "Now get in the car, and I'll make sure the old guy doesn't clock you again."

We drove to the forensic lab and Tyrone was right. It was in the same direction as Blissful Acres. As the sun lowered toward the horizon, we passed the security guard and made our way to the clubhouse for the second time.

Joe Rossi was once again at the same table, but when he saw it was us, he looked away and said, "I got nothing to say to you."

This did not intimidate Tyrone. "That's fine, Mr. Rossi. But since you assaulted Doctor Wise, I might ask a couple of officers to escort you downtown. We can do this here and now, all friendly, or I can make a phone call."

Rossi threw down his hand, and the others at the table complained as he rose. "You got five minutes and none of the crap like before."

We once again headed into the nearby meeting room, and he sat in the chair with his arms crossed, glaring at me.

I remained standing several feet away in case Rossi lunged at me a second time. If I ended up with a black eye, as predicted, it would be a lonely night on the sofa of my hotel suite.

I decided just talking about it directly was the best approach. "I know about the scam fifteen years ago."

"Well then, enlighten me," Rossi said, unimpressed.

"The tournament where Sal got you the gimmicked dealer's shoe. The devices in your footwear so you could signal him. Sal was an excellent poker player, but you gave him the edge he needed to win three million dollars."

The look on his face shifted slowly from cocksure to confused to downright scared.

His mouth opened and closed like a fish, then his jaw grew hard and he glared at me. "I didn't have nothing to do with what went down. I just did what Sal told me." He glanced at Tyrone. "You havin' me arrested?"

"Not over a card game that happened fifteen years ago," Tyrone said. "But I want to know what happened because it may have bearing on the murder of your cousin."

As he spoke, I saw the shame and regret in his eyes. "Sal only did it because he was in a hole, owed money. The whole thing worked flawlessly, and Sal was good to me. He gave me twenty-five grand for my part of it, which got me out of the debt I was in with my ex-wife. Sal said it was a good take, and he never wanted to do it again. I thought that was the end."

"But that wasn't the end, was it?" I asked.

"The friggin' magician was the problem."

"Jack Cole?" I said. "Why? What did he do?"

"Not him, his wife," Rossi said. "Cole got us these things we put in our shoes, so I could signal Sal when to bet and when not to."

"The mentalism gimmick," I said.

"Yeah. He paid Cole, like, ten grand. After all, Cole only fixed us up with the gimmicks. I had to be at the tournament, dealing for hours and helping Sal the whole time."

"Get to the point, Rossi," Tyrone said.

"The magician told his wife, and when she hears Sal won three mil, she wants a bigger cut," Rossi said. "She don't know that you don't pull that shit on Sal Lombardo."

I saw where this was going, but I wanted to hear it from Rossi. "So Sal told Big John to do something."

He nodded. "Big John was just supposed to scare her, run her off the road, and put the fear of God into the stuck-up bitch. But she was going faster than Big John thought and she ends up in a car crash and dies."

I thought of the young girl, Vicky Cole, having her mother torn violently from her so early in life. That would be the motive to seek vengeance.

Rossi went on. "So Cole can't do his show with his wife dead, so Sal gives him some severance and fires him."

"And six months later, he dies of an overdose," I said. "Did Big John help with that as well?"

"From what I hear, he did it to himself," Rossi said. "You can't blame me for any of it. All I did was keep my mouth shut."

"How does Sarah Lewis fit into this?"

Rossi frowned. "The reporter? I don't know nothing about that."

"How about the daughter?" I asked. "What happened to the daughter?"

"How the hell do I know?" Rossi confessed. "They coulda put her in child services or sent her off to live with an aunt, I don't know."

"One last question," I said. "Do you know a dealer named Will Anderson?"

He frowned, surprised by this question. "Sure. Young guy, a dealer at the Sphinx same as me. I think he worked as a bartender, too."

"Did you tell him anything about how Sal won the money or how he did it?"

"I told you, I didn't say nothing to no one. After the Cole broad died, Big John paid me a visit and warned me I needed to be sure to keep quiet about the whole thing."

"Did he threaten you?" Tyrone asked.

"He didn't need to. I knew the man Lombardo was, and what my cousin was capable of. That's why I've told no one." He looked up at me. "But how did you find out about it?"

"I have my ways," I said.

Rossi glared at Tyrone. "You ain't gonna arrest me, are you?"

"Not at this time, but I may need you to tell this to the DA," Tyrone said. "Go back to your game."

"I think I've had enough for one day," he said and, with a nasty glance at me, left the room.

Tyrone sighed. "Well, that was interesting, but not much help for our case. How did you find all of that out?"

"I did some research, and put two and two together," I said, not wanting to admit I'd peeked at Joe Rossi's memories.

"What are your impressions, Len? You think Will Anderson found out about the cheating scam and wanted to try it?"

"He had that dealer's shoe at his apartment, remember?" I said.

"He said he wanted to practice."

I smiled. "He's been a dealer for twenty-five years. Why would he need to hone his skills? Unless he was practicing with a partner to learn how to cheat."

"You think he's been practicing with the thing they put in their shoes?" Tyrone said, nodding.

"That's my thought. A Victoria Cole is in the tournament as a player. She was on that list you gave me. If she's the daughter of Jack Cole, she might have the very equipment Sal Lombardo and Joe Rossi used and is planning to use the same technique to cheat at the upcoming tournament."

"That's a stretch."

"It makes perfect sense. Will was the bartender. He could easily have added the poisons to the drinks."

Tyrone stood and stretched. "Sorry, Len. I talked to forensics when we dropped off your clothes. They found the glass Big John drank from and it contained traces of muscarine—"

"There you go!"

"But they didn't find any traces of muscarine on any of the bar equipment."

"Not any?" I said, stunned.

"They tore the bar apart, and it all came back clean."

"Even the ice cubes?"

"As well as the container he stored the ice in. They even went through the garbage and found nothing. If you think Will poisoned the victims, how did he handle it and administer it?"

"I don't know, but I'm sure he knows something."

Tyrone frowned. "Let's say he did it. Why kill Lombardo and Rossi? Will Anderson has no motive."

"If he's working with Victoria Cole, she has a motive. Big John killed her mother and Sal Lombardo ordered him to scare her." I headed for the door. "I think we should talk to him right now."

"Slow down, Len," Tyrone said and glanced at his watch. "Will Anderson works now, and they don't allow the dealers to carry cell phones on the casino floors."

"Damn," I grumbled. "Can we interview him at work?"

"If we had more evidence than your theory, I'd have him picked up right now," Tyrone said. "But so far, it's all conjecture. We don't have probable cause."

"We have reasonable suspicion."

"That we do. But you have that dinner you have to go to, and I want you to go with me when I question him. Let's do it tomorrow in the morning."

I paused. The wedding didn't take place until late afternoon, so I would have the time.

"All right," I said. "If you can drop me off at my hotel, I can get ready for the rehearsal dinner. I just don't like letting it go until tomorrow."

"Sometimes you have to wait, Len," Tyrone said as we headed for the car. "I'm sure you know that from working with McGee."

"I know it. That doesn't mean I like it."

Back in the hotel, I found Jyanette in our room at the sink in the bathroom, working on her hair. She was turning it into a bun with a combination of hair products and magic. She wore only her bra and panties, but when I approached she warned, "Distract me and you die."

Having risked my life enough the last few days, I retreated into the bedroom to change into a fine gray suit I brought along with the rehearsal dinner in mind.

I wondered if I was going to get that other sports coat back.

Knowing Jyanette might be a while, I went out into the sitting room. My laptop stood open. Someone had opened the folder with the photos.

"Hon, did you go through my laptop?" I yelled out.

"I was just looking at the photos from the séances," she yelled back. "I didn't reveal any of your deep dark secrets or look at your browser history."

I opened the folder and looked at the photos, wishing something would jump out at me and solve this case.

Jyanette came out, her hair done, and she had donned a lovely turquoise cocktail dress that had traces of sequin accents.

I rose. "You look spectacular."

She held up a warning finger. "Don't muss me. I want to look perfect as we go into the dinner."

"Can I muss you later?"

She narrowed her eyes. "We'll see. What are you planning for the bachelor party?"

"What?"

She raised her head. "The bachelor party? Tonight? After the rehearsal dinner?"

An icy feeling raced up my spine. "I completely forgot about it."

She faced me. "How could you? The bridesmaids and I are taking Julia out to see a male review. What are you and the men doing?"

I grabbed my phone and searched frantically for the embossed card for Emily Patterson, the party planner.

Jyanette shook her head. "I don't know what you're going to do at this point."

I dialed the number. "I was supposed to arrange things with the party planner, and I got busy."

The phone rang, and she answered with a curt, "This is Emily... go."

"Ms. Patterson, it's... um... Leonard Wise. I'm sorry, I forgot to contact you about the bachelor party—"

"Everything is arranged."

"Really?" I replied, my mouth hanging open.

"Yes, I chartered a bus to pick up the gentleman after the rehearsal dinner and all of you to go to a show which should offer the amount of undressed femininity to meet the requirement of a bachelor party, while keeping everything controlled enough to not be too uncouth."

"I-I can't thank you enough."

"You seemed out of your depth," she said.

"Quite a bit, I'm afraid," I said as relief washed over me.

"And I certainly couldn't let you ruin part of the event by neglecting an important tradition."

And there it was, her attitude I encountered before. However, she saved me, so I let it go.

"What show are we going to see?"

"I believe it's called *X-tacy*."

She was sending us to the show where Desirée performed.

"Now, I have arrangements to make for the rehearsal dinner," she said dismissively.

"Oh! Sure," I said. "Thanks again—"

She already ended the call.

Jyanette was sitting on the couch in front of my open laptop. I sat next to her, putting my phone away. I could smell her perfume. She was wearing the one that always drives me wild.

"You should be grateful to that woman," she said. "She saved your ass."

"I just wish she didn't make me feel like my ass was just spanked." I noticed she was studying the photos. "What do you think?"

"These photos are amazing. Especially considering both events were pretty terrifying."

"Yes, I was hoping to find a clue, but I've got nothing."

"Anything turn up your special way?"

I shook my head. "I got a buzz about the drinking glass, but that's it."

"Really? Could it be when that girl grabbed the wrong one?"

I looked at my lady. "What?"

She opened several photos on the screen. "When the girl grabbed the wrong glass," she stated, and pointed at one photo of the group at the table. "See? Big John has the glass with a clear liquid and ice cubes."

"Yes, so what?"

"In this photo," Jyanette went on, switching to another photo. "This girl, I think her name is Rosie? She grabs the glass with the ice cubes and leaves her glass there in front of him."

She blew up the image on the screen. She was right.

It was Rosie who picked up a water glass and said to Big John, "We'd better move these." Then Big John said, "Oh, yeah," and drained the glass before putting it on the floor. Looking at the photo, Rosie is holding the glass, and it is obvious the ice cubes are in it.

Rosie switched glasses with Big John, and he was dead ten minutes later.

Jyanette said. "We have to go, Len."

"Yeah," I said and closed my laptop, still trying to understand it. Could Rosie have poisoned her own glass of water? But if she switched them, how did she know he'd finish it?

Or maybe in the concentrated version of the poison, he didn't need to finish it.

But what did Rosie Graham have to do with all of this?

17. ENTICING WORSHIP

W e headed down to the meeting room level of the hotel, joining guests heading to the banquet room. There was also a large group of reporters and as Jyanette and I approached, they descended on us like vultures on a kill.

"Doctor Wise! Is it true the police have a suspect in custody?"

"Doctor Wise! Is it true a ghost has been leading the investigation?"

"Doctor Wise! How did you find out that poison was involved?"

On and on, yelling questions at me, with camera strobes going off. It surprised me they were so aware of the recent updates in the investigation.

I was glad that I was well-dressed and had a beautiful woman on my arm. Jyanette and I patiently made our way through the gaggle and into the banquet room. At the doorway, several hotel security guards were checking people's names against a list on a clipboard as we went in.

"Pretty crazy out there," Jyanette said to the guard.

The man nodded, not looking up from the clipboard as he scanned for our names. "Yes, some out-of-towner was involved in a murder or something. Makes our job a pain in the ass."

We moved past the man into the grand banquet hall, which was decked out in lavish red and gold decor, with tables dressed in crisp white linens and adorned with flickering candles.

I saw Ms. Patterson milling about, escorting a photographer and speaking to someone from one of those celebrity news shows, with a camera focused on her as she spoke.

Apparently, she granted access to certain reporters.

The groomsmen wore clothing that looked more like costumes, sporting top hats and glittering jackets. That's when it hit me.

They were all magicians!

We all sat down to dinner, which offered choices of prime rib, Chicken Wellington, poached salmon and truffled risotto. An assortment of side dishes accompanied each choice.

Jyanette talked and mingled as I attempted to be polite and engaging. But throughout the meal, my mind kept going over the case, as I tried to find the connection between Rosie Graham and Sarah Lewis.

Dessert was a Viennese table with assorted trays of French miniature pastries. Once everyone made their selections and returned to their seats, Jeff McBride moved to a platform, wearing his fanciful red and black tailcoat with oriental designs and his remarkable top hat.

A lovely woman with dark hair set out several items behind him. He removed the top hat and put on a short cape that went just to his waist.

"Welcome all, to this festive occasion. Here in Las Vegas we have a strong magical community, and we are here to celebrate our friend Thomas Wise, the Great Wizini, on his nuptials!"

That drew applause from the assembled crowd.

Jeff went on. "Some of you were sad to hear that our groom's show is on hiatus during your visit. So, as his friends, we wanted to give you a special magical experience."

The lights in the room went down as two bright white lights, like eyes, flashed from the platform. The lights came back up, and Jeff had turned his back to the audience, and a mask with flashing eyes was on the back of his head. As dramatic music played, he spun around and a golden mask covered his face.

In a few quick moments, and from where I did not know, he suddenly held a second gold mask on a stick and that became three masks, and then a fourth, which, in a flash of fire, became six. Finally, the gold mask on his face changed into a black and white mask.

My mouth fell open. I did magic with Thomas back when we were teenagers, but this was at a level I'd never imagined.

With ease and proficiency, McBride placed the gold masks into a black table behind him. He went through a series of breathtaking changes to the mask on his face, each one unique and sometimes frightening. For the finale, he changed his mask from red to green, and then removed that final mask to uncover his true face.

With roaring applause from the audience, McBride introduced another groomsman and friend. This man was a mentalist who presented his routines laced with comedy. He wowed the crowd with his unpredictable routine, making the audience laugh at every turn.

The entire show went on for at least an hour, with different groomsmen each doing about five minutes. The acts ranged from the classic routines like the Chinese Rings to eccentric illusions using fire and smoke. There were card tricks, coin and rope magic, and the levitation of a small table. Not a single person in the room could resist the charm of the magicians' presence, and each one had a unique style and technique.

McBride finished the show by doing the most astounding card manipulation I ever witnessed. He made fans of cards appear out of the air again and again with his sleeves rolled up. He flicked the pasteboards with one hand, making them soar into the audience and over our heads, and bounced them off the floor. The most impressive moment came when he produced a stack of cards straight from his mouth, leaving the crowd astounded.

Everyone, including the other magicians, rose to their feet and applauded loudly. Jeff returned to his seat and kissed the woman who assisted him at the beginning.

"Who's the woman with Jeff?" I asked Thomas.

Thomas smiled. "That's his wife, Abigail. She's a musician, choreographer, and dancer, as well as Jeff's assistant. Very talented lady."

Julia spoke up. "Tom, you know my help will always be backstage support."

Thomas looked at his bride lovingly. "As long as you're with me, Jules, I'm fine with that."

Soon, the bridesmaids, led by Jyanette, whisked Julia out of the room. They were off to see their show of beefed-up male dancers. Julia was a good sport and waved at Thomas as they pulled her out of the room.

"So what's the plan for us guys?" Thomas said to me.

"The group is going to *X-tacy*," I admitted lamely — after all, I had nothing to do with it. "There's a bus downstairs to drive us over."

My father, who was at the table, said, "You young men have fun. I'm staying here with your mother. We'll make our own romance."

My mother turned red and slapped his arm, but she was smiling. "Sam, stop! Not in front of the children."

He leaned over and kissed her. It was a lovely moment. My parents and the Tannenbaum's left the room, as well as Mark and Rayna, who were passing on the bawdy festivities, leaving the night to the mostly single young men.

Thomas announced in his booming stage voice, "All right, gentleman. We are going to see the show *X-tacy* tonight. I haven't seen many shows, because I'm too busy doing my own, twice a night!"

"You'll be doing twice a night tomorrow as well, buddy!" yelled one magician, to laughs and hoots from the group.

Thomas continued. "I believe this show is of a highly artful type, with skilled dancers, and very professional variety acts."

"And topless women!" yelled another magician, and most of the men all hooted and hollered.

"Some of you are married and may not wish to join us," Thomas said and placed his hand over his heart. "And if so, you are free to go, with no repercussions—"

The crowd grew quiet.

"Except we'll be calling you a wimp for years," he bellowed, and everyone laughed. "Now downstairs, there's a party bus waiting to take us to the show!"

The group headed for the door and I grabbed Thomas' arm. "I have to tell you, I didn't arrange any of it. Your party planner did."

"I figured. Len, you're a great brother, but you really know nothing about hiring strippers or anything like that."

"Are you disappointed?" I said, concerned.

"This is perfect. We see a show! I wanted nothing too wild. Besides, there's a bar on the bus, and we can drink as none of us are driving."

"I'm also sorry for all the reporters that are outside."

"Are you kidding? This will keep my name in the paper for weeks! Ticket sales, Bro."

We walked out of the banquet room, and the reporters were there, flashing photos as Thomas put his arm around me and helped me keep up with the group. Some of the more intrepid reporters followed us down into the lobby and out a side entrance where a large bus waited.

Covered in a bright blue plastic, tall letters claimed the bus was THE ORIGINAL PARTY BUS.

Inside, there was a full bar set up with a lady bartender and a pair of gorgeous waitresses in bright blue sequin outfits. They held trays of champagne and handed them out as the men came in.

One of the waitresses walked up to me holding a flute glass with a sparkling liquid that looked extremely tempting.

"None for me," I said, waving her away.

She stepped close so only I could hear her. "It's not champagne, it's sparkling apple juice. I was told when I saw the man with the cane I should bring it to him."

I smiled. Leave it to Thomas to think of everything. I realized I'd never told Thomas I was a recovering alcoholic, but leave it to my twin to figure it out for himself.

I took the glass, thanked her, and felt tears of gratitude in my eyes. This was my brother saying he knew about my problem and accepted it without question.

I saw he was watching me. I raised my glass in a salute, which he returned.

During the ride, the magicians ended up performing tricks for the cute female servers, who clapped and squealed in delight. It was a role reversal where they got to be the guests, and I am sure they didn't expect it.

We were let off at the Three Kings Casino where I was the other day when I spoke to Rosie Graham. I was unaware the show she crewed for was *X-tacy*.

I still wondered about the suggestion Jyanette made about Rosie switching drinking glasses with Big John. Could she have administered the poison? But how would she have been able to make the poison, or get it? It's not like she could pick it up at a pharmacy. Plus, would she put muscarine into her own drink? That seemed insane.

Then again, this entire case was insane.

We were soon up the stairs and into the theater. Our seats were in the front row, close to the performers.

When the show started, a dozen women filled the stage. They came down an enormous staircase wearing rhinestone covered bikinis, large, feathered backpacks, and headdresses. One woman wearing a red leotard embossed with rhinestones, fishnet stockings, and high boots with a fanciful red top hat sang a song about beautiful girls.

Next, the curtains opened to mist and blue lights. On a table center stage, a figure sat in silhouette. It was Desirée Longing, bare-breasted and only wearing a tiny G-string. On the table was a collection of plates and sticks.

She picked up a plate and a stick and, with a quick flick of her wrist, the plate spun rapidly on top of the wooden implement. She slid off the table onto the floor and threw the plate into the air, only to catch it on the stick several times in succession.

She grabbed a second stick and plate with her free hand, and balanced the spinning plate on her chin as she started the second one. She repeated the tossing and catching until she was balancing the plates on both of her index fingers alone.

With the plates still spinning, she did an elaborate series of movements, bringing the plates under and over her arms while they balanced only on the one finger of each hand.

The crowd applauded wildly, and she carefully returned each plate, intact, to her table. She took a bow and at that moment made eye contact with me.

I was suddenly inside her mind, and I was backstage at this very theater, but it wasn't during the show.

The work lights were on and the women standing around wore dance warm up clothes instead of costumes, and the crew was on stage.

Facing me was Rosie Graham, who was listening as I was finishing up explaining how the lights needed to be set for the plate-spinning routine. With Desirée's voice, I asked, "So, what's your name again?"

"Just call me Rosie. Everyone does," Rosie said with a smile.

"What's that, a nickname or something?"

"Yeah, my real name is Vicky, but everyone calls me Rosie. I prefer it," she said and her face froze in my mind.

I cursed myself for not seeing it before. The daughter in the newspaper article about the Coles — Vicky Cole — had appeared familiar to me. I now knew why. She was the young Rosie Graham.

It was perfectly clear who murdered Sal Lombardo and Big John Rossi.

Now I knew why.

18. PROCEDURAL PURSUIT

Turning to my brother, I said, "I have to go. I've got a break in the case."

"What?" Thomas said, as the next number was starting.

I moved past the groomsmen, up the aisle and out to the hall, pulling my phone as I did. Tyrone picked up on the third ring.

"Aren't you supposed to be at a dinner or something?" he groused. "I was hoping for a night at home with my wife."

"Tyrone," I said. "Rosie Graham isn't Rosie Graham—"

"Then who is she, the Great Pumpkin?"

"She's Vicky Cole, the daughter of Jack and Olivia Cole, the magicians who helped Lombardo cheat."

"How do you know that?" he demanded. I could tell he wasn't pleased.

"I saw an article from years ago about the Coles and they photographed them with their daughter. Rosie is just a nickname because she does rigging."

I stopped in the lobby of the Three Kings, the noise of Fremont Street beyond the nearby doors.

"Okay, but that doesn't explain the poison or how we found it all over the Cryptic Collection back room."

"I think I have the answer, but I need to talk to Celeste. Is she still in holding?"

Tyrone sighed. "Yes, until tomorrow, when her lawyer is going to post bail. I suppose you want to bum a ride?"

"If I can. I'm at the Three Kings Casino."

"Does McGee have to drive you all around hell and creation?"

"In New Jersey, I have my own vehicle."

"That's convenient for him. All right, meet me at the entrance."

I ended the call and paced at the entranceway until Tyrone pulled up.

He headed toward the LVPD station. "This better be good."

"It is. If Rosie is Vicky, it means that Big John killed her mother."

"If what you're saying is true, why would she kill Sal Lombardo?"

"Lombardo gave the order to scare Olivia Cole, which caused the accident. But it's more than that. I think Rosie wanted to use the same trick to cheat in the upcoming tournament. That's how Will Anderson is involved."

"Why would she do that?"

"Maybe she still feels the casino owes her for taking her parents and making her an orphan."

"Look, this is all pretty flimsy. We only have Joe Rossi to verify that Big John told him he killed Mrs. Cole. That makes it hearsay."

"I might have more once I talk to Celeste."

We pulled into the lot, and the pair of us rushed to the door. Tyrone guided me back to an interview room, and arranged for two officers to bring in Ms. Moon.

I paced the room. I was tired from the day's exertions, but too energized to sit. After what felt like an eternity, they brought Ms. Moon in and she sat behind the table.

"Doctor Wise," she said. "I hope you have some good news for me."

"I might if you can help me. Who set up the lighting for the Cryptic Collection, all those spotlights and fake candles?"

This question surprised Celeste. "Oh? A lighting designer friend of mine did the work."

"By any chance, is he the lighting designer at the Three Kings Casino?"

"Yes," she said. "How did you know?"

"Just a guess," I said. "Did he bring his crew from the casino?"

"Only two people."

"Was one of those Rosie Graham?"

She frowned, lost in thought. "It was, now that you mention it."

"Did you have to give them keys to the entire building?"

"No, I was there for most of the renovation, about four years ago. They stored the lighting fixtures in the potions room. They had the equipment in one place and could get to the display through the bookcase door."

"Did you supervise the work?"

"As much as I could."

"And the lighting crew you hired had a key for that room?" I insisted.

"Yes, but they returned it once the work was done and approved."

After Rosie made a copy, I thought.

"When was the last time you used the potions room?"

She considered this. "The last time I made a supply was about four months ago. But I cleaned up after myself. I don't know how it ended up in such a mess."

"And when did Mr. Wells approach you about running the séance at the Golden Era?"

"About six months ago. They've been doing massive publicity for the last three months."

This fit the timeline Wells told me. Rosie heard about the show, and she probably saw an article about Sal coming to that first séance. That must have been when she put her idea into action. She had the opportunity of getting close to him. She had the means, which was a place she could make the poison, and she had motive, the death of her parents.

But how did she manipulate her way into doing the work and getting the invite to *Mystic Shadows*?

"This is good, Ms. Moon. You've filled in some gaps for me."

"Will you be able to find out who did this terrible thing?" she asked.

"I can't promise, but if everything works out, they will drop all charges made against you."

That made her smile.

As officers returned her to lock up, I went to the detective's bullpen and sat at a chair next to Tyrone's desk.

"I listened in," Tyrone said. "Rosie Graham put in the lighting at the Cryptic Collection."

"My guess is that she made a copy of the key to that back door to the potions room."

"You think she made the poison using the equipment there?" Tyrone said.

"Which is why it all tested positive for muscarine."

"Where did she get the mushrooms?"

"The Ivory Funnel is a common mushroom in North America," I said. "My guess is she took a trip and found them herself. They're easy enough to recognize and grow wild in almost every forest."

"If what you think is true, how did she administer the poison?"

"Both times at the séance, she wore a ring with a large amethyst. Her parents were magicians and mentalists. I think the ring has a compartment to hold the poison."

Tyrone shook his head. "That's a hell of a risk. She would have to be very careful not to get it on her hands."

"Maybe she felt the risk was worth it if she killed the men who murdered her parents," I said.

Tyrone faced his computer. "Okay, the *X-tacy* show has two performances tonight, and the later show is going to end in about an hour. I'll assign some uniforms to find her backstage once the show is over."

"Can I ride along with you?" I asked.

"You've gone this far. Might as well see it to the end."

Tyrone assigned four officers to come with us, and we soon arrived at the Three Kings Casino. At the casino, Tyrone positioned three men on the theater exits while he, I, and the fourth officer stationed ourselves at the stage door.

The show ended, and we saw the audience, which was overwhelmingly male, exiting the theater.

Tyrone went in the backstage entrance and was talking in a low tone to a woman who was about five feet-ten with short gray hair. I hastened to join him.

"You can't go in there. The ladies haven't dressed yet," the woman said.

Tyrone explained. "I need to speak to one of the crew, Rosie Graham."

"Rosie? She'd be up on the catwalk adjusting the lights," the woman said. "There's a convention using the theater tomorrow."

"How do we get to the catwalk?" Tyrone demanded.

"Which ones?" she replied. "We have several sets." She pointed down a hallway away from the dressing rooms. "Head down there, and past the stage there are metal ladders which will take you up to them."

Tyrone turned to the uniformed officer. "You wait here and if she comes out, arrest her."

"Yes sir," the officer said.

Tyrone and I headed down the hall, past openings that led onto the stage at several points. We continued behind the audience seats toward the back of the house.

We reached three solid metal ladders mounted on cement in the floor that went up to the catwalks.

"Okay, I'll go up this ladder," he said. "You monitor that one over there, in case she comes down."

"I could go up," I said.

"With your bad leg?" Tyrone said. "I don't think so."

I gazed up at the ladder. Each rung was solid and secure, and the entire conveyance was bolted to the floor, ensuring it remained steadfast. It went up through an opening in the hallway ceiling and up several stories to connect seamlessly with an imposing catwalk looming high above the audience.

Tyrone exhaled heavily. "I'm usually okay with heights, but this sucks."

He grabbed one of the sturdy rungs and pulled himself up. He was soon through the opening and climbing higher.

I stared up my ladder to the catwalk, stretching high overhead with lighting instruments and equipment hanging from the metal supports above it.

I saw someone dressed in black moving up there.

The surrounding air grew suddenly colder, and a shape came into view next to me. I turned to see the semi-translucent body of Sarah Lewis. She was looking up at the ladder and the figure high overhead with anger in her eyes.

"Sarah?" I said, puzzled by her appearance.

She glanced at me, then focused up again, her expression growing fierce.

"You can't blame Rosie. She didn't hurt you. She's a victim, like you."

Paying no attention to me, the spirit rose into the air and moved toward the catwalk.

"Sarah, no!" I said aloud, fear gripping me. This was a spirit that had more than once thrown me across the room. If she were up there with Rosie on a precarious catwalk and was angry at her, Rosie was in immediate danger from something she couldn't see.

Leaning my cane against the wall, I started up the ladder, pursuing the specter.

I don't have a fear of heights, but climbing that ladder and going so high over the audience seats in this large theater was harrowing. I could easily imagine a fall from this distance would kill or incapacitate me permanently.

My right leg was aching badly from the climb, which did not add to my confidence. If I made it to the top, could I get down again?

My concerns became secondary as I stepped onto the catwalk high above the showroom, my heart pounding. I moved along the narrow metal service platform, my eyes searching for the figure I glimpsed. I tried not to look down, as I felt a rush of vertigo from the vast showroom below, but I had to focus on my quarry.

The catwalk was one of many interconnected metal walkways that snaked above the audience and stage. I saw Tyrone walking on a different walkway many feet away from me. I waved to him and he shook his head in annoyance.

I gestured in the direction I thought I saw Rosie from the ground and he made his way to find the interconnection to meet me.

I crept along the metal walkways, my senses on high alert, reaching out to detect anyone. The maze of catwalks high above the showroom was disorienting, and I carefully navigated them. I saw a figure ahead, dressed in black. The person was down on their knees tightening the support bolt on a lighting instrument.

"Rosie," I said, and the figure looked up in surprise.

Connor Maxwell turned to face me, holding the guardrail. "What are you doing here?"

"I could ask you the same," I said.

His countenance grew dark. "Picking up extra work. I have to get my own apartment now. Since you told Desirée I was cheating on her, she threw me out."

"I'm looking for Rosie. Did you see her?"

"She's working the back catwalk. It's kinda unstable, and she's the only one who'll work on it."

Just what I needed, a catwalk that was more unstable.

"How do I get to it?" I asked.

He pointed. "Go this way and take the walkway to the right."

I worked my way past him. I made my way to the branching walkway and headed further toward the back of the theater.

I saw Rosie on a separate thinner catwalk that branched off from the one I stood on.

I was relieved to see she was alone. The ghostly Sarah was nowhere to be seen. I wondered if it had all been a trick by Sarah to make me climb up here.

"Rosie," I said, raising my voice.

She raised her head, saw me, and lifted her arm. "Stop, don't come on this walkway. It's not stable."

"You need to come with me down to the floor," I said.

She looked at the lighting instrument she was manipulating, and then at me like I was crazy. "Why?"

I fixed her with my gaze. "We know, Vicky."

She drew in a stunned breath and looked at me, and then down at the seats below us.

"What are you talking about?"

"We know about the poison, how you got the key to Celeste's back room, where you made it. That enormous ring you wore held it. You put it in your drink and switched glasses with the victims. You killed Lombardo because he gave the order to have your mother run off the road, and Big John was the one who did it. We also know about the poker scam. You used your real name for the tournament."

I stepped on the walkway, which rattled and shook, so I retreated. Rosie was right. It was unstable.

Rosie looked at me, and I saw tears in her eyes. "I knew Sal cheated and that my father helped him do it. After my mother died, my father fell apart and told me the entire story. But he told a reporter all about it, and she was going to reveal the entire plan on TV."

"Was that Sarah Lewis?" I asked.

"Yes. I took a bus to that damn hotel, the Sphinx, and found Big John, who took me to Sal Lombardo. I told him that Sarah Lewis was going to expose him for the fraud he was."

"Wait," I said, as a chill went up my spine. "You told Lombardo about Sarah?"

She stared at me fiercely. "I wanted to see the look on his face, but he just laughed at me. He said I'd had enough tragedy and should just go home. Then he had Big John escort me out."

It all fit together. Rosie revealed the story and got Sarah murdered. Big John probably abducted Sarah, brought her to that office, and Sal finished her. I wondered what he did to Sarah before he killed her.

"When Sarah Lewis disappeared, my father warned me never to say anything to anyone. Then, when he died, child protective services took me in, even though I was fourteen."

"How did you end up working on shows?"

"A stagehand who knew me became my foster parent. I worked the shows with him, and one day I saw Joe Rossi and Big John talking in the theater where I was working, but they didn't see me up on the catwalk above them. Big John told Rossi he killed my mom and that Joe had to keep quiet about the cheating."

I reached out my hand to her. "Vicky — Rosie — whatever you prefer, the police are here. Surrender yourself."

"They deserved it, both of them. I only regret it took so long to kill them. It took me years to find a place to make the poison—"

"You were going to let Celeste take the blame?"

"I don't owe her anything, with her stupid collection of junk. I heard of the séance show, and that Lombardo was going to be there. The ring could only fit enough of a dose to kill one of them, and I used it on Lombardo. When they thought he died of a heart attack, I knew I'd gotten away with it."

"You disposed of the glass the first time, but you couldn't the second time because the detective was there," I said. "The police found the muscarine. They know it was murder."

Tyrone appeared to my right, having found the correct walkways and figured out a route to me. He had his weapon drawn, but seeing Rosie out at the end of the catwalk, he slipped it back into his holster.

"The catwalk's unstable," I told him. "We have to bring her to us."

"Give it up, Rosie, there's no way out," Tyrone shouted.

I felt the air grow suddenly colder.

I stepped forward, but the catwalk shuddered. I pulled back, taking my weight off it.

A shape came into view, and Sarah stood next to Rosie, eying the young woman with fury in her eyes.

"Don't do this," I said to Sarah.

"What is she doing?" Tyrone said, his hand returning to his weapon.

Rosie saw where I was looking, turned and stepped back with a gasp. "No, it can't be."

"Rosie!" I shouted, trying to get her attention as she backed away on the catwalk.

She stepped back against the guardrail, stumbled, and plunged over it, falling backwards off the catwalk. For a moment, she seemed to hang in mid-air before plummeting to the ground.

She fell without a sound, as I yelled, "No!"

There was the terrible noise of breaking bone and flesh as her body struck the stage below.

There were screams, and the officer from backstage ran out and over to the limp body.

I knew the truth. She was dead.

"Shit," Tyrone said. "Len, are you all right? I have to go down there and call this in."

"I couldn't stop her," I said, miserable. I glared at Sarah, who stared back at me with a grim smile.

"I know," Tyrone said. "Can you get down by yourself?"

I nodded curtly, and he headed off.

I was still looking at Sarah.

"Now your revenge is complete," I hissed.

She stared down at Rosie's broken body, then with a glance at me — she merely faded away.

Sarah had wanted vengeance even more than Rosie.

Despite my shock and sadness, there was one thing more I needed to do this night.

19. SPIRITUAL SACRAMENT

Once at the bottom of the ladder, feeling more dead than alive, I retrieved my cane. In the time it took me to get downstairs, they brought in emergency personnel and more uniformed officers, but there was little they could do. Now it was a job for the coroner and the morgue.

I cursed myself for thinking Sarah was helping me to find the truth when what she really sought was vengeance.

Sarah used me as her energy source to tag along and find the person who gave her name to Sal Lombardo — but I knew where Sarah's ultimate source of power was.

The séance room at the Golden Era Casino where she'd broken through and freed herself.

The night of the second séance, the exploding planchette and the opening of the portal, allowed Sarah to leave her one room, her prison. I had been her ticket out.

It was time to shove that genie back into its bottle, and tired as I was, I was more than ready to do it.

I walked over to Tyrone, who was talking to one of the EMTs, and took him aside. "I'm going to call Bonnie Summers at the Golden Era and get into the séance room."

"What, now?" Tyrone said. "Len, it's midnight. Why do you want to go there at this time of night?"

My jaw was tight. "I need to clean up a few things."

"Look, Len, this case is over. I'm getting a warrant for her apartment. If we can find that ring you talked about and it has the poison, this case is closed."

"I know. That's why I need to get into the séance room. I need to close my part of the case. I opened something. Let's call it a door or a portal. It needs to be shut."

Tyrone sighed. "Do what you need to do."

I could only imagine what Sal did to Sarah before she died. Her death twisted her, corrupted her. She became what was called a *ruach ra'ah* in Hebrew or a *dybbuk* in Yiddish. Both terms meant an evil spirit.

There are many religious traditions to exorcise a spirit, the most well-known being the Catholic ritual, because of movies like *The Exorcist.* However, Judaism has rituals to remove spirits as well, but requires ten men in a synagogue to perform them. I obviously would not put that together in the middle of the night.

My mentor, Doctor Kohl, however, put the entire concept of spirits in terms of energy. Sarah received energy from the séance room where she first manifested. She used the energy of the participants in the first séance to move the gun and the second séance to break free of the limitations of that one room. Using my energy, she manifested in my hotel room, and she used the energy of the Cryptic Collection to appear there. She used both me and Rosie to manifest up on the catwalk.

Everywhere she appeared, Sarah required a source to maintain herself.

In a way, the spirit of Sarah Lewis possessed me.

She didn't take control of my body or anything like a demonic possession, but she could leave her one room to go with me as I studied the case. And since I wanted answers, I'd unknowingly allowed myself to be used.

It was time to get rid of my hitchhiker.

I pulled out my phone and dialed the number Ms. Summers had given me.

It surprised me when she answered on the first ring and sounded awake. "Bonnie Summers."

"Ms. Summers, this is Doctor Leonard Wise. I hope I didn't wake you."

"It's the casino industry, Doctor. Working nights is part of the job. Can you tell me anything?"

"I have some bad news. Rosie Graham fell from a catwalk."

"What?"

"Before she fell, she admitted to poisoning Sal Lombardo and John Rossi, so the Golden Era is not legally responsible."

There was a long pause, and I heard the slot machines behind her.

She finally spoke up. "I'm sorry she fell, but it is a relief from a liability point of view."

"I need to get into the séance room. Now, tonight."

"Why?"

I needed an excuse, and I went with the first one that came to mind. "Will Anderson may have been working with her. I need to check the bar."

It was a lie, but telling her I was going to battle a ghost might have limited me getting in.

"How long do you need to be up there?"

"Maybe all night," I said.

She exhaled heavily. "All right. When will you get here?"

I looked at my watch. "I'm at the Three Kings Casino and I'm going to walk over. Give me fifteen minutes."

"I'll meet you in the stairwell at the false wall. Does that work for you?"

"Yes, thank you." I ended the call and walked over to Tyrone.

"What's up?" he asked as I drew near.

"I'm going over to the Golden Era."

"I should come as backup."

"I appreciate that, Tyrone. But I'm going there to get rid of a ghost, and I need to do it alone."

"Sometimes, you say things that make me doubt your sanity," he said, shaking his head.

"Thank you for everything."

"Can you not make it sound like you're going to your death?" Tyrone said. "You're creeping me out."

"Let me know what you find at Rosie's apartment, will you?"

"Okay, that I can do."

Fremont Street was completely different at this time of night. The LED canopy overhead was dark, the street-performers were gone, and the DeeJay booths and the outdoor stages were closed down.

I quickly texted Jyanette, hoping she was asleep and would see it in the morning.

I'm fine and uninjured

I have to do some more work tonight

I'll be there in the morning, I promise

I soon arrived at the Golden Era and walked through the casino. The room was quieter than during the day. The players were a mix of die-hard locals and a few tourists, seeking the thrill of a late-night gambling session. There were only a few slot machines manned by players and only two table games with dealers. A tired-looking cocktail waitress stood at the bar, looking like she wanted nothing more than her shift to end so she could go home.

One dealer was Will Anderson. He followed me with his eyes, and I saw them grow wide when I entered the elevator. I took it to the top floor and walked down the now familiar hallways to the stairwell.

Bonnie Summers stood in front of the fake wall. "You made good time."

"Thanks."

She opened the wall. "You said Rosie Graham fell?"

We climbed the stairs. "I'm afraid the fall killed her."

"And you think she was working with Will Anderson to kill Mr. Lombardo and Mr. Rossi? Should I have security take him off the floor?"

"I believe they were working together to cheat your casino at the tournament you're having next week."

"What?" she said, shocked. "How could they do that?"

"Using a mentalist device," I said as she unlocked the séance room door. "I don't want to go into it right now. Not until the police have questioned Mr. Anderson."

"Of course," she said.

I slipped past her into the séance room. "If you want to leave, I can close up when I'm done."

"What are you going to do? Perhaps I can help?"

"There is something you could check on," I said. "For their cheating scam to work, Will and Rosie would both be at the tournament, with her playing and him dealing. Can you find out who schedules the players and the dealers for the tournament?"

She nodded. "I'll do that right now."

"It can wait until morning. Just let Detective Washington know once you find out," I said and gently closed the door with her on the other side.

I gazed around the room and noticed that forensics had taken all the glasses, but the bar still had bottles of alcohol displayed. The fake candles sat on top of the table, as well as the ouija board that caught my attention the first time I'd entered the room. I still saw pieces of the exploded planchette on the floor and table, and several chunks embedded in the wall.

The display case that held the old pistol was empty.

The gun that floated at the first séance was gone.

I forced myself to relax. Obviously, it was a display item and forensics may have taken it when they went through the room.

I also took it as a warning to remember what the spirit I was facing was capable of.

I wished I could light candles, but the only ones were the fake ones. I sat in the seat Celeste Moon had used in both séances.

I closed my eyes and focused my mind, knowing if I wanted to see the spirit, I needed to get down to her level. I wanted to understand, really understand Sarah. That meant I would have to take the fight down to the realm of the purely spiritual.

That idea frightened me.

I am trained in using what is called the astral form. It is a state where I am pure spirit and I actually separate from my body. I have used the technique at haunted houses to interact with entities trapped there. My concern is while I am in that state, I don't have the same amount of safety as I do within my body.

Yet, in that form, I took on actual demons and cast them out.

With my eyes still closed, I focused on my breathing.

In... out, in... out.

I felt myself relax, but I needed to go deeper, to move into a theta state. Too little and I would remain in alpha, too much and I could easily slip into a delta state and fall asleep.

My mind produced colors and sounds as I went deeper... deeper...

It's an odd sensation, and I am only familiar with it because I trained with Doctor Kohl to achieve astral projection. I learned through practice to feel when my soul frees itself from the limited physicality of my body.

I opened my eyes, but not really my eyes. From my visual angle, I was hovering above the table and saw my body sitting in the chair, my eyes tightly closed. A translucent cord about the thickness of a clothesline linked my astral body to the sitting one. Mystics call this the silver cord that tethers the spirit to the physical body. If something breaks that cord, I cannot return and my body will die.

I realized I was not alone.

Sitting at the chairs around the table were the figures of Big John Rossi, Sal Lombardo, and Rosie Graham aka Vicky Cole, each in the seats they used at the séances. I saw them clearly as if their bodies were there, and only a slight translucence let me know they were ghosts.

Their eyes fixated on me, and I came to understand that they were trapped in the room against their wills.

My gaze moved to the room's corner, where Sarah Lewis was standing.

With only a thought to propel me, I moved across the floor to stand face to face with her.

"You used me," I told her.

She gazed at the floor in response.

"You can talk to me," I explained. "We exist as beings of pure spirit. You can transmit your thoughts to me."

She glared at me and opened her mouth wide. I saw the stub in the back of her throat.

Her tongue was missing.

As I gazed in disbelief, my mind raced, desperately seeking answers to the ghastly questions that now consumed me.

I turned to the sitting figure of Sal Lombardo. He was no longer the image of the old man I saw in my vision, but the younger version that I glimpsed in Joe Rossi's memory.

"What did you do?" I wanted to yell at him, but our communication was purely mental.

"I did what I had to do," Sal said, his jaw tight. "I was a tough man in a tough business."

"Cutting her tongue out?" I demanded. "Did you rape her as well? Desirée told me what you did to her."

I wanted to delve into Sal's mind, to make him deal with the horror of the things he had done. He always believed his power and wealth gave him free rein over people's lives, even their bodies and souls. But now, released from his own physical body, I imagined he struggled to make sense of his own horrifying actions. For years, he did not face the truth. Now he had no choice.

"I've never forgotten her, or what I did to her," Sal said. "That's why I walled up this room, because I couldn't bear to be in it anymore."

Big John's movement caught my attention.

"Can you get us out of here?" he said, raising his hand. "I wanna be with my Isabella. I can feel her. I just can't get to her."

I looked at Rosie. "Do you want to go, too?"

She looked at me with concern. "I don't know. I killed two men." She looked at Sal and Big John. "Is Hell real? Is that where I'll end up?"

I glanced back at Sarah. She watched us but said nothing.

"You need to let them go," I said. "You're the force holding them here."

She shook her head, and a photograph exploded off the wall, crashing to the floor.

"Enough of your tricks," I demanded. "You can talk. Your tongue was part of your body. You are a spirit and are no longer limited by what happened to your body."

She turned away and worked her mouth, then faced me. "No," she said. She was amazed and touched her throat.

"Why would you keep them here?" I said.

She stared at me, her mouth working, and finally she pointed at Lombardo. "He left me here all these years." She paused, as if she was re-learning how to speak. She pointed at Big John. "He's the one who abducted me and brought me here." She pointed at Rosie. "And she's the one who told them I was investigating them."

She glided back away from me. "Don't you see? My death is their fault. Sal tortured me to death, but the other two are guilty as well."

"It is not your place to judge."

"I can judge and I find them guilty! I want them to know what it's like to be trapped in this room, only being aware when there is someone with the right energy to bring you awake."

"It was cruel when it happened to you. Why do you want to torture them?"

She faced me. "I want them to know what it feels like." She gritted her teeth and pointed at Sal. "Especially him, that monster..."

She glared at Sal, who sat at the table, unable to look at her.

"Don't you see? Trapped in this room, alone, by myself. Now I've got the bastards who took me, took my life and the woman who told them about me." She drifted over to Rosie and bent so she was face to face with her. "You got me killed."

Rosie turned away from her, sadness in her eyes. "I didn't mean to. I wanted to scare them."

"You scared them so badly that they murdered me."

Rosie bent over, her face in her hands.

"Sarah, it's time to stop this," I said. "You have the power to move on."

She stood up straight and glared at me. "What are you going to do about it?"

"You don't get it," I said. "I have the power in this situation."

"Why? Because you're still alive?" She pointed at the bar, and several bottles flew off the shelf and smashed to the ground. She pointed at my still body sitting at the séance table with eyes closed. "I can make one of those bottles smash against your head — and you'll be spending eternity here with me."

I looked over at my body. My breath came out as a fog. I couldn't feel it, but the air in the room was frigid.

"You're using up what energy you have. You think you can do anything because of the gun and the planchette. Celeste and I, and everyone sitting around the table, fed you the energy you needed. You need something to supply your energy." I pointed at my body, sitting head down, looking like I was asleep. "My body can't supply you what you need. While I'm in this state, you can't use my abilities or physical energy to power yourself."

"You are wrong," Sarah yelled. "There is a darkness here that I can use!"

She lunged at my astral body, as dark energy swirled around her, reaching out like tendrils.

I was stunned. What was the source of this dark power, and how could she manipulate it so easily?

She shoved into me and the pair of us fell into and through the bar. Several bottles fell to the floor.

"Sarah, you don't need to do this. You can find rest, you can find peace," I projected to her. I grabbed her ghostly wrists with my spectral hands. The black tendrils from Sarah were surrounding me, reaching like hungry serpents to grab and hold me. I shoved her away.

She faced me, the dark energy still around her, as I fought to figure out what created it. Was she powering herself with the anger of her premature death, and her desire for vengeance?

She would need a solid object from which to draw the energy. We floated a foot off the ground when something else caught my attention.

I saw the surrounding room, but it appeared dark and far away. When I went to this level, reality faded, and the spirits glowed, their luminescence taking my focus.

But I was facing the door to the room, and I saw it open, slowly.

I was sure I had locked it behind me.

Sarah frowned, and turned to face the door, as did the others.

Bonnie Summers stepped stealthily into the room. At first, I wondered what she was doing there — then I saw the large Colt

Peacemaker in her hands, the one that had been in the display case. She looked at my body, apparently asleep in the chair.

She was wearing rubber gloves to prevent fingerprints ending up on the gun and gunshot residue from marking her hands.

She gently locked the door and quietly stepped closer, raising the weapon as she did.

20. PRO FORMA FIGHT

A s a psychic, I often believe the answers will always come to me, and warn me in advance so I am always protected.

But I was stunned by Bonnie's appearance, and more by the pistol, which appeared enormous in her small hands.

Then I understood.

In order for Rosie and Will to pull off their plan to cheat at the poker tournament, they would need someone on the inside who could schedule them to be at the tables at the same time. Bonnie Summers was in charge of promotions. Who else would they put in charge of arranging the players and the dealers?

It all came to me in a rush — the article claiming I was a fraud, the misinformation of Sal and Big John dying of natural causes — this needed someone who knew publicity and could influence the press.

The clues had all been there. Bonnie said she hired Rosie to do the lighting in the séance room. Did Rosie's story of her slaughtered parents launch the plan to rip-off the casino? I wondered how Rosie would have approached Will, and now I knew. Bonnie was the middleman.

And I told her about the next person I wanted to investigate, warning her I was a danger!

As she drew closer to my inert body, I sensed what she planned. Shoot me, leave the gun, and blame the ghost. After all, there were photos and witnesses to the gun moving by itself. I was the only one who knew the truth, and with me eliminated, no one could trace the plan to cheat back to her.

I glanced at Sarah, but she was backing away, fear in her eyes. I thought she would be jubilant at my destruction, but she focused on the gun Bonnie held.

"Is that the gun Lombardo killed you with?" I asked.

She nodded. "I became aware when the workers found it."

I looked over and saw a black aura surrounded the pistol like a black hole. It was this weapon and the dark energy around it that powered Sarah's recent attack on me. Even not in the room, that weapon gave her enough power to strike.

Glancing at the gun, I sensed it had been used to kill more than just Sarah. It had been used to kill for years until Lombardo hid it in this room, only to be found during the renovation.

I faced Sarah, "Don't you see? You're using the power of that gun, the weapon that killed you, to attack me. It twisted you, turned you into something you're not."

Bonnie maneuvered closer to my unmoving body, the gun raised. I frantically tried to think of what to do. Pulling myself out of this deep level would take me a moment or two, not enough time to stop her from blowing my head off.

I had energy in this form like Sarah did, so I floated over to the bar and pushed a bottle.

My hand went right through it.

Sarah still looked at the gun, but projected her thoughts to me. "You must focus all your emotions."

"What?" I said.

"All of them. It is the only way you can move things."

I concentrated, put all of my energy, my anger, my determination, and my love for Jyanette into my hand, and pushed the bottle. This time, the bottle tumbled from the bar and crashed to the floor.

Bonnie turned, her eyes wide, and she crouched low, the barrel of the gun pointed at the bar. Her eyes flashed to my body to make sure I hadn't stirred.

I had not, of course. The real me was out here watching her as a witness.

Bonnie moved to the bar and glanced over the edge, convinced by the fallen bottle there was someone here.

I turned to Sarah. "You don't have to seek revenge anymore. You don't have to use the dark energy from that gun. Help me. Together, we can stop her."

Sarah still looked at the pistol, fully aware of the darkness surrounding the weapon. The history of violence and death that clung to it even now. The very energy she had been using.

Bonnie returned to the séance table, stood across from me, and aimed the gun at my chest in a clumsy two-handed grip.

Sarah turned away from me, and the dark energy surrounded her. A bottle flew off the bar and struck Bonnie on the shoulder, throwing her off-balance as she pulled the trigger.

The gun went off with a massive explosion, unbelievably loud, in the small room.

A framed photo on the wall exploded from the impact of the bullet. Bonnie fell to the floor, the gun slipping from her hand.

I grasped the silver cord and concentrated on forcing myself back into my body.

My training taught me to come out of an altered state slowly and carefully. Forcing yourself into full consciousness too quickly can lead to a feeling akin to a scuba diver rising back to the surface too quickly, which can lead to nausea, severe headaches, and disorientation.

But I had little choice.

Back in my body, I took a deep breath, raised my head, and gave it a shake to clear it. A cloud of smoke with an acrid smell filled the air.

Bonnie was on the floor holding her shoulder, struck by the bottle. As I rose from the chair, she rolled over and reached for the fallen gun.

I had a numbing headache and felt dizzy as I arose. She was only about a foot from the weapon. I clumsily stumbled around the table, my eyes on the gun.

She grabbed it and rolled to bring it up to point it at me. My training in Aikido kicked in. I grabbed the gun near the handle, pointing it away from me, and used a move called *tenkan kiri-oroshi* which means 'to cut and turn like a sword'. I twisted her hand and made her release the weapon.

Once freed from her grip, it fell to the floor and I kicked it away. The gun slid across the floor to the bar.

She screamed in anger and frustration, clawing at me with her fingernails, but her rubber gloves kept the nails from sinking in. I pulled my arm back and hit her with a simple strike called an *atemi* on the side of her neck and she fell unconscious.

I stumbled to my feet, my head spinning, and I lurched to the gun, sitting heavily on the floor as I picked it up. Pointing the barrel toward the ceiling, I opened the loading gate and carefully revolved the rotating cylinder, dumping the remaining bullets to the floor. Once done, I dropped the weapon, as it was too heavy for me to hold any longer.

I heard a pounding at the door, but I was too tired to get up and go to open it. After a moment, I heard a key in the lock, and the door opened.

I was relieved to see Kofi Johnson and Detective Washington. Tyrone had his gun drawn and scanned the room with it in a two-hand grip.

"Shooter down!" I croaked, drawing in deep, ragged breaths.

"What did you do to Ms. Bonnie?" Kofi asked, going to the fallen woman.

"She tried to shoot me." I pointed at the gun on the floor.

Tyrone put his service weapon back into his shoulder holster. He approached me, looking at the debris on the floor. "I thought it was an unloaded gun, merely for display."

I nodded. "Apparently, she found the bullets it needed." I pointed at the unconscious Bonnie. "She came in while I was meditating and tried to shoot me." I met Tyrone's eyes, remembering he wasn't supposed to be in this hotel. "What are you doing here?"

"Questioning Will Anderson," Tyrone said and shrugged. "We finished up at the Three Kings. I realized Anderson's shift was almost over and figured, what the hell? So I called Kofi and asked him to monitor Anderson until I got here."

"You were lucky," Kofi said, checking Bonnie's pulse. "We were in the meeting room downstairs and heard the gunshot."

Tyrone met my eyes. "You look like death warmed over. Are you all right?"

"Yeah. Bonnie was the person who put the scam together. She met Rosie and figured out how she could cheat the casino. I think she knew about Rosie's plan to poison Lombardo and Rossi."

"Anderson already told us that," Tyrone said. "We sat him down, told him that Rosie was dead and that we knew about the cheating scam. He confessed Bonnie approached him and asked him to be part of it, and that he would get a one-third cut if he co-operated."

"At least Bonnie was more generous than Sal Lombardo," I said, my head finally clearing.

"Come on downstairs, I am arresting the pair of them," Tyrone said, pulling out a pair of handcuffs.

"I can't," I said.

"Len, you're a witness. I need your statement."

"Get it in the morning," I said. "I need to finish this."

Bonnie was regaining consciousness, and Kofi helped her to her feet. She stood, looking woozier than me, and pointed at me. "Thank God you two are here. He attacked me."

"Give it up, Ms. Summers," Tyrone said, as he turned her around and snapped on the handcuffs. "We already talked to Will

Anderson, and he confessed to the entire scheme. Kofi, take her downstairs and hold her in the meeting room with Anderson."

Bonnie glared at me as Kofi led her out.

"I need the gun as evidence," Tyrone said as he pulled on a pair of gloves from an outer pocket.

"Is it okay that you leave me here?" I asked.

"I don't like it, but if you have to do it, get to it," he said, picking up the gun and the bullets. "You want me to stay?"

"No, I need to be alone."

He nodded and headed for the door. He stopped after he opened it and asked, "Are you safe up here? I could post an officer at the door. Are you sure there isn't anyone else coming up to get you?"

"Bonnie was the last piece of the puzzle," I said sadly.

He nodded and closed the door. I locked it.

Returning to the séance table, I sat down again and meditated. It took a few minutes, but I brought myself to that deep place and separated my astral self once again.

I saw Sal Lombardo, John Rossi, and Rosie Graham sitting around the table again.

Sarah came out of the corner of the room, becoming more solid as she floated toward me. I was glad to see she was no longer surrounded by the black aura.

"You were right," she said. "I used the energy of that gun. It made me want vengeance, to kill."

I faced her. "Sarah, I don't want to fight you. I want you to be at peace."

She looked at the ground. "How can I find peace? I lost everything. Lombardo tortured me, shot me with that very gun."

I glanced at Sal. "The gun was his?"

"Yes," Sarah said. "Then I saw that woman, and how the gun was twisting her to want to kill." She looked at the ground. "I realized I was no better than Lombardo."

"And you saw how it manifested."

"Yes, and I knew I didn't want to use such energy anymore."

"You can be free, Sarah," I said and gestured at the three other figures. "Your guests have no desire to stay here and I don't think you want to stay, either."

"Look, lady," Big John said, and rose from his seat. "I'm sorry for grabbing you out front of your house. I thought Sal was just gonna scare you. It wasn't until I saw you dead on the office floor that I realized what happened." He glanced at Sal and then back to Sarah. "I wanna be with my Isabella."

Rosie stood as well. "Sarah, I never should have told Lombardo about you. But staying here in this room? How does that help any of us?"

Big John looked at Rosie. "I did enough bad things in my life. Kid, I'm sorry about your mom. I only wanted to scare her so she'd lay off. I didn't want her to die, not her or your dad. Those two were always good to me."

Rosie nodded.

"I'll stay," Sal said, not looking up.

"What?" I said.

"It's the haunted hotel, right? Well, I'm haunted too. All the things I did in this room, they stay with me." Sal turned to Sarah.

I saw my opportunity and turned to Sarah. "If you really want to move on, I can help."

Sarah frowned. "Can you?"

"Let me show you," I said and faced Big John. "Focus on your wife and look into that corner of the room," I said and pointed at the wall where I'd seen Sarah the first time. I was sure it was where we created the portal.

"What do I do?" John asked.

"Think about your wife," I said, "and how you want to be with her."

I focused as well, hoping…. believing…

A faint white light appeared in the corner. Slowly, the light grew brighter, until it formed a shimmering circle hovering in mid-air. Within it, blue lights swirled with otherworldly energy.

This was the portal Celeste and I accidentally opened at the second séance. It was still there. I wanted to use it to help the spirits move on, and then close it so it would no longer be a bridge between the living and the dead.

"Where will that take us?" Sarah glared at the opening with trepidation.

"It will allow you to move on," I said. "I don't know where you'll end up, but I know you'll be free of this place."

"Did you hear that?" Big John said, looking at the others. "It's Isabella. I hear her calling me."

Big John moved toward the glowing circle, but I called out. "Wait! Where is Sarah's body? If I can find her, I can get her a proper burial."

"That's only right." He met my eyes, and an image flashed in my mind. I saw a parking lot in the desert at night, and a red stone with writing on it I read from a powerful lamp overhead:

Red Rock Canyon

Welcome to the

Late Night Trailhead

Big John spoke. "There's a brown sign post, a bulletin board. You'll find her buried right behind it."

He stepped into the circle and a smile appeared on his face as he faded away and was gone.

Rosie turned to me. "May I go, too?"

I glanced at Sarah, who stood in awe of the spinning circle. She moved her eyes to Rosie and nodded.

"You can," I said. "If you're ready."

Rosie stared at the circle in amazement. "I hear them. I hear my parents."

Rosie glared at Sal, then rushed past him and into the circle where her ghostly shape faded away.

Sal looked at Sarah. "Go on, Sarah. You spent enough time trapped here."

Sarah stared at the opening, an expression of apprehension on her face. "I don't know if there is anyone waiting for me."

I moved to her. "Listen. Try to hear who would call you."

Sarah lifted her head, and a smile appeared on her face. "It's my mother and my father. I hear them calling me."

"Then go to them."

With a glance at me, she stepped through the portal and faded away.

I faced the one spirit that remained. "You can leave too, Sal."

Sal shook his head. "No." He looked around the room. "For years, this place was my life. Don't they need a ghost here to make it a haunted hotel? So I'm gonna haunt this place until they tear the whole thing down."

"If that is your choice," I said.

"It is," he said. "But tell you what, if I cause too much trouble, maybe you'll come back and offer me a way out, huh?"

"You don't need me, Sal," I said. "You can leave any time you're ready."

Sal nodded. "Right now, I ain't ready."

I wanted to close the portal, and I turned to face it.

A voice I knew spoke, far away and faint, but I knew it well. "Len? Is that you?"

My throat tightened. "Cathy?"

"Yes, my darling. I'm here." It was the voice of my dead fiancée, Cathy Garber, far away and yet near at the same time.

I moved toward the circle of light, reaching out my hand. A barrier stopped me. I felt it with both hands, but it would not let me through.

"You can't come here, Len, not yet," she said. "It's not your time. Go back to your life. Marry Jyanette, Len. Be happy."

"But Cathy, I have to know—"

The spinning circle shrank before my eyes, and her voice faded. There was a small burst of energy as the portal became no bigger than a pinhole, the light fading away as quickly as it appeared.

I moved to my body, felt myself reconnect, and carefully brought myself back to a waking state.

I opened my eyes and looked around, seeing nothing but the surrounding room. I pulled my coat closer. The room was chilly, but it was rapidly heating.

I still sensed Sal was there, but I could no longer see him.

The others were gone.

Utterly exhausted, I dropped my head to the table and fell asleep.

21. WEDDING RITES

I heard a noise and lifted my head. I was in the séance room. Sunlight poured in through the window. I groaned as I sat up.

The noise was my phone.

"H-Hello," I said, my mouth so dry I could barely form the words.

"Thank God," Jyanette said. "Are you all right?"

"I'm fine," I said. "What time is it?"

"Nine in the morning." Her tone changed. "You wanna tell me where the Hell you've been all night?"

"I'm… uh… in the séance room at the Golden Era. I had to set some ghosts free."

"If you were any other man, I would call that one lame-ass excuse," Jyanette said. "But in your case, that would be something you'd do."

I attempted to rise, groaned, and fell back into the seat.

"Where did you sleep?" she asked.

"I passed out on the séance table," I lamented. "And now I'm paying for it." I took a deep breath to center myself. "We caught the killers — there were three of them."

"That's good, right?"

"No," I muttered. "The ghost frightened one, and she fell to her death."

"Len, that's terrible," Jyanette said, and I could tell she was serious. "You weren't... y'know... drinking, were you?"

"Not a drop, darling, I swear. But I could sure use some painkillers right now."

"Come back to the hotel and you can catch a few hours' sleep before the wedding."

I made my way downstairs and arranged an Uber. I was exhausted and really not ready for a joyous occasion like a wedding.

It occurred to me I hadn't looked at the best man speech I wrote back in New Jersey. If I had just had a few hours in an actual bed, I would be much better off.

My ride arrived, and as it headed toward my hotel, I texted Tyrone:

Sarah Lewis

Red Rock Canyon, Late Night Trailhead

Body buried behind the brown bulletin board

The driver travelled the wide Las Vegas streets, and in a few minutes, he dropped me off at the Majestic Odyssey.

"Darling," Jyanette said, rushing to me as I walked into the room.

She hugged me, and I just broke. All the feelings from the last night, losing a life, and the purging of the spirits — it was all too much. I held Jyanette and sobbed like a child.

"Shh, it's okay, it's okay," she said and guided me to the bedroom. She sat me on the bed like a child to pull my clothes off, and lay me down in my underwear and held me as the storm passed and soon sleep took me.

That damn ringing pulled me out of sleep, and I looked over to the nightstand to find my phone. It was past four in the afternoon, and Jyanette was gone.

I grabbed the phone.

"Hello?" I felt better. The sleep was exactly what I needed.

"Len? How are you feeling.?" Jyanette asked.

"A lot better," I said. "Where are you?"

"Where am I? Len, the wedding is in two hours. I'm getting made up and my hair styled and shoehorned into my dress, as well as helping Julia."

"Of course, sorry."

"If you're going to be ready on time, you'd better get started."

"Yes, dear," I said in a singsong.

"Keep talking to me that way and you could still end up with a black eye," Jyanette joked. At least I hoped she was joking. "Be downstairs no later than five thirty."

"I'm on it," I said and ended the call. Before I could get myself motivated, I called Tyrone.

"Len? Are you back in the land of the living?" Tyrone answered.

"More or less," I said. "Did you get my message about the body?"

"Got it and sent a forensics team out there this morning. You gonna tell me how you knew the body was there?"

"What if I said Big John told me?" I explained.

"That's as good as any other story. There was identification with the body, and although they don't have a positive ID yet, it looks like it was Sarah Lewis."

"Hopefully her family will get closure," I said.

"LVPD went through Rosie's apartment early this morning. They found that ring you mentioned. And you were right, it had a little tube, and when you pushed the side it released liquid. The lab said it contained muscarine, and it matched what they found in the glass and the stomach contents. The coroner, Doctor Peters, says he can't imagine how you knew."

"I can't give away all my secrets," I said.

"Get this, when we went to the basement of her place, the police found a planter — she was growing the damn Ivory Funnel mushrooms."

"So much for where she got them," I said.

"We got Will Anderson downtown, and he confessed to the entire plan, saying it was all Bonnie's idea. Ms. Summers shut her mouth and asked for a lawyer, but we got a warrant for her apartment and found the electronic signaling device that fit in the shoes. A run on her financials showed she paid the fee for Rosie to join the tournament. When can you come down and give me a statement?"

"Not today. I have a wedding to attend."

"Tomorrow then. Len, I'm afraid your name is going to be all over the newspapers for the next few days, but hopefully not the hatchet job they did the other day."

"Why? I didn't give any interviews or tell anyone what I was doing."

"You don't need to. We released Ms. Moon, and she has been going on and on about how you saved her."

"Great! One more thing I don't need."

"Sorry, but I'm sure your fifteen minutes of fame will be over pretty quickly."

"Thanks for calling me in. I'll tell McGee that you and I work together well."

"You're an unusual asset, Len. I hope we get to work together again someday. But not too soon. I could use a rest and some normal cases."

"Thanks, Tyrone."

I ended the call and headed in to take a hot shower. I followed it with a shave and it pleased me that the bump on the back of my head had gone down, and the cut on my scalp was unnoticeable.

I dressed in my white tuxedo jacket with the black formal pants and vest. My outfit had patent leather shoes that fit my size fourteen feet.

With my hair properly combed, I cut a handsome figure. Not bad for a guy who spent the week getting kicked around like a soccer ball and almost shot the previous night.

With ten minutes to spare, I took the elevator down and went to the room set aside for the groomsmen.

As I walked down the hall, guests were already filing into the meeting rooms that acted as the chapel. I saw a familiar face or two.

The efficient Ms. Patterson was walking up and down the hallway, escorting several reporters and talking about the advantages of using the Majestic Odyssey as a wedding venue. She excused herself to catch up to me.

"Doctor Wise, I see you're right on time," she said, glancing at her watch.

I chuckled. "My fiancée made threats." I turned to her. "Thank you so much for arranging everything last night. You really saved me."

She smiled, a genuine smile for once. "I just hope you enjoy today's service."

"I'm sure I will," I said.

She headed off toward the reporters. I had that strange feeling again, like there was a joke and I wasn't in on it.

I headed into the groomsmen's room where the men were sitting around, all in their tuxedos. Jeff McBride was there as well and looked good in a plain tux. After the previous night, I missed the fancy top hat he usually wore.

Thomas turned to me and handed me a white kippah, which I put on my head. "Are you all set?"

"I have the simple part," I said and pulled out the prepared speech. "I just have to read this at the reception."

"We'll see," Thomas said, a twinkle in his eye.

I frowned and pulled Thomas aside. "Is anything wrong? Everyone has been treating me kind of weird. Even the dragon lady smiled at me."

"Ms. Patterson? She was probably just happy you showed up on time," Thomas joked. "Len, you've been working with the police for too long. You're becoming paranoid."

The groomsmen were all sipping champagne, and there was a bottle of sparkling cider as well, so I poured myself a glass.

Thomas clapped his hands over his head. "Now, everyone, we are taking posed photos in the chapel soon after the ceremony while the guests go to the cocktail hour. Try not to set your clothes on fire or anything."

"No promises," said one magician, which made the others laugh.

Ms. Patterson peeked in. "Gentleman, this is your five-minute call."

Cries of "Thank you, five!" went around the room, which puzzled me.

McBride saw my look of confusion and stepped next to me. "That's what a stage manager does in a show. They announce the five-minute call, and everyone responds that way."

I nodded, getting it. "Best way to get a bunch of performers prepared." I headed over to Thomas. "Ready, Tom?"

"Ready and happy about it," he said, and looked me over. "I'm glad you could be part of it."

"Wouldn't miss it," I said.

Thomas and I led the group to the entrance of the temporary chapel as the last few people headed in, and we met Rabbi Goldstein at the doorway.

The Rabbi smiled. "Do you have the rings?"

I think I went white, but Thomas glanced at Jeff, who nodded with a smile, and I calmed down.

"Should I have been holding the rings?" I said.

"Relax," Thomas said with a huge smile. "You'd think you were the one getting married."

The groomsmen chuckled, but I was grateful someone handled the situation.

There was a harpist and pianist in the room's front and they played a Yiddish tune I remembered from my childhood. Rabbi Goldstein walked into the room up the five steps of the raised platform and stood under the chuppah, smiling and nodding at the gathered group. The groomsmen went next, one at a time, spaced perfectly, just as we rehearsed it. The nice thing about stage performers, they remember their choreography and know how to hit their mark.

Our father and mother joined Thomas and I, escorting us to the dais, where they moved out for their seats in the first row. The pair of us walked up the steps and joined the Rabbi under the chuppah. The music changed, and the bridesmaids started down the aisle, again all moving in perfect precision and keeping the pace going.

Julia, in her flowing white dress, entered at the end of the group, with Aaron and Leah Tannenbaum on either side of her, following the Jewish tradition of parents escorting the bride. The music shifted into the traditional bridal march and everyone in the audience stood. Julia came down the aisle, a transparent white veil over her face, beaming, looking almost ethereal as she approached. I couldn't help but smile, as multiple photographers in the audience snapped photos.

She reached the bottom step of the platform, and her parents went to their seats in the first row. She turned and faced the entrance to the room, which surprised me.

As the bridal march continued, Jyanette appeared in a flowing white bridal gown with long sleeves and a transparent veil over her face. On either side of her were her parents, George and Deka Emery. Her tall father was on one side and her mother on the other, both of them beaming.

My mouth fell open.

"You'd better close your mouth before something flies in," Thomas muttered to me.

"How?" I murmured.

"You said you wanted to get married, and Julia thought it was a great idea. I mean, unless you've changed your mind."

I stood up straighter and looked at my beautiful woman as she drew near.

"Absolutely not," I gasped.

George and Deka smiled up at me, and I saw tears of joy in Deka's eyes. The two brides ascended the stairs and the pair of them faced their grooms.

"Surprised?" Jyanette whispered.

"Very," I said back.

"Pleased?" she asked, her eyes wet.

"Extremely!" I said, and felt my eyes become teary as well.

Rabbi Goldstein directed us where to stand and started the ceremony. First, he explained the chuppah, that it symbolizes the home the two couples would make, filled with love, hospitality, and welcoming to all.

The Rabbi filled two cups of wine in silver Kiddish cups, the type of goblet used in all Jewish festivals and Jyanette leaned close. "Should I have gotten grape juice?"

"Don't worry," I whispered. "A little alcohol will keep everyone out of my head. I'm willing to risk it."

The Rabbi did the blessing over the wine, and Thomas and Julia drank. He handed me my cup, and I turned to Jyanette and we each took a sip. As with all forms of alcohol, I immediately felt my psychic abilities fade.

Jeff McBride handed a ring box to each of us. Thomas took out his ring, looked at Julia and declared, in Hebrew, "You are sanctified to me with this ring, according to the law of Moses and Israel."

I pulled out a lovely, simple band for Jyanette, and knowing Jyanette wasn't Jewish, offered the variant, "You are sanctified to me, with this ring, according to the traditions of Israel."

Both brides put the rings on our fingers as well, making it a double ring ceremony. Thank goodness Thomas and I were twins, because the ring fit perfectly.

The Rabbi handed Thomas a pair of papers which I knew had to be the Ketubah, which is the covenant of the marriage and signed by the officiant, bride, groom, and witnesses. He handed me one and a pen and took the other.

I unrolled the scroll, which was embellished with artwork and fine lettering. I signed on the blank line meant for me, and Jyanette signed in the correct place.

Two of the groomsmen pulled out cloth bags and placed them on the floor next to Thomas and me. These contained glasses for us to break, a tradition that goes back centuries.

Thomas eyed me and counted, "One… two… three."

We stomped on them and to the sound of breaking glass, everyone in the room yelled, "Mazel tov!"

I lifted Jyanette's veil and planted a kiss on her lips as the harpist and the pianist played the traditional exiting march. Thomas and Julia went first, and we followed. As we headed out to the hallway, smiling, the impeccable Ms. Patterson guided us into two separate rooms.

"I'll come get you for the photos in ten minutes," she said.

We went into our room, and I helped Jyanette sit, as her wedding gown was unwieldy.

"Okay, this part I don't get," she said. "We sit in a room by ourselves alone. What does that do?"

"According to Jewish custom, it makes the marriage official," I explained. "How did you arrange all this?"

She sat back in her chair, a smug look on her face. "I mentioned to Julia that you wanted to run off and get married, and all of this was her idea. We picked out the dress while the bridesmaids were getting fitted. I called my parents and my sisters and they all flew out. Even Margery came."

"Mrs. Higgins is here?" I said, stunned that our Irish landlady had flown out to be part of the event.

"She said she wouldn't miss it."

"But how did you get the license? I mean, I was busy on the case all week."

"Oh, that," she said, waving dismissively. "I simply went into your wallet and removed your driver's license. Thomas went with me to sign the papers.." She leaned forward conspiratorially. "He's very good at forging your signature."

"He always was."

"Then I snuck it back into your wallet. I guess if you ever wanted to divorce me, you could claim we tricked you into it," she said.

"Seems petty after all this trouble."

"Agreed. I want to get the photo of your face when I walked into that room, and have it blown up into a poster," she said with a chuckle.

"I felt very surprised."

She glanced around the room. "So how does us being alone for ten minutes make the marriage legal?"

"In ancient days, the newly married couple would consummate the marriage."

She raised her eyebrows. "No way, you're not messing up my makeup before photos," Jyanette said, taking my hand. "We'll have to do our consummating tonight."

"I look forward to it," I said and kissed her.

Soon Ms. Patterson came out to collect us, and we spent the next thirty minutes posing. We took photos together with the group.

Finally, the party moved into the Grand Banquet room as Jyanette and I lined up with the rest of the bridal party. I had time to get to George and Deka, and hug them.

We filled the night with dancing, sometimes couples, sometimes just the men, sometimes just the women, but the food was great and the mood joyous. I got to do my best man's speech, and to my surprise, Thomas gave a speech to me and Jyanette.

I sat across the head table next to Jyanette and thanked Thomas and Julia, who were all smiles.

It was the happiest day of my life.

22. EPILOGUE

The next day, I awoke in our hotel room, after a night of some pretty amazing consummating. My bride filled the massive tub, and the sound woke me.

"Good morning, Mrs. Wise," I said.

"Good morning, Mr. Wise," she said. "Or do I have to call you Doctor, like Margery does?"

"Mrs. Higgins and I have established habits, but I think you can be informal."

I pulled her close to kiss her and caressed her back.

"Don't get started. We have to meet the families for brunch in an hour, which is just enough time for a bath."

"Not if we take it together."

"Mr. Wise, have mercy on your bride," she said in a mocking tone. "For she has led a sheltered life and is not used to a man's rampant desires."

"After brunch, I have to go to LVPD and give my statement," I said.

"Not until you tell me what happened. I want to hear every detail."

We took the bath together, and as the tub filled, I told her everything I knew. Rosie's desire for revenge, Bonnie's greed, and Will Anderson being in on the plan. I mentioned hearing Cathy's voice and her wish for me to marry Jyanette.

As we dressed, she said, "If you hadn't been involved, no one would have thought it was murder at all. Do you think they would have gotten away with the cheating plan?"

"We'll never know," I said.

Brunch was a relaxed affair, and George and Deka Emery were there, as well as Jyanette's two older sisters, Natisha and Shanika. It was fun to see the sisters because all three of them are almost six feet tall, like Jyanette. Both sisters had skin tones like their father, and only Jyanette possessed her mother's ebony coloring.

The sisters hugged and chatted as I sat at the table next to Mrs. Higgins.

My landlady was a short woman, gray-haired, with a few auburn highlights mixed in the neatly done bun on her head. She was wearing a very nice dress, and she looked radiant.

"So you flew out alone?" I said, hugging her.

"Aye. I'm a grown woman and can get on a plane all by meself, Doctor," she said with her lovely Irish brogue.

"Sorry, we got little chance to talk last night."

"T'was a beautiful ceremony, Doctor," she said. "I'm so glad Jyanette called and told me to come."

George said, "Glad we could make it out, Len — I guess I should get used to calling you, son."

Deka put herself in the seat next to me on the other side of Mrs. Higgins. "You certainly looked surprised."

"I was," I admitted. "I had talked about running off and getting married, but I expected nothing like what Jyanette and Julia pulled off. And having all of you here made it even more special."

As we ate, my mother gave a rambling speech about how all of her children were now married, and she had her heart set on more grandchildren. People rose and said lovely things about Thomas and me, as well as Julia and Jyanette.

Finally, my father got up. "I know that Thomas and Julia have plans for their honeymoon, but for my other son and newest daughter, we have gotten together and—"

"With some help from a sister property of the Majestic Odyssey," Thomas added.

"We've arranged for a two-week stay for you two at the Edgewater Resort in Lake Tahoe."

Missing…

The announcement elicited applause around the table, but I heard the buzz in my head. I didn't know if it was a warning or a bit of information I needed to know, but it sent a shiver down my spine.

I looked at my bride, who was several seats down from me. "Is that okay with you?"

She shrugged. "I'm currently unemployed, and you're on summer vacation from the university. To me, it sounds great."

"You should go, Doctor," Mrs. Higgins said. "Ye'll ne'er know what ye'll find."

"I agree, Len," Deka said. "I believe they need you there."

Jyanette's eyes grew wide, and we took several steps away from the table. "What did my mother mean by that?"

"What? Nothing. I just — uh — might be needed."

She shook her head, a threatening tone in her voice. "We are not going to some resort for our honeymoon and you run off to play detective and leave me alone."

"Of course not," I blurted.

Jyanette eyed me with suspicion. "Okay then, just so that's clear."

I thanked my father — and everyone — profoundly. It turned out we would have to fly up to Reno and drive down to the resort, and Jyanette and I talked about leaving after the weekend.

As I talked with her, I got the buzz a second time.

Missing…

I was trying to determine what it was. Could it have been something I needed to know?

Or was it a warning?

FREE PREVIEW

VANISHED IN THE MIND

DOCTOR WISE BOOK 13

ARJAY LEWIS

MIND
BENDER
PRESS

PREVIEW

I sabella Fontaine stabbed at her phone, her perfectly manicured nails clicking furiously as her voice rose in frustration.

"How could you leave me in this place? There is absolutely nothing to do!"

Her father's voice remained infuriatingly calm. "Isabella, my darling." His composed tone only stoked her anger. "You've created quite the stir in Hollywood with your... shall we say... headline-grabbing relationship with that actor—"

"Georgio is going to be famous one day," she snapped.

"Fame or not," he continued smoothly, unfazed, "the fact remains that gossip sites splashed images of the two of you — drunken and disheveled — all over the internet. And let's not forget the unfortunate incident with your dress—"

"That was an accident... a wardrobe malfunction!" she huffed, but couldn't help a small smirk. The memory of that night — blazing camera flashes, the roar of paparazzi, the rush of knowing all eyes were on her — felt like a dream compared to her current predicament.

She faced the full-length mirror. She knew she was striking — her tall, statuesque frame exuding effortless grace. Silky waves of chestnut brown hair tumbled over her shoulders, framing her piercing green eyes and high cheekbones. It wasn't vanity. It was simply a fact — she belonged in the spotlight, not hidden away in some remote location.

Her father sighed, the weary, long-suffering sigh that only a diplomat and father of Isabella Fontaine could muster. "Seeing my daughter sprawled across a sidewalk in a less-than-dignified state has caused me no end of distress."

"I don't understand why I have to be a prisoner here!" she protested, her voice edging toward a full-blown tantrum.

"Listen, Isabella," he said, his patience thinning. "My reputation depends not just on my actions, but my family's as well. If I embarrass our country, they will recall me, and then you will have to either return home or fend for yourself."

She scoffed, still admiring her reflection. "I could manage. I could start a brand — become an influencer, start a blog or a podcast... or something."

Her father chuckled indulgently. "My dear, you wouldn't be able to run a lemonade stand even if someone else squeezed the lemons and handed you the money."

She scowled.

"All I need from you is to stay at the Edgewater Resort for a few weeks. Lie low. Let the media frenzy settle—"

"There's nothing to do here!" She flung herself onto the plush sofa, tossing a throw pillow for good measure.

"There are plenty of activities," her father countered, clearly unimpressed. "Perhaps fewer than the ones available at your usual Hollywood soirées, where you... shall we say, 'bared it all'."

Isabella let out an exaggerated sigh, willing herself not to scream.

Her father pressed on. "And if this Georgio fellow truly cares for you, he can visit. Lake Tahoe isn't the end of the world — you're only a few hours from L.A."

"We broke up!" she shot back, bristling. "And how do you expect me to meet anyone new? I'm stuck on a goddamn mountain in the middle of nowhere!"

"The Edgewater is a five-star resort with exquisite amenities, and you have your own private chateau," he reminded her.

"Oh yes, and my only company is Victor, the world's least talkative bodyguard," she grumbled.

"Victor is there to ensure you don't find yourself in another compromising situation. First, the dress incident, then the beach —"

"The beach wasn't my fault!" she protested. "I thought it was a nude beach! In Europe, no one cares!"

Her father groaned. "Just stay put until I say otherwise. Can you do that for me, my little one?"

Isabella clenched her teeth, gripping the pillow tightly. "Fine," she bit out. "But I'm not happy about it."

"Neither am I. But I have crucial meetings this week, so please try not to flood my inbox with complaints. I promise I'll visit soon and take you shopping."

She exhaled sharply. "Yes, Poppa."

"That's my good girl." His tone softened. "I'll call when I'm on my way."

Isabella tossed her phone onto the sofa, where it fell in between the cushions. She let out a long, exaggerated groan.

A knock at the door brought her to her feet, irritation bubbling back to the surface.

"Now what?" she muttered, stalking to the door. If Victor was bothering her with something pointless again, she was going to scream.

She yanked the door open—

And froze.

A tall man in a server's uniform stood in the doorway, a black skull mask covering his face.

Before she could react, he shoved his way inside.

She stumbled backward. "What the hell are you—"

The click of a pistol's safety disengaging cut her off. It had been hidden under the tray the man had carried.

Her heart slammed against her ribs as the man aimed the gun — sleek, black, with an intimidatingly long silencer attached to the barrel.

Three more masked men burst through the door, their heavy footsteps shattering the fragile stillness. Between them, they dragged a figure — Victor. Isabella's heart clenched, a cold pit forming in her stomach as they brutally hurled him to the floor. Victor — the man who had been her shield, her silent guardian through countless dangers, the one who had stood by her side long enough to become more than just a protector. He was her friend. And seeing him like this, vulnerable and broken, sent a wave of fear and helplessness crashing over her.

He groaned weakly, blood soaking into the plush carpet.

"Victor!" she gasped, but the moment she tried to move, a hand clamped over her mouth.

"*Silencio*," one of the masked intruders ordered, his breath hot against her ear.

She thrashed against him, but a quick jab of the gun's muzzle against her temple stopped her cold. The gun felt warm — too warm — as if someone had recently fired it.

"You're coming with us," another voice said, low and devoid of emotion. "Make a sound, and I'll make sure you never make another."

Tears burned at the edges of her vision. She nodded, her body rigid.

The hand over her mouth finally lifted, and she sucked in a shaky breath.

"Come," the man commanded.

Rough hands seized her arms, dragging her toward the door. The cool mountain air hit her like a slap as they shoved her into a white, windowless van idling at the curb.

"What do you want with me?" she croaked.

One man turned his masked face toward her, his eyes gleaming with something dark— something cruel.

"*El Conjurador Oscuro* wishes to speak with you," he said, his voice like gravel.

Her blood turned to ice.

TO BE CONTINUED IN

VANISHED IN THE MIND

DOCTOR WISE BOOK 13

AUTHOR'S NOTE

Good to see you, admirer of the odd.

Ritual In the Mind was my attempt at a new way of writing. I love the classic murder mystery trope, where someone murders a person in a roomful of people, making all the other guests suspects. I wanted to try my hand at this classic technique with the Dr. Wise weirdness thrown in.

I even flew out to Las Vegas and stayed at the Apache Hotel, famed for being a "haunted hotel." I didn't meet any ghosts, but I got some great background information, and everyone who worked there was very helpful in my research.

My first draft didn't work as well as I'd hoped, but fortunately, my editor made suggestions that fixed many of my problems, and I increased the pace of the events. I even used a little known technique for the murders.

Jeff McBride, who appears in the book, is a real person, and an actual magician and magic teacher. I have also known him for about a half a century. He gave his permission to appear as a character in the book, and I think it added a level of realism.

The one thing that is different at the end of this book from every other Wise book is that it is a cliffhanger. Since the next book takes place during Len and Jyanette's honeymoon, I will get it out quickly, and the two books are "paired" together.

Vanished In The Mind will be a much bigger story, affecting an entire resort and perhaps an entire town. I hope to see you then!

—Arjay Lewis

ABOUT THE AUTHOR

K nown as the "Wizard Of Odd", Arjay Lewis is an actor, magician, and multi-award-winning author.

I write tales of the strange and the horrifying.

I have spent my life as an entertainer, amusing people as a street-performer in the 1970s; a Broadway and casino artist in the 1980s; a party performer in the 1990s and 2000s; a cruise ship performer in the 2010s.

Stories have always been in my mind, and I have been writing since the 1990s. My reason to write is simple: to entertain. I write the type of books that I like to read: murder mysteries, strange tales of unnatural gifts, odd happenings and horror.

Please visit my web site and sign up for my mailing list to be "in the know" for upcoming books. Visit me on Facebook, Twitter, or my Amazon Author page.

And thank you for reading. You are the reason I write.

www.arjaylewis.com
www.facebook.com/arjaylewis
www.twitter.com/arjaylewiswrite
www.amazon.com/Arjay-Lewis

ALSO BY ARJAY LEWIS

Doctor Wise Series
Fire In The Mind
Seduction In The Mind
Reunion In The Mind
Haunted In The Mind
Devotion In The Mind
Asylum In The Mind
Specter In The Mind
Vengeance In The Mind
Echoes In The Mind
Infection In The Mind
Justice In The Mind
Ritual In The Mind
Vanished In The Mind

Horror
The Muse
Kept In The Dark
The Vanishing
Digger

Romantic Suspense
(with Debra Snow)
A Study In Murder

NYPD Wizard Detective
The Wizards Of Central Park West
The Vampires Of Greenwich Village
The Werewolves Of Washington Square

www.ingramcontent.com/pod-product-compliance
Lightning Source LLC
Chambersburg PA
CBHW021504240626
47154CB00002B/496